PENGUIN BOOKS

MY SON'S STORY

Nadine Gordimer was born and lives in South Africa. She has written ten novels, including *A Sport of Nature*, *Burger's Daughter*, *July's People*, and *The Conservationist* (cowinner of the Booker Prize in England). Her short stories have been collected in nine volumes, and her nonfiction pieces were published together as *The Essential Gesture*. Gordimer has received numerous international prizes, including, in the United States, the Modern Literature Association Award, and, in 1987, the Bennett Award. Her fiction has appeared in many American magazines, including *The New Yorker*, and her essays have appeared in *The New York Times* and *The New York Review of Books*. She has been given honorary degrees by Yale, Harvard, and other universities and has been honored by the French government with the decoration Officier de l'Ordre des Arts et des Lettres. She is a vice president of PEN International and an executive member of the Congress of South African Writers.

MY SON'S STORY

Nadine Gordimer

PENGUIN BOOKS

PENGUIN BOOKS
Published by the Penguin Group
Viking Penguin, a division of Penguin Books USA Inc.,
375 Hudson Street, New York, New York 10014, U.S.A.
Penguin Books Ltd, 27 Wrights Lane,
London W8 5TZ, England
Penguin Books Australia Ltd, Ringwood,
Victoria, Australia
Penguin Books Canada Ltd, 10 Alcorn Avenue, Suite 300,
Toronto, Ontario, Canada M4V 3B2
Penguin Books (N.Z.) Ltd, 182–190 Wairau Road,
Auckland 10, New Zealand

Penguin Books Ltd, Registered Offices:
Harmondsworth, Middlesex, England

First published in the United States of America by
Farrar, Straus and Giroux, 1990
Published in Penguin Books 1991

1 3 5 7 9 10 8 6 4 2

PUBLISHER'S NOTE

This is a work of fiction. Names, characters, places, and incidents either are the product of the author's imagination or are used fictitiously, and any resemblance to actual persons, living or dead, events, or locales is entirely coincidental.

LIBRARY OF CONGRESS CATALOGING IN PUBLICATION DATA
Gordimer, Nadine.
My son's story/Nadine Gordimer.
p. cm.
ISBN 0 14 01.5975 4
I. Title.
[PR9369.3.G6M9 1991]
823—dc20 91-17273

Printed in the United States of America

For Reinhold

You had a Father, let your son say so.

WILLIAM SHAKESPEARE
Sonnet 13

My Son's Story

How did I find out?

I was deceiving him.

November. I was on study leave—for two weeks before the exams pupils in the senior classes were allowed to stay home to prepare themselves. I would say I was going to work with a friend at a friend's house, and then I'd slip off to a cinema. Cinemas had been open to us only a year or so; it was a double freedom I took: to bunk study and to sit in the maroon nylon velvet seat of a cinema in a suburb where whites live. My father was not well off but my parents wanted my sister and me to have a youth less stunted by the limits of an empty pocket than they had had, and my pocket-money was more generous than their precarious position, at the time, warranted. So I was in the foyer waiting to get into a five o'clock performance at one of the cinemas in a new complex and my father and a woman came out of the earlier performance in another.

There was my father; the moment we saw one another it was I who had discovered him, not he me. We stood there while other people crossed our line of vision. Then he came towards me with her in the dazed way people emerge from the dark of a cinema to daylight.

He said, You remember Hannah, don't you—

And she prompted with a twitching smile to draw my gaze from him—for I was concentrating on him the great rush of questions, answers, realizations, credulity and dismay which stiffened my cheeks and gave the sensation of cold water rising up my neck—she prompted, Hannah Plowman, of course we know each other.

I said, Hullo. He drew it from me; we were back again in our little house across the veld from Benoni and I was being urged to overcome the surly shyness of a six-year-old presented with an aunt or cousin. What are you going to see? he said. While he spoke to me he drew back as if I might smell her on him. I didn't know. They managed to smile, almost laugh, almost make the exchange commonplace. But it was so: the title of the film I had planned to see was already banished from my mind, as this meeting would have to be, ground away under my heel, buried along with it. The Bertolucci—an Italian film—it's very good, he said, delicately avoiding the implications of the natural prefix, 'We thought. . .' She nodded enthusiastically. That's the one to see, Will, he was saying. And the voice was an echo from another life, where he was my father giving me his usual measured, modest advice. Then he signalled a go-along-and-enjoy-yourself gesture, she murmured politely, and they left me as measuredly as they had approached. I watched their backs so I would believe it really had happened; that woman with her bare pink bottle-calves and clumsy sandals below the cotton outfit composed of a confusion of styles from different peasant cultures, him in his one good jacket that I had taken to the dry-cleaner for him many times, holding the shape of his shoulders folded back over my arm. Then I ran from the cinema foyer, my vision confined straight ahead like a blinkered horse so that I wouldn't see which way they were going, and I took a bus home, home, home where I shut myself up in my room, safe among familiar schoolbooks.

He was a schoolteacher in one of the towns that had grown up long ago along the reef of gold-bearing rock east of the city—Johannesburg. Where his great-grandfather or grandfather had come from nobody had recorded—the rough hands of those generations did not write letters or keep notes; brick-layers and carpenters, the only documentation of their lives was their work-papers and the various, much-folded slips entitling them to be employed in the town and to live in the area, outside the town, designated by the municipality for their kind. He thought his great-grandfather might have come from the diamond diggings in Kimberley; a photograph had survived while oral family history had gone to the grave. Among a work gang holding sieves of the kind used in panning for alluvial diamonds, there stood beside the white overseer a toothless grinning face with a family resemblance. No identification on the back of the photograph.

The schoolteacher's own father, acquiring one of the traditional trades of the maternal, Cape Town side of the family, had set up in a garage as an upholsterer. There was no car; his sonny-boy bounced instead on the exposed springs of chairs and sofas, and had lint in his curls. The boy was the first in the family to leave earth, cement, wood and kapok behind and take up the pen and book. He was the first to complete the full years of schooling. Sonny became a teacher. He was the pride of the old people and the generic diminutive by which they had celebrated him as *the* son, the first-born male, was to stay with him in the changing identities a man passes through, for the rest of his life.

He taught in the same school, earning regular increments for service and improving his position by ability and gradual seniority during the years when he married his wife, Aila, and their two children, a girl followed by a boy, were born. The girl, like her father, having been fondly welcomed as *the* baby, kept the generic and continued to be called Baby, would never be known as anything else, through all the circumstances of her life. The boy was Will, diminutive of William. He was named for Shakespeare, whose works, in a cheap complete edition bound in fake leather, stood in the glass-fronted bookcase in the small sitting-room and were no mere ornamental pretensions to culture. Sonny read and reread them with devotion; although the gilt lettering had been eaten away by fishmoth, and the volume he wanted had to be selected blindly, his hand always went straight to it.

The pride the old people took in him was not just the snobbery of the poor and uneducated, that rejoices in claiming one who has moved up out of their class, and which, although their hubris hides this aspect from them, contains also, always, the inevitability of sorrow: his desertion. The pride came from an instinct, like the water-diviner's for the pull of his twig, for Sonny's distinction. And this in spite of the fact that he had turned out darker- rather than lighter-skinned than the rest of the family—something that, normally, might have down-graded him among them. Everything he was and did evidenced distinction. The definitive face that begins to emerge with adolescence was long, slender, and tenderly responsive beneath thick-browed, great black eyes ringed with dark skin as if in physical manifestation of deep thought. Even the hands that emerged from the pudgy paws of early childhood were at once extraordinary, the fingers growing very long in proportion to the curve of the palm, nervous in their alert touch and deftness, yet bestowing calm when resting in handshake or as a caress. It was proper, it was his *right* in the fitness of all he did and attracted to him, that he should marry a girl who seemed to have been set apart, for him. Not that it was an arranged marriage in what had been the custom of her ancestors and still lingered among her family, although the religion that went with it had been neglected or abandoned by the younger generation. Aila was so quiet it was irritably felt by others that her beauty was undeserved. Wasted; boys, men did not know what to say to her that would draw a response. Her coiled river of shining black hair looked as if it would never flow down for one of them. It was not possible to have thoughts about what her small body was like under her clothes. Her lovely lips and teeth formed a smile that greeted a man exactly as it did an old woman or a child; she did not seem to understand what the approach of a man was telling her.

Sonny was the one who knew what it was she rejected in the only way possible for someone like her: by silence. She spoke, with Sonny; when he came to see her for the first time, having been introduced a few days before by one of her brothers (the correct way to approach a girl, in her kind of family), they seemed to take up a conversation that had already begun, with him, in her silence among others. They mistook her gentleness for disdain; perhaps he mistook it, too, in another way, taking the gentleness for what it appeared to be instead of the strength of will it softly gloved. No-one knows the reserves that remain even in the most profound understanding between a man and woman. Aila had not known how to flirt, had never given a moment's attention to the thought of any other man as the singular being, lifelong friend and lover, a 'husband' meant for her; if she gave Sonny everything else of herself, it would have been worth less if she had not kept to herself some fibre of personality as a separate identity. Perhaps without his knowing what the element was, it was that which added to their love for each other his particular, unspoken respect for her—a sacred quality outside the subjectivity of passion and affection.

There was passion and affection. They married after a formal engagement—he even bought her a ring with a chip of diamond—and were not lovers until they were husband and wife. They never used endearments in public or displayed the behaviour expected of people to prove they are in love with one another, but there was a real body under her clothes, a lovely body with all its features there for him: the dark nipples like grapes in his mouth, the smooth belly with its tiny well of navel, her entry satiny within as the material of the nightgown her mother had provided for her bridal 'bottom drawer'. All their long dreamy talks about their lives before they knew each other, their life as they were going to make it together, ended with him almost stealthily moving into her, and the pleasure that came to them both always as if a surprise. They were greatly moved, each by the other. The emotion expressed itself in sensitivity, telepathy. They arrived, often without discussion, at the same decisions affecting their lives; and in discussion, in daily responses, a way they wanted to live timidly evolved between them. Domestically they adjusted to one another as cats curl up in accommodation before a fire.

They decided to have children, but not more than two. The fecklessly begotten families of the poor, from which they came, were not for them. Yet they did not plan to privilege these children beyond the decencies of opportunity and healthy, happy growth they believed were a child's right. One of the early sweet intimacies between them was that both had rejected any religious beliefs, although to please the old people she occasionally followed public rituals. They found that for them both the meaning of life seemed to be contained, if mysteriously, in living useful lives. They knew what that was not: not living only for oneself, or one's children, or the clan of relatives. They were not sure what it was; not yet. Only that it had to do with responsibility to a community; and that could only mean the community to which they were confined, to which they belonged because the law told them so, in the first place, and that to which the attachments and dependencies of daily life and the shared concerns that came from living within it, made them belong, of themselves.

Sonny felt his way was obviously through a special responsibility to the children in the school: it opened out from conscientiousness in teaching his own classes to an accountability for the welfare of all the children at the school. He saw the need to bring together the school and the community in which it performed an isolated function—education as a luxury, a privilege apart from the survival preoccupations of the parents. He bought books that kept him from Shakespeare. He read them over and over in order to grasp and adapt the theory that recognized social education of the community, the parents and relatives and neighbours of the pupils, as part of a school's function. He started a parent-teacher association and an advisory service for parents, collected money for special equipment for handicapped children, took groups of senior boys and girls to do repairs in the yard rooms of pensioners. What else might he do? For the uplift of the community he enterprisingly approached the Rotary Club and Lions' Club in the white town with respectful requests that they might graciously send their doctors, lawyers, and members of amateur theatre and music groups to lecture or perform in the school hall.

It was not so easy to find a way for Aila. There she was, in the watchful quiet of her readiness. She, too, had matriculated, but she had married from the close female domain of her parents' home at eighteen, and never worked in the world. He did not want a bed-and-board wife and she wanted to become what he wanted, so she took a secretarial course and studied psychology by correspondence as preparation for a useful working life. His poor salary was reason enough for her to need to earn; but that was not their primary concern. While she was pregnant with their first child they spent the evenings over her material from the correspondence college, he helping her with her assignments. When Baby was born, the young mother would sit at her books between feeds and household tasks, and the young father would be on the other side of the table, correcting his pupils' papers. He read out howlers to her and they softly laughed together, parenthetic to their concentration; sometimes Baby interrupted them with colic cries, sometimes his long-fingered caress on his wife's neck, across the table, or the touch of her hand placed momentarily over his, led to love-making.

They bought their furniture on hire purchase. On Saturday mornings went by bus and later in the car they had saved for, to shop in town. Baby was dressed up in white frill-topped socks and Will had his safari suit with long pants, a miniature of his father's Saturday outfit. Sonny and Aila carried their week's supply of groceries in the plastic bags whose O.K. Bazaars logo identified families like them everywhere in the streets, wage-earners who had to buy in the cheapest store, with the weekly indulgence of ice-cream cones or peanuts for the kids and the luxury of queueing up for weekend beers on the side of the liquor stores segregated from where white people were served.

Like some sudden growth pushing up after rain, these people appeared in the town on Saturdays, covering the streets with trailing children and window-gazing men and women studying the advertised down-payments on bedroom 'schemes' and lounge 'suites' named to bring to cramped and crumbling hovels the dimensions of palaces, 'Granada', 'Versailles'. During the week the throng vanished, obediently banished back to the areas set aside for them outside the town. The workers were in the factories, the schoolteacher went to his designated school; men, women, children—everyone kept to the daily pathways worn within that circumscribed area. In the town, the lawyer and estate agents and municipal officials moved unjostled about streets expanded, spacious, swept of the detritus of Saturday's common usage. A white town.

Sonny and his wife did not covet 'Granada' or 'Versailles'; with an understanding of Shakespeare there comes a release from the gullibility that makes you prey to the great shopkeeper who runs the world, and would sell you cheap to illusion. (False values—but that was what he was to call them only later.) Yet the couple were not set apart in any outward way from the crowd of their kind who came into the town every Saturday to buy from the white people. With their children by the hand, they passed the town's two cinemas without particular awareness that they had never entered, could not enter. When Sonny's family was hungry he bought chips from the Greek's shop and he and Aila carefully put the crumpled paper, wet with vinegar, into the municipal trash baskets when the children had finished eating as they walked; the Greek had a few tables set out with fly-spotted artificial flowers and tomato sauce bottles, at which people could be served, but not this family. If—as always—the children needed to go to the lavatory, the parents trotted them off down to the railway station, where there were the only toilets provided for their kind, although the department store had a cloakroom for the use of other customers. As some lordly wild animal marks the boundaries of his hunting and mating ground which no other may cross, it was as if the municipality left some warning odour, scent of immutable authority, where the Saturday people were not to transgress. And they read the scent; they recognized it always, it had always been there. There was no need for notices spelling it out; there were only a few of these in the town, on public benches, for example. There was none at the library; but no-one would have pretended not to know what there was to know about that building from which the scent came, disguised this time as the smell of books, the cool must of yellowing paper, scuffed leather, and the wood-fragrance absorbed from the shelves where they were held, as brandy takes flavour from the casks in which it matures.

The lover of Shakespeare never had the right to enter the municipal library and so did not so much as think about it while white people came out before him with books under their arms; he did not recognize what the building represented for him, with its municipal coat of arms and motto above the pillared entrance: CARPE DIEM.

She is blonde, my father's woman. Of course. What else would she be? How else would he be caught, this man who has travelled so far from all the humble traps of our kind, drink, glue-sniffing, wife-beating, loud-mouthed capering, obsequious bumming (please my master ag please my baas), and all the sophisticated traps of lackeyism, corruption, nepotism, that wait for men who take privilege at the expense of the lives of others, and of their own self-respect. Self-respect! It's been his religion, his godhead. It's never failed him, when he wanted to know what course to take next: his inner signpost, his touchstone. Do what will enable you to keep your self-respect. That is the wisdom he has offered to us—my sister and me. It came with the warm flow of assurance that floods you when you receive something to live by whose proof is there in the person of the donor. If someone whose self-respect has demanded and received so much from him—loss of the work he was dedicated to, transformation from contemplative privacy to public activity, speechifying, imprisonment and trial—if *he* is to be caught of course it's going to be by the most vulgar, commonplace, shopworn of sticky traps, fit for a dirty fly that comes into the kitchen to eat our food and shit on it at the same time.

Of course she is blonde. The wet dreams I have, a schoolboy who's never slept with a woman, are blonde. It's an infection brought to us by the laws that have decided what we are, and what they are—the blonde ones. It turns out that all of us are carriers, as people may have in their bloodstreams a disease that may or may not manifest itself in them but will be passed on; it has come to him in spite of all he has emancipated himself from so admirably—oh yes, I did, I do admire my father. People talk of someone 'coming down' with a fever; he's come down with this; to this.

Of course 'we know each other'. She entered our house when he was in detention. I let her in. I opened the door to her myself; I always went to the door, then, the schoolboy was the man of the house for my mother and sister, now that he was not there. Each time, I prepared my expression, the way I would stand to confront the police come to search the house once again. But it was a blonde woman with the naked face and apologetic, presumptuous familiarity, in her smile, of people who come to help. It was her job; she was the representative of an international human rights organization sent to monitor political detentions and trials, and to assist people like my father and their families. We didn't need groceries, my school fees were paid; my mother and Baby (after school) were both working and there was no rent owed because when we moved to the city my father had bought that house in what later was called a 'grey area' where people of our kind defied the law and settled in among whites.

So we didn't need her. She sat on the edge of our sofa and drank tea and offered what is known as moral support. She talked about the probability of my father being brought to trial, the iniquity of the likely charges, the foreboding Defence lawyers always had, in such cases, that one would get a 'bad judge', a secret member of the *Broederbond*. She was showing—but not showing off, she was all humility before our family's trouble—inside knowledge she must have gathered from interviews with the lawyers and furtive exchanges in court with the accused in trials she had already attended, exchanges made across the barrier between the public gallery and the dock during the judge's tea recess. She was so intense it seemed my quiet mother, her hair groomed and elegant legs neatly crossed as if her husband were there to approve of the standard—the self-respect—she kept up, was the one to supply support and encouragement.

Of course I know her. That broad pink expanse of face they have, where the features don't appear surely drawn as ours are, our dark lips, our abundant, glossy dark lashes and eyebrows, the shadows that give depth to the contours of our nostrils. Pinkish and white-downy—blurred; her pink, unpainted lips, the embroidered blouse over some sort of shapeless soft cushion (it dented when she moved) that must be her breasts, the long denim skirt with its guerrilla military pockets—couldn't she make up her mind whether she wanted to look as if she'd just come from a garden party or a Freedom Fighters' hide in the bush? Everything undefined; except the eyes. Blue, of course. Not very large and like the dabs filled in with brilliant colour on an otherwise unfinished sketch.

And even if I hadn't known her, I could have put her together like those composite drawings of wanted criminals you see in the papers, an identikit. The schoolboy's wet dream. My father's woman. But I had no voluptuous fantasy that night. I woke up in the dark. It's hard for an adolescent boy to allow himself to weep; the sound is horrible, I suppose because it's his voice that's breaking.

The schoolteacher had a yearning—he thought it was to improve himself. This was not in conflict with usefulness. He could only improve the quality of life for the school, for the community across the veld from the town, if he himself 'enriched his mind'—as he thought of it. He could not belong to whatever political debate there was in the town. Not that that was much loss, he was aware, since from accounts he read in the local paper it consisted of squabbles for control of the municipal council and the office of mayor between two groups prejudiced against each other, the Afrikaans-speaking and the English-speaking, with common purpose principally in keeping their jobs, benches, cinemas, library—the town—white. He could not belong to whatever cultural circles the town had—the amateur players' theatre, the chamber music society started by German Jewish refugees who had arrived during the war, bringing culture as well as the brewing of good coffee to a mining town that knew only Gilbert and Sullivan and a boiled chicory mixture. He could not belong to the Sunday bird-watchers' group, although he was interested in nature and sometimes took his children by train to the zoo in the city on the weekly day when it was open to their kind, and into no-man's-land, the stretch of veld between where his community lived and the town, to learn the habits of the mongoose and the dung-beetle, who lived there among the mine-dumps. He could not belong to the chess club (another initiative of the German Jews to create intellectual life in a town without any).

He could not afford to buy many books. He thought he ought to have some guidance towards those that were important, which might feed the yearning for whose satisfaction he was not sure what was really needed. Or rather what was wanting. He, too, enrolled in a correspondence course. He chose comparative literature and discovered Kafka to add to his Shakespearean source of transcendence—a way out of battered classrooms, the press of Saturday people, the promiscuity of thin-walled houses, and at the same time back into them again with a deeper sense of what the life in them might mean. Kafka named what he had no names for. The town whose walls were wandered around by the Saturday people was the Castle; the library whose doors he stood before were the gates of the law at which K. sat, year after year, always to be told he must wait for entry. The sin for which the schoolteacher's kind were banished to a prescribed area, proscribed in everything they did, procreating, being born, dying, at work or at play, was the sin Joseph K. was summoned to answer for to an immanent power, not knowing what the charge was, knowing only that if that power said he was guilty of something, then he was decreed so.

This philosophizing reconciled Sonny, a profoundly defeatist way of staunching the kind of slow flux which is yearning. He was able to find satisfaction in the detachment of seeing the municipality and the Greek tearoom where his family could not sit down, in these terms. He became fascinated, as an intellectual exercise, with the idea of power as an abstraction, an extra-religious mystery, since religions explained away all mystery in the person of mythical beings, one religion even awkwardly offering a half-god, half-man, born of a virgin woman, so as to make that particular myth somehow more credible. And although Kafka explained the context of the schoolteacher's life better than Shakespeare, Sonny did not go so far as to believe, with Kafka, that the power in which people are held powerless exists only in their own submission.

He knew better. There were the local law-makers, proconsuls, gauleiters in the town's council chamber under the photographs of past mayors and the motto CARPE DIEM.

I think they were happy when my sister and I were little, in that township we lived in outside the Reef town. So far as children can know what their parents are; considerate, discreet parents like ours, not the drunken violent ones, some of our neighbours whose ugly lives came reverberating through our walls, and whose kids ran to our house out of fear of what was being revealed to them. Sometimes a woman would ask my father to 'speak to' her husband. I hung around my father, climbing on the back of his old armchair or leaning against his legs when strangers were there and understanding snatches of what was being said: the man had beaten her, he was drunk every night, he was going to lose his job with a builder. I stared in curiosity at the fear-distorted, snivelling face I never saw in my own home.

It wasn't only self-respect my father had; people respected him, not even a drunk would curse him. I don't know what made all sorts of men and women feel he would find for them their way out of the bewilderment of debt, ignorance, promiscuity and insecurity that giddied them, so that they lunged from one sordid obstacle to the next. It was partly, I suppose, because of what he did at the school, and then later when he got the township manager to let him start up the youth club; people saw him as one of themselves—powerless—who nevertheless had the special kind of self-respect (yes, that again) that makes it possible to influence others—take on responsibility for their lives in a way different from that of those, the masters, in the administrative offices, courtrooms and police stations. He did things for other people the way he did things for us—his family. That was it; to give came to him naturally, as it came to them to take.

Yet my parents didn't have a lot of friends. Not what the neighbours would call friends. The Sunday gatherings we children saw at other people's houses when we went to play with their children were not customary in our house. There were no beer and brandy bottles lying about our yard and no shuffling and giggling to music so loud it made the transistor radio balanced on the stoep steps buzz and tremble. Uncles and aunts and cousins sometimes came to us for tea, and once in a while to Sunday lunch when my mother would have spent the whole of Saturday preparing the traditional foods that had come down to her, like her oriental beauty half-hidden by neat blouses and skirts, while the rest of that side of her ancestral heritage had been buried in generations of intermarriage and cross-cultural alliances of other kinds. Mostly we did things alone together—my mother, my father, and we children. Before Baby got interested in boys, she would help my mother make dresses for her. There was a horseshoe magnet I loved to use, first spilling the tin of pins on the floor and then drawing them in prickly bunches to the metal, getting in the way of the girls (as my father affectionately called them). My father taught me how to change fuses and replace the cord on my mother's steam iron. He kept everything in the house in good order; we couldn't afford to call in professional repair men. But he didn't teach me to service our car and he never learnt to do so himself—there was a young apprentice mechanic, a cousin who came at weekends, earned a bit of extra pocket-money and kept the old second-hand Ford going. I liked the smell of the greasy pouch of oily black tools he opened out on the dirt floor of the shed my father had put up to house the car; it reminded me of the axles of great steam engines my father had taken me to see in an open-air museum. He promised to find a line on which they were still in use, and take me for a ride; that was the one promise I can remember he didn't keep. Probably he found that people of our kind weren't permitted to enjoy the treat, and he didn't want to tell me.

We didn't have any particular sense of what we were—my sister and I. I mean, my father made of the circumscription of our life within the areas open to us a charmed circle. Of a kind. I see that I don't want to admit that, now, because it comes to me as a criticism, but the truth is that it did give us some sort of security. He didn't keep from us, in general, the knowledge that there were places we couldn't go, things we couldn't do; but he never tried to expose us to such places, he substituted so many things we could do. My sister had dancing lessons and he taught me to play chess. I was allowed to stay up quite late on Friday night—no school next day—and we'd sit at the table in the kitchen after supper was cleared away, his great black eyes on me, encouraging, serious, crinkling into a smile back in their darkness, while I hesitated to make my move. Every Saturday when we went to town he bought a comic each for me and my sister—not the kind where the vocabulary was limited to onomatopoeic exclamations by supermen (those I borrowed secretly from my pals), but publications from England with stories of brave fighter pilots and King Arthur's Round Table, for me, and romantic fables retold in pictures for my sister.

Why do I say 'he' made the charmed circle in which we lived in innocence? My mother, too, drew it around us. But although they planned everything together and if there was a decision to be made affecting us, or any other matter that could be discussed in front of us, we would see him looking at her (the way he looked at me over the chess board) while he awaited her opinion, I am right in attributing the drawing of the safe circle of our lives, then, to him. It was always as if he knew what she wanted, for him and us, and that she knew he would find the way to articulate the components of daily life accordingly. For what she wanted was, in essence, always what he wanted; and that is not as simple or purely submissive as it sounds. I didn't—don't—pretend to understand how. It was between them, and will not be available to any child of theirs, ever.

What did it matter that the seaside hotels, the beaches, pleasure-grounds with swimming-pools were not for us? We couldn't afford hotels, anyway; a fun fair for the use of our kind came to our area at Easter, the circus came at Christmas, and we picnicked in the no-man's-land of veld between the mine-dumps, where in the summer a spruit ran between the reeds and my father showed us how the weaver birds make their hanging nests. There, on our rug, overseen by nobody, safe from everybody, the drunks next door and the municipality in the town, my father would lay his head in my mother's lap and we children would lie against their sides, under the warmth of their arms. A happy childhood.

But at fifteen you are no longer a child.

Halfway between: the schoolteacher lived and taught and carried out his uplifting projects in the community with the municipal council seated under its coat-of-arms on the one side of the veld, and the real blacks—more, many more of them than the whites, 'coloureds' and Indians counted together—on the other. His community had a certain kind of communication with the real blacks, as it did with the town through the Saturday dispensation; but rather different. Not defined—and it was this lack of definition in itself that was never to be questioned, but observed like a taboo, something which no-one, while following, ever could admit to. The blacks appeared in the community hawking tomatoes and onions, putting up a fence, digging a trench, even hanging out the washing in those households a rung more affluent than that of a schoolteacher. Their languages, their laughter yelled from block to block, sounded unceasingly through the day as cicadas thrum during hot hours. They went back to their own areas when the work was done; removed from the community as the community was from the white town. Out of the way. Better that way. The sight of them was a stirring deep down: it was because of *them* that the schoolteacher's community was what it was: cast outside the town. Needing uplift. It was because of *them* whose pigment darkened the blood, procreated a murky dilution in the veins of the white town, disowned by the white town, that the community was disqualified for the birthright of the cinema, the library, the lavatories and the coat-of-arms. To be confronted with the monumental, friendly high-riding backsides of the women, the dusty felted heads of the men, the beauty of the lolling babies on the mothers' backs—it was surely only to see and know that if you wanted to claim a self that, by right, ought to be accepted by the town, you had another self with an equal right—one that was a malediction, not to be thought of—to be claimed by *them*. With that strain of pigment went more interdictions, a passbook to be produced tremblingly before policemen, dirtier work, even poorer places to live and die in. Better to keep them at a distance, not recognize any feature in them. And yet they were useful; the self that recognized something of itself in the franchised of the town inherited along with that resemblance the town's assumption that blacks were there to do things you didn't want to do, that were beneath your station; for nothing was beneath theirs.

The schoolteacher always had been aware of the blacks in another way; well, this was nascent in that vague yet insistent sense of responsibility he had. In the years when he was getting the lint of his father's trade out of his curls, carrying his books to the light from the moted gloom where the pouffes and sofas from big houses in the town were pinned into new velvet like women for whom his father, on his hunkers, was the dressmaker, the blacks were clustering around enormous ideas. Equality. At so much a day; while he was a child it was expressed that humble way: a pound a day, that's all. The people in his community were underpaid, too. As an adult, he earned less than a white teacher with the same level of qualification. But he was set on sitting up at night studying for a higher qualification, maybe even getting a university degree; that was how he would better himself, not by going to meetings or getting arrested on the march. Equality; he went to Shakespeare for a definition with more authority than those given on makeshift platforms in the veld. The trouble was, he didn't feel himself inferior—inferior to what, to whom? He was so preoccupied with an inner life that he took little notice of the humiliations and slights that pushed and jabbed at him the moment he ventured outside the community. If, like the rest of his kind, he was a Sebastian, the arrows did not penetrate his sense of self. If they had—if he had been really black?—he might have joined, waved a fist. Admiring the real blacks from this sort of distancing, he left it to them. It seemed more their affair; they had no family resemblance that might somehow, someday, promote them to acceptance among the townspeople. And in this spectator status he was not alone; the community had hopes of the blacks, and also scepticism about these hopes. There was fervent stoep and yard talk, *they going to moer the lanies you'll see ou they quite right make the Boers shit their pants there in Pretoria what you think you talking about they going to get a rope round their necks that what they putting up their hands for, bracelets man bullets up the backside you can't win against whitey.* Only a few would cross the veld to join them.

He had cousins in the Cape who belonged to a resistance movement of their kind's own, and one of them came up with his mate to stay in the old people's house for a weekend while trying to get a branch going in the community, but they could see that somehow, although he was so intelligent, and at first they were encouraged by his clear grasp of their aims, Sonny would not be the one to take on the task. He told himself—seeing their expressions, hearing snatches of their remarks in his mind, a day or two afterwards—that he must first get his higher certificate and then he'd see. On the train going back to Mannenberg the cousins dismissed him between themselves as useless, a sell-out, interested in getting some piddling bit of paper that would make him the paid agent of handout education.

He followed political trials in the newspaper; he didn't know any of the accused personally although their names had become familiar as brand names around stoeps and yards. He had read a copy of the charter that had come out of a great meeting while he was himself not yet twenty, and that you could go to prison for possessing. There came a point, not possible to determine exactly when, at which *equality* became a cry that couldn't be made out, had been misheard or misinterpreted, turned out to be something else—finer. *Freedom.* That was it. Equality was not freedom, it had been only the mistaken yearning to become like the people of the town. And who wanted to become like the very ones feared and hated? Envy was not freedom.

After he was married, while the children were still small, although he knew that the instinct of responsibility extended beyond his part in maintaining the safety-net of families a marriage brings together, he thought he had found the instinct's natural bounds in the time, energy and imagination he put into his projects for the community and the participation of his family in these. The Rotary Club and the Lions granted money for Aila and the committee of housewives she had mustered to set up a crèche, impressed by the respectability of the schoolteacher from across the veld—his distinction, if they could go so far as to use that surprising term in description of one of those who made Saturday a day to avoid shopping in town. Baby was a member of the Junior Red Cross (community branch, segregated from that of the town) and went solemnly, holding hands with a small companion, from door to door with a collection box. And little Will was a keen Scout Cub (community troop) by the time another small boy, running with a crowd of older schoolchildren towards the police, was shot dead, and a newspaper photographer's picture of his body, carried by another child, became the *pietà* of suffering happening everywhere across the veld where the real blacks were.

When did distinction between black and real black, between himself and them, fade, for the schoolteacher? That ringing in the air, 'equality' beginning to be heard as 'freedom'—it happened without specific awareness, a recognition of what really had been there to understand, all the time. All his time. In the year after the *pietà* (he had a photograph of the one in Rome, reproduced in one of the books in his bookcase) was re-enacted in the black areas that were everywhere across the veld outside the towns, the children at his school began to stay out of class and stand about in the schoolyard with bits of cardboard slung from their necks. The lettering generally ran out of space before the message was completed, but it was so familiar, from pictures and reports of what was happening in the schools of real blacks that it could be read, anyway. WE DONT WANT THIS RUBBISH

EDUCATION APARTHEID SLAVVERY POLICE GET OUT OUR SCHOOLS. They were copying the real blacks, the headmaster told his staff meeting, and he would have none of it. They would not grow up to carry passes, their schools were better than the blacks', they were advantaged—no, he did not say it: they were lighter than the blacks. But the hardest-working, best member of his staff was thinking how children learn from modelling themselves on others, mimicking at first the forms of maturity they see in their parents and then coming to perform them cognitively as their capacities grow; why should they not be learning something about themselves, for themselves, by mimicking the responsibilities recognized precociously by certain other children—their siblings. To recognize the real blacks as siblings: that was already something no irritated, angry headmaster could explain away as a schoolyard craze, wearing bottle-top jewellery, passing a zoll round in the lavatories.

The schoolteacher walked back to his empty classroom; stood there at his table alone; then picked up a red marker with a broad tip and went out among his boys and girls. They stirred with bravado and fear; they had had many calls for silence from teachers who came to harangue them with orders and even to plead reason to them. But he went from cardboard to cardboard correcting spelling and adding prepositions left out. Giggles and laughter moved the children now, like one of the gusts that kicked dust spiralling away in the trampled yard. —Let's take your placards into class and rewrite them. When you want to tell people something you have to know how to express it properly. So that they will take you seriously.— And they followed him.

But it was not always so easy. Knowing *he* took them seriously they expected much of him. Not only his own class, but the rest of the senior school. They quickly picked up a kind of pidgin terminology of revolutionary rhetoric that was the period's replacement for schoolboy slang, and their demands as well as their actions became more and more strident. They came to him, they expected him to stand between them and the principal. He persuaded the principal to let him go with them when they determined to march across the veld to show solidarity with the children who had been locked out of their school by the police, after a boycott of classes; black solidarity. He took responsibility for keeping stones out of their hands. And he succeeded. For the first time, the old people saw his distinction ratified in a newspaper: not one of the important dailies, only a weekly published for the interests of people like themselves, but there he was above the bobbing corks of children's heads, tall and thin with dark newsprint caves where his eyes would be. The picture was cut out and passed round cousins, aunts and uncles. It was very likely the first time his photograph went into police files, as well. And when the police did come to his school because some of the children had set alight a bus in frustration that found release in ugly elation at destruction, the children expected him to stand between them and the police; he had not been able to keep petrol and matches out of their hands as he had kept stones. He went to the police station when seven among them were detained; but all that was achieved was, in trying to find out where they were being held, he had to give his name and address, and so the police had that confirming identification to file along with the newspaper photograph; he received no information.

He was doing it all for the school, for the children of the community. Aila knew that. He didn't keep anything from her. She knew some of the parents had complained about his having marched with the children over the veld to the blacks' school: a teacher should not be allowed to encourage such things. She knew that when the principal informed him of this it was a warning. The principal looked as if he were about to say what his fifth-form teacher was expecting from him; but his authority always wavered before this particular member of his staff; he added nothing. And Aila did not need her husband to spell out realization that including the community in one's concerns was bringing something the innocence of good intentions hadn't taken into account: risk to the modest security of the base from which that concern reached out—his job, the payments on the car and the refrigerator, the stock of groceries brought home every Saturday. After such signals as the interview with the principal they went matter-of-factly about the occupations of the day. But in their bedroom, the sight of her folding their clothes away, brushing the jacket he wore to school, told him that this was, that night, a ritual defending her family, asserting the persistence of the familiar against any unknown; and the awareness, for her, that he had lowered his book and was looking at her (she met his eyes in her mirror, he was behind her, lying in bed) while she plaited her hair, was a compact in which they would together accommodate the unforeseen. They were not really afraid; only on behalf of the children. And if it had been only a matter of being able to continue to feed and clothe them! Baby was nearly twelve; some her age were already running excitedly with the crowd, stones in hand, as the first child to be shot had done. Baby displayed no interest in such solidarity—she was absorbed in her dancing lessons, pop-star worship and bosom friendships, but who knew for how long? Will was too young to be at risk—in this community, unlike the black ones across the veld where no-one was too young to be out in the streets, caught between crossfire.

No wonder parents wanted removed from the school a teacher, one of their own kind, who led their children over there.

What made him allow himself to be seen with his woman in a public place? What made him go with her to that cinema, in a smart complex of underground shops and restaurants, moving stairways and piped music? Well, what made me go there: I thought no-one'd see me. No-one would know me. A suburb where well-off white people lived, always had lived; at a cheap cinema in one of the grey areas where we'd moved in there'd be bound to be people who would have recognized me. Recognized him. Seen him with her.

So we both went across the city, tried to get lost in foreign territory, deceiving each other. Though I flattered myself; he certainly didn't have me in mind as I, fifteen, had *him*, the parent, in mind when I bunked study leave that afternoon. Do you ever forget about them, the parents, for a moment? They are always there in the hesitations—whether you will obey or defy—the opinions—where did you get them from?—that decide what you're doing. Because even while you defy the parents, deceive them, you believe in them.

And then there he was. What are you going to see? he said. But I had seen. He kept his distance from me because he thought he must smell of her arm and shoulder pressed against his. Perhaps he'd been touching her in the dark. His hand worming up her sleeve and feeling her breast. We try it with girls at parties when someone turns off the lights.

He had shown me something I should never have been shown.

I came into the kitchen for supper when the others were already at table. I had stopped outside the door before I went in, my whole body shying away. He was there in his usual place, as if he were my father again, not the man with his blonde woman in the foyer of the cinema. I slid into my place beside my sister on the bench he had made himself—and I had helped him—when he was assembling the do-it-yourself 'breakfast nook' unit for my mother. In the ease of the family presence we often didn't actually greet each other at meals; it would have been like talking to oneself. So I didn't have to speak. He was shaking the salt cellar over his food, I saw his hand and I did not have to see his face. My mother was talking softly, commenting on something or other Baby must have mentioned, as she went between stove and table as a bird flies back and forth with food to drop into the open beaks of her young. —Sit down and eat. He can help himself.— My father spoke of me like that; he spoke with gentle consideration to my mother. Then I looked up at him, perhaps he was willing me to do so. We saw each other again.

Nothing happened; as if nothing had happened. My mother said I looked tired. —I think he ought to be taking Sanatogen.—

—Oh Aila, you don't believe that nonsense!— He was smiling at her.

—Well, everybody took it for exam nerves when I was at school. Will, won't you have a glass of milk? Don't you think he's done enough, he's been at it all day, Sonny, he should close his books and have an early night. Tell him.— Although my father was no longer a schoolteacher she kept the habit of referring to him as the expert in matters affecting our education. And those deeply-recessed eyes gazed at me across the table: —Now that's a good idea. Sleep's the best tonic. What's the subject you write next week?—

I spoke to him for the first time. —Biology. On Tuesday.— And so there was complicity between us, he drew me into it, as if he were not my father (a father would never do such a thing). And yet because he was my father how could I resist, how could I dare refuse him?

It might even have been that the principal protected the schoolteacher for some time. Conscience—the principal's own, that he didn't follow—or loyalty to his own kind against the power of the town's and the government's authority might have moved him; in the community there was no-one so determined to stay out of trouble that he would not secretly admire one who was not afraid to get into trouble. The schoolteacher did not lose his post during the period when the children were disrupting the school just as if they were really black.

But he had ventured outside the harmless activities of good works for which funds could be begged from the Rotarians and the Lions, and approved by them at their weekly lunches in the town's appointed hotel. People in communities like his own, in other areas of the Transvaal, got to hear of him—probably it was the newspaper photograph that started it. Proclamations in the *Government Gazette* were being enacted in these areas—

literally, as the script of a play is enacted by the voices and movements of players, by government trucks carting away people and their possessions and by bulldozers pushing over what had been their homes. Shopkeepers who were not really black but not white, either, were being moved out of the shops they had occupied for generations in the white towns. There were people like him in these communities, people who felt responsibility beyond their families, and they were eager to recruit anyone who showed a sign: he had marched across the veld; he was marked. Although no family was losing its home as yet in his community it was obvious he was the kind of man who would realize that all communities of his kind were in fact one and if that one were threatened by a white town this month or year, this one could be the next. He was approached to form a local committee, he was elected to a regional executive, he studied government white papers in the tin-trunk archives of township proclamations, and title deeds old people had kept; he stood on the creaking boards of a church hall and made his first speech.

He had stayed the children's hands when they picked up stones. But words, too, are stones. Now he had taken up the sling, another David among many singling themselves out to be marked—again, by the eyes of Goliath.

Unexpectedly, he proved to be one of the best speakers in the movement and at weekends was needed to address gatherings around the province. His name appeared on posters in dorps where they were scrawled over obscenely or torn down by local whites. 'Sonny', in quotes, was printed between his first and surnames, in the lists of speakers, the childish appellation became a natural political advantage, stressing approachability and closeness to the people he would address. And when there were combined meetings with real blacks, his own dark skin, in contrast with the lighter colouring of most of his kind, surely helped reduce superficial differences between those who were entirely black and those who had something of the white man in their veins. Colleagues, more politically sophisticated than he, saw the usefulness of these attributes. He himself was innocent of the fact that they could be used in any way; was only gratified that his years of reading—that individualistic, withdrawn preoccupation, as he was beginning to think of it—were being put directly to the use of the community in providing him with a vocabulary adequate to what needed to be said. Words came flying to his tongue from the roosts of his private pleasures. When he was told he was good he laughed and said embarrassedly that he was a teacher, a public speaker in the classroom every day of his working life.

The principal came to the teacher's house on a Saturday afternoon. Aila opened the door and in her face (the principal always had thought her beautiful, but in the way of one of those national costume dolls brought back from foreign countries, too typical) he saw such instant comprehension and dread that, having never ever dropped in, before, what he came out with was something ridiculous: I was just passing. . . She led him in, in silence. She went to fetch her husband from the back yard where for privacy, under the shelter of the grapevine he'd grown, he was in a meeting with his new associates. They saw her face. They rose quickly to their feet.

—No, not the police. The principal.—

The associates sat down again; one gave a gesture of relief, excusing the teacher for the interruption, as he himself might have given a pupil permission to leave the classroom.

The education department responsible for people of their kind had informed the principal that this teacher was to be dismissed.

The teacher smiled as one does at something expected, feared, and already dealt with at four in the mornings, lying quite still so as not to disturb the sleeper sharing the bed.

—Man, what can I do. I tried to stop it.— The principal's lower jaw jutted and pushed his lips and moustache up towards his nose; that comic grimace so familiar to his staff whenever he had something unpleasant to say and the muscles of his face sought to disguise his nervousness by assuming a fearsome aspect, the way a defenceless animal changes colour, or bristles.

—It's all right.—

—Sonny, I held them off. . . I told them, you're one of my best. I told how popular you are with the kids. What you've done for the school.—

But he had said the wrong thing again. It was exactly what the teacher had done for the school that had opened the dossier which had led to this: dismissal. In distress the principal unburdened himself of the worst. —You know. . . don't you . . .man, it's bad. The Department won't allow any other school to give you a post.—

Aila came in with a tray of tea.

She did not look up at either of the men and left without breaking the silence, for them.

Benoni—son of sorrow.

My father, who didn't have a university degree (unlike that woman he admires so much) used to have the facility for picking up incidental knowledge that only intelligent people whose formal education is limited, possess. He drew fragments of information to himself as I drew my mother's pins to the horseshoe magnet. One time he told me what the name of the town meant. I don't know where he learnt it. He said it was Hebrew.

I was born in that town, his son. I think now that this sorrow began when we left it. As long ago as that. Even before. When he had to stop being a teacher and his profession and his community work were no longer each an extension of the other, something that made him whole. Our family, whole.

They found a job for him in an Indian wholesaler's—the people of the committee against removals which was now his community work, taking him all over the place, speaking on platforms and attending meetings outside the community of our streets, our area. He no longer had a profession; his profession had become the meetings, the speeches, the campaigns, the delegations to the authorities. The job—book-keeping or something of that kind he quickly taught himself—was not like teaching; it was a necessity that fed us and that was got through between taking the train to the city every morning and returning every evening. It had no place in our life. He did not bring it home, it was not present with us in the house as his being a teacher always had been. I was eleven years old; he went away every day and came back; I never saw that warehouse at the other end of the train journey. Men's and boys' clothing, he said: I had asked what was in it. Imagine him in cave after cave of shoes without feet, stacks and dangling strings of grey and brown felt hats, without heads or faces, he who had been surrounded by live children. He used to read to us at night, Baby and me, whenever there were no meetings. Baby didn't listen, she would go into the kitchen with her little radio. He had taught me to read when I was less than five years old but I still loved best to be read to by him. Sometimes I made him read to me from the book he himself was in the middle of, even though I didn't fully understand it. I learnt new words—he would interrupt himself and explain them, if I stopped him. When grownups asked the usual silly question put to children, Baby answered (depending on whether she was out to impress the visitor or be saucy) she would be 'a doctor', 'a beauty queen', and I said nothing. But he—my father—would say, 'My son's going to be a writer'. The only time I had spoken for myself everyone laughed. I had been taken to the circus at Christmas and what I wanted to be when I grew up was a clown. Baby called out—bright little madam, everyone dubbed her—'Because your feet's so big already!' My mother didn't want to see my feelings hurt and tried to change the derision to a rational objection. But clowns are sad, Will, she said.

The faces they draw over their faces, the big down-turned mouth and the little vertical points below and above the middle of each eye, that suggest shed tears. When he sat opposite me at supper that first night what face did he see on me. What face did he make me wear, from then on, to conceal him, what he was doing—my knowledge of it—from us: my mother, my sister, myself.

Perhaps if we had never left our area outside the small town it would never have happened? We should never have been there, at that cinema. She would never have found him, us—his blonde woman. I've thought of all the things that would have had to be avoided if I were not to have met my father at that cinema on an afternoon before the exams. I've lived them over in my mind because I did not know how to live now that I had met him, now that I had seen, not the movie I bunked swotting for, but what our own life is.

Although he worked in the city we had gone on living in our little house on the Reef for a time. My parents were paying off monthly instalments against the municipal loan with which they had bought it; my mother had her job running the crèche, for which eventually there had been granted a municipal subsidy by the town councillors. So we stayed where we were. Except for him, everything was in its place. The swing he had put up in the back yard when we were little, the kennel I'd helped him build for our Mickey, the dog he'd taken me to choose at the SPCA. While he was away with his committees and meetings at weekends my mother tried to do with us the things we all used to do together. And the last Sunday picnic before we left our home was in the winter. The last time; the end of winter. The veld had been fired to let the new growth come through, the sun burned off the night's frost, vaporized as a cool zest on the smell of ashes. A black landscape with only our mountains, the mine-dumps, yellow in the shadowless light. My mother spread a sheet of plastic under our rug over the sharp black stubble that puffed like smoke under our feet and dirtied our socks. There were the things we liked to eat, naartjies whose brilliant orange skins Baby arranged in flower patterns on the blackness. Did he say, my daughter's going to be an artist? Because he was there. At that last picnic we had on our old patch of veld between the dumps, he was with us. He and I rambled off, I poking with a stick at every mound and hole for what treasures I did not know, and he showed me some, he discovered them for me; he always did. There was the skeleton of a fledgling caught by the fire, and he said we could take it home and wire it together. Then he spied for me the cast of a songololo thick as my middle finger, I held it up and could see the sky through it at the end of its tiny tunnel. Ice-blue sky, yellow dumps, black veld, like the primary colours of a flag. Our burnt-out picnic. She would never have known where to find us, there.

But when she came to the house in Johannesburg she had already found him. On her errands of mercy and justice she had visited the prison.

The ex-schoolteacher and his wife discussed the decision as they always had done everything, before they left the Reef town. They talked over months, as people who are very close to one another do, while carrying on the routine, whether of tasks or rest, that is the context of their common being. He was replacing the element in the kettle and she was cutting up vegetables for one of her delicious cheap dishes; she was in the bath and he came in and took up what he had been saying after Baby and Will had gone to bed; he and his wife were themselves in bed, had said goodnight and turned away, then slowly talk began again.

It was the biggest decision of their lives so far. Marriage? Love had led them so gently into that. To leave the place where they had courted, where the children had been born, where everybody knew them, knew she was Sonny's wife, Baby and Will were Sonny's children. Aila's silences said things like this.

—But what is this house? A hovel you've slaved away to make into something decent. How much longer can we have Baby sharing a room with her brother—she's a big girl, now. Paying the town council interest for another twenty-five years, thirty years, the never-never, we can't even give our kids a little room each. We don't have a vote for their council but they take our money for the privilege of living in this ghetto.— He had never before used this term to her, for their home. A changing vocabulary was accompanying the transformation of Sonny to 'Sonny' the political personality defined by a middle, nickname. She knew he was leading her into a different life, patiently, step by step neither he nor she was sure she could follow. Her spoken contribution to their discussions was mostly questions. —But we won't find anything much better where we're going, will we? Where are we going to live?— None knew more than a member of the committee against removals about the shortage of shelter for people of their kind, decades- generations-long. 'Housing' meant finding a curtained-off portion of a room, a garage, a tin lean-to. Then there was the matter of her job. Where would she find work in Johannesburg? Her kind of work. —I suppose I could do something else. . .get taken on in a factory.— Aila was referring to his connections with the clothing industry, he knew; it alarmed him. Unthinkable that through him Aila should sit bent over a machine. Jostle with factory girls in the street. He would find some solution, he would not show his alarm. Suddenly he saw exactly, precisely what she was doing, before him, at that moment: slicing green beans diagonally into sections of the same length, cutting yellow and red bell peppers into slivers of identical thickness, all perishable, all beautiful as a mosaic. Aila's hands were not coarsened and dried by the housework she did; she went to bed with him every night with them creamed and in cotton gloves. The momentary distraction was not a distraction but a focus that thrust him, face down, in to the organic order and aesthetic discipline of Aila's life, that he was uprooting.

She sat in the bath soaping her neck. Her hair was piled up and tied out of the way in the old purple scarf that had its place on a hook among towels. He was already drawing breath to speak when he came through the door. —Why should you be 'grateful' for the measly subsidy they give so you can run a crèche for them.—

—Not for them, for the children.—

—Ah no, no, for *them.* So they can sit in their council chamber and congratulate themselves on 'upgrading' living conditions in the ghetto where our kids are brought up. Where we're supposed to live and die. The place where they confine us. Zoo. Leper colony. Asylum. It's humiliating to take from them, Aila. Let them have it.—

Her questions were never objections; they were the practical consequence of acceptance. She did not oppose the move. She was careful to present it to their children as something exciting and desirable. And the children were ready to quit with heartlessness their friends, their school, the four walls and small yard where they had played. Baby had the teenager's longing for the life she imagined existed in the city; Will cared only about taking the dog along. To Johannesburg, Johannesburg! Nobody asked exactly where. The husband, the father, was taking care of that.

When he knew where they were going to live the slither of the commuter train over the rails, taking him home from the warehouse, raced his bravado excitement, but as he walked the familiar streets each night, back to the old house, through the greasy paper litter outside the fish and chips shop, past the liquor store with its iron bars and attendant drunk beggars, past the funeral parlour where the great shining black car stood always ready to take the poor grandly on a last ride, past his old school with its broken windows and the graffiti of freedom that still had not come—as he deserted this, he realized that a certain shelter was being given up, for the family. Shabby, degrading shelter—but nevertheless. He himself had the strength of a mission to arm him; his family—Aila—it would be different for them. So he calmed his euphoria before he told her. And it was not in front of the children.

—We're going to move in among whites. It's a tactic decided upon, and I'm one who's volunteered. If you agree.—

She smiled indulgently, disbelieving. The committee had debated many tactics of resistance that did not come to anything. —What are you talking about. Tell me. How?—

—It's been done already. It'll be in one of the southern suburbs, of course, not where well-off whites live. Working-class Afrikaners want to move up in the world and they'll sell for a high price.—

—We can't afford to buy anything! In Johannesburg! Where will we get the money?—

—The money's being put up for us. We'll pay off a rent, same as we do here.—

—But it's illegal, how can you own a house in a white place?—

—That's the idea. We don't accept their segregation, we've had enough of telling them, we're showing them.—

—Us?— A pause. —So that's the idea.—

It was the nearest she came to challenging a committee's presumption in directing her family's life.

—It's a really nice house. Three bedrooms, a sitting-room,

another room we can use for your sewing and my books—imagine! I'll be able to have a desk. We'll do up the kitchen, I'll build you a breakfast nook. And there's a big yard. A huge old apricot tree. Will can make a tree-house.—

Aila was inclining her head at each feature, as if marking off a list. She stopped when he did, looking at him with her black liquid gaze, appreciatively. Aila understood everything, even the things he didn't intend to bring up all at once; he could keep nothing from her, her quiet absorbed his subsumed half-thoughts, hesitations, disguising or dissembling facial expressions, and fitted together the missing sense. Because she said little herself, she did not depend on words for the supply of information from others. It was as if she had been there when he had been walking home from the station through the dreary streets and he had spoken aloud about their degradation as also some kind of shelter. Aila said: —Afrikaner neighbours.—

—Oh kids quickly get together. Dirty knees all look the same colour, hey. He'll make friends. The parents will avoid us. . .if we're lucky, that's all they'll do. But then we don't need them.—

—No.—

A single word had weight, from her. The subdued monosyllable was pronounced with such certainty; the habit of each other had made them even less demonstrative than they had been at the beginning of their marriage, but he was moved to go over to her. She turned away to some task. Awkwardly—she touched him only in the dark, in bed—she put up a hand to rest a moment on the nape of his neck. The spicy-sweet steam of Friar's Balsam came from the jam jar into which she had poured boiling water. —Who's that for?—

—Will's got a chest cold.—

—I'll take it to him. Is he in bed?—

He went off to tell his son about the tree-house they were going to build together. At their new home, high up, leaving the ghetto behind.

I don't understand how Baby doesn't know. Of course the fact that my father is away at all hours and sometimes for several days in itself doesn't mean anything. Long before he went to prison he had to get used to leaving us alone a lot. We had to get used to it. He wasn't a schoolteacher anymore, home every evening. He hasn't worked in the warehouse since the end of the first year in Johannesburg because the committee needed him as a full-time organizer. And then the committee made alliances with the new black trade unions which had just been allowed to be formed, and I don't know what else. All sorts of other people; groups active against the government. He was always one of those who wanted unity among them, always talking about it. When he *was* at home there were meetings sometimes the whole of Sunday, blacks, and our kind—lucky this house was built as a white people's house and there was room for them to shut themselves away.

And as soon as he came out of prison it started again—my father isn't the man to be scared off his political work because he's been jailed for it. Or he wasn't the man; now I don't know what he is. He goes out, away, and when he comes back, walks in, does the things he used to (pouring himself a glass of iced water from the fridge, hanging keys on one of the hooks he put up when we first moved here, asking us what sort of day we've had) he is *acting*. Performing what he used to be. Can't my sister feel that? It isn't something to see—the point is, it all looks the same, sounds the same. But the feeling. The body inside his same clothes. Whatever he touches, it's with the hand that has just left *her*. He smells different. Can't my sister smell it? Not of scent or anything, it's not that. I suppose he'd surely be too ashamed, he's become too sly for that. His own smell—of his skin—that I remember from when I was little and he'd cuddle me, or that used to be there until quite lately, when we'd share the bathroom. It's gone. I wouldn't recognize him in the dark.

Why should I be the one who had to know. Is it supposed to be some kind of a privilege? (What does he think!) She's older than I am, why should she be running around happily with her boy-friends, going off to her commercial college with silver-painted nails and Freedom T-shirts, secretly smoking pot every day.

I want to tell her, so she'll know what it's like to know. Why shouldn't she. I've tried. I said to her, he's different since he's out of prison—I mean, do you think Dad's all right? She laughed, impatient with me. She's always in a hurry. —All right! Who wouldn't be feeling good to get out! D'you expect him to be moping around like you?—

And of course she doesn't have anything to do with his body, any more, she's touching boys. My mother doesn't know about her either. I'm the only one.

Another thing he used to do, like going straight to the fridge for a glass of water, he used to call, Aila? Aila? if she wasn't in the first room he entered. He doesn't do that. If she's busy in another room he's sometimes home for half an hour or so before she knows he's there. In her innocence she takes this as one of the benefits we've won for ourselves, for the cause, for freedom: this house has privacy, it's not like the old one in the ghetto where we were together all the time. It's a space he deserves. *It's something we have to be grateful to him for*. He's been to prison for principles like this. When they came and took him away she kept looking around where she stood, as if a cleaver had come down as I'd seen it split a sheep carcass when she sent me to the butcher, lopping away a part of her she couldn't feel, yet. I went and took her hand but mine wasn't what was lost. I think they'd always been together in everything, she couldn't believe he was going off calmly (as he did) to an experience neither could ever have imagined would happen to them when they were young. (She was only eighteen when they married, just about the same age as my sister is now.) All the times away at meetings hadn't prepared her for this; from those he had always come home and called, Aila. And then he came out of prison with an experience she hadn't gone through with him, the way I suppose they'd had us—the children—together, and made the move to Johannesburg, and taught Baby and me to be polite but not to be afraid of the whites living in the same street because to be afraid was to accept that we didn't have the right to live there. It isn't exactly that my mother seems to want to find a way to make up, to him, for the unimaginable experience he has had on his own. (Visiting someone in prison you only have them shown to you for a few minutes, Baby and I went with her sometimes and he had been taken out of his cell, we never saw it, he talked through glass.) It's more that having been in prison for the cause of freedom has made him someone elect, not to be followed in his private thoughts by ordinary people. Like herself. Like us. She once told Baby and me she remembered, when she was very small, her grandfather looking so different, wearing a white turban when he returned from Mecca, that she ran away and hid.

What I'd like to know is does prison give my father the freedom to do what he's doing. Is it all right so long as she doesn't know. *That* is what he was getting me to agree to when he made me look at him across the table that night after the cinema. But it works both ways. I can play hooky whenever I like; he can't ask where I'm going, where I've been. Because I know where he's going, where he's been. He can't order me, during the holidays, to finish reading the set-works for next term. He sees me with *Sportsday*, under his nose, instead of *King Lear* that he can quote reams of. An ungrateful child is sharper than a serpent's tooth. I don't want to be *in the know* with him. I don't want to ask him for anything. . . in case he can't refuse. I'll bet I could bring up the question of a motorbike again now, and maybe I'd get it.

It's easy to refuse to ask for things. But he knows I can't speak—to my mother; I can't refuse to be in the know, with him.

I'm not a child. If people come out of prison, if they've been lopped off, lost; there's love. Isn't there? It's a way to make up for anything, so people say, from the time you're a kid. Adults. In church, in school; in sex magazines. How to love, all kinds, all love. She comes out of the bathroom and smiles goodnight at me, I'm too old to be kissed unless it's a birthday or some other occasion, and she goes into their bedroom with her hair in her shiny plait down the back of her dressing-gown. They sleep in the same bed, but does he love her, after he's come from the other one? I never used to think about them—him, my mother—that way. I don't want to think about it now. I don't want to think he pretends she's pink and thick and soft; as I pretend, in dreams, that I'm doing things to them, the blondes in full-page spreads I tear out.

Sonny was not prepared for a visit granted to someone monitoring for a human rights organization. Friends and even relatives who had applied to see him had been denied permission; political comrades dared not show themselves for fear they'd be locked up, as well. For three months he saw no-one from outside. Then he saw only Aila, and once or twice the children were allowed to accompany her. That was as he had expected. He knew he was on his way to prison from the days back in the coloured location of his home-town on the Reef when he had led his pupils across the veld to the black location—as he still called those places, then. Or if he didn't know it, he should have; he realized this as, instinctively taking up one form of political action after another, he understood that the mystery of the meaning of life he and Aila had vaguely known to be contained in living useful lives was no mystery. For them, their kind, black like the others, there was only one meaning: the political struggle. (As he loved the magnificent choices of Shakespearean language, the crudely reductive terms of political concepts were an embarrassment to him, but he had to use them, like everybody else.)

Family matters. It was the rule in prison that only family matters could be discussed during visits. Well, these were what always had been discussed between Aila and him. He asked if Will was managing to keep up, in maths. If Baby was being helpful or spending too much time at parties. Aila reassured him; everything was all right. The very look of her conveyed that to him; at home, indeed, everything was the same; her black hair smoothly coiled, a necklace chosen to pick out a colour in the elegant tweed jacket she had sewn for herself. Her beautiful lips carefully drawn. The same; that sameness seemed to recede from him the more they talked about it, about family matters. And he had expected to yearn for home. The silences between Aila and him that were so comfortable, natural in their closeness, at home, were now a real silence without communication of any kind. He had been taught, in the tactics of the struggle, that it was possible to use a private, oblique language to receive information from intimates, but Aila didn't seem to catch on. She was calm but he noticed she held her arms close to her sides as if to draw away from the presence of the warders who flanked him. What private language? They had had love-names, tender and jokey euphemisms for what was hard to express, key words that recalled events in their life together or the antics of one or other of their children—who could expect Aila to put love-talk to the use of a prison code?

The stranger from the human rights organization had no family matters, with him, to confine herself to. He didn't know how she managed to get permission for such visits, but it was clear she had somehow obtained it and already seen several of his comrades. She conveyed this ingeniously in an abstract vocabulary that the two warders, blinking dully and even yawning, could not follow and clearly soon ceased to listen to. He didn't know what she had been told she would be allowed to talk about; presumably only to ask him if he was receiving adequate food, exercise periods and medical care. Talking about food she was actually letting him know that in another prison some of the comrades were on a hunger strike, and apparently innocently relating the weather report she was able to indicate—remarking which cities were receiving heavy rainfall—where many other comrades were held. When she began saying how very stuffy it was, by contrast, in Pretoria, she quickly noticed he was bewildered, straining to follow, and gazing at him in a pause, a silence of greatest aliveness reaching out to him, drew him to realize she was telling him she had been to the Supreme Court where others who were detained when he was were now charged. —And in crowded places it's going to get hotter.— She had narrow blue eyes, the kind that do not have much depth or variety of expression, like the glass-bright eyes fixed so realistically in furry stuffed toys yet which hold attention by their surface colour. He eagerly understood she was passing a message that he might expect to be charged soon.

A stranger has no love-talk, but she was the one who unknowingly found the way to connect him with home, with the possibility of home. It was a casual remark following on a question about how he was passing the time, which he could not answer because a warder woke and intervened, saying talk of prison matters was not allowed.

—Well, I suppose you find sermons in stones.— A bit breathless at having managed at least to hand on some of the information she had been given by others, she jerked her head shyly at the confines of the walls.

He grinned to receive this, another kind of message, she

was almost certainly not aware of; elated to be able to recognize it. —And good in your kindness in coming to see me.—

The young woman was not graceful or well dressed—not in the way he liked, in a woman, that gave a woman like his wife class and breeding, even in the ghetto. But what does that matter. Sonny had had to change his mind about so many things, as his life changed, as the very meaning of his ridiculous name changed—first a hangover from sentimental parents, then a nickname to reassure the crowds at rallies that he was one of them, then an addendum to his full names in a prison dossier: 'also known as "Sonny" '. A common criminal with aliases.

Hannah. She introduced herself like that at once; a prison visiting room is no place for formalities. It was only later, when he met her outside prison, that he saw how she had been the first time she came to visit. Head and shoulders, the portrait was, that he kept with him everywhere, in his mind, as a photograph is carried between identity documents in a breast pocket. It must have been a cold June day outside—but prison always gave the impression of cold, anyway, swept clean, bare, with only hairy floating filaments in a cone of light, alive; from the breasts up, as she appeared behind glass above the wooden barrier, she had prepared herself with layers of garments, loose-sleeved knitted things over some sort of canvas waistcoat and several T-shirts whose clashing colours overlapped at the neckline. She had eased a striped scarf and freed her broad, matt-white neck in a gush of warmth (a retouch of the picture that came from subsequent experience of her presence without the separation of glass and wood). Her lips were quilted by the dry cold and paler than a soft pink face whose colour changed with a kind of patchy radiance as she steered double-talk past the warders. A big face whose bone structure was not evident. Two small cold-reddened pads of earlobes appearing and disappearing under rough-cut curly hair. Blonde. Of course, with that skin colouring. Very blonde. But not consciously so (as so many women with that attribute tend to be); her attention on more important things. He could not reconstruct how she had looked full-length, walking away from him after a warder. The lightly freckled calves that remained sturdy right down to the ankle, bringing her towards him, were not any fixed image, but recurring through the pattern of their meetings, moving; always *now*, not *then*.

She came to the trial. It was her professional duty. She was often there; when he and the others with whom he was charged filed up from the cell beneath the court and turned smiling to look for relatives and friends in the gallery, she lifted a hand in reliable greeting. Aila could come only occasionally, she was receptionist to an Indian doctor at his city rooms in the lower end of town, and on Saturdays, when he did not consult there, the court did not sit. The doctor was generous in offering her time off, but Aila was conscientious, it was an article of faith between Sonny and her, part of her loyalty and support for him, in prison, that they would not let the State destroy the discipline of their daily life. When she could come she brought him jackets and trousers fresh from the dry-cleaner—as no longer a detainee but an accused on trial without bail he was allowed such humanizing privileges, and it was a tactic, displaying high morale to the judge, to confront him day after day with alleged revolutionaries looking like businessmen. Aila knew Hannah Plowman, who was monitoring the trial—the young woman had kindly come to the house once, while Sonny was still a detainee, to offer her organization's help—but they did not sit together in the visitors' gallery; the young woman had her colleagues, people from the churches, representatives from foreign embassies, a colloquy exchanging mouth-to-ear observations and analyses of how the Defence's case was going. Aila sat among the other wives, mothers, fathers of the accused, big peasant women in crocheted hats who rested deformed feet out of shoes worn lopsided, young pregnant women with defiant profiles under beaded lovelocks, grey-woolled old men wearing Church of Zion badges. Sonny would pick her out at once, there in one of her white blouses with the bow looped through her string of seed pearls, the plastic folder from the dry-cleaner neatly arranged across her lap so as not to crease his clothes.

At the tea-break, when the court had risen for the judge to retire, the colloquy of observers surged forward sociably along with the relatives. Couples embraced across the barrier of the witness box but it was not Aila's and Sonny's way to kiss on the mouth in public, their intimacy always had been too private for exposure. She leaned on the barrier and he held her hands folded together in his; and then she released herself, her eyes so brimming with dark, so shining and solemn, and handed over the dry-cleaner's bag with explanations of stains that couldn't be removed, as if this were the most important exchange between them. And they talked of family matters, although there was no restriction except political discretion on what they might say softly to one another, for these few minutes, here. Every other moment they were interrupted by his putting an arm out behind her to shake hands with a fellow prisoner's relative, or he would have to turn away—gripping her wrist or upper arm, through the cloth, to keep the precious contact with her hidden self—to talk to one of the observers about some point they ought to make when seeking support for the Defence among influential people abroad. Sonny had to share out the brief interval of the judge's tea-break like this because he had become spokesman for his fellow accused: the studious ex-schoolteacher had a way with words.

Will came, and Baby, when the trial continued through the school holidays, and Will, so tall already, eyebrows beginning to grow together in a crossbow, just like his own, kissed and hugged him, laughed, didn't want to let go. But Baby cried, and an extraordinary distress came over Sonny. There in the babbling company of the tea-break, the court where police stood at every exit deceptively sluggish as dogs who will attack at the first move, he was overcome by what he had done, got himself into this prisoner's dock, going to be shut away in a cell at the end of the day's hearing; suddenly possessed of an urge—jump the barrier, take this poor girl-child of his and break out. Aila was at work; the children had been brought to court by one of the lawyers. The young woman who was monitoring the trial, who had been once to the family house, appeared at the girl's side and comforted her, smiled away Baby's embarrassment; and Sonny's panic died down without anyone noticing his moment of weakness, more shameful than the natural emotion of a daughter whose struggle was only with adolescence.

As the picture of the first time he saw her—the young woman monitoring the trial—was reconstructed only later, so the meaning of the moment when she came to comfort his daughter was interpreted by him only later, growing in its power over him, a sign. It was then that it began, that it was inescapable. *Needing Hannah.* He could not think of what had happened to him as 'love', 'falling in love' any more than, except as lip-service convenience, political jargon expressed for him his decision to sacrifice schoolmastering, self-improvement, and go to prison for his kind. A spontaneous gesture quite in the line of her professional concern for prisoners and their families: she walked across the gallery of Court A into a need that clanged closed, about the two of them.

It was the creation myth of their beginning. That it was not recognized as such at once, by them, added to its beauty. He was a political activist on trial for promotion of boycotts and participation in illegal gatherings. Police videos were shown by the State prosecutor where the accused was speaking on the platform. In other gatherings his identification was disputed by the Defence: Counsel made everyone but the judge laugh when he dryly drew attention to the fact 'plain to see on his face' that this accused had a distinctive feature—his eyebrows. But the lighter moments in evidence and the cheerful atmosphere of airport reunions at tea-break were the 'humanized' part of a process whose purpose was to send these men, who already had spent many months in detention, back to prison as convicts; part of the processing of all opposition to the State pulped into prison. Sonny, like his comrades, was preoccupied with writing notes for the lawyers to use in his defence. Under the effort to recall precisely, exactly, where one had been, whom one had seen, what one had said on occasions over the three years on which the State based its case, all immediate impressions, however indelible, extraordinary, were thrust away.

Sonny was sentenced to five years. On appeal, before another judge, sentence was reduced to two.

—It's bearable.— The first thing he said to Aila when she was allowed to visit him before he was transferred to maximum-security prison. —It'll pass before we know it.— There had to be objectives to make it pass. —Baby'll be working for her matric—I'd like her to have some extra coaching when the time's near. I'll certainly get permission to do some study, myself.— He gave instructions on many practical matters—but didn't want it to sound like making a will, he was leaving her for only two years, not a lifetime. She took the instructions as supports to hold, until his return, the life they had made together. They filled the visit with a rapid, determined exchange of plans. —Not five, remember; only two years.— They smiled at each other continually. When it was time for Aila to go he discarded the ritual—expressions of confidence that she would manage, admonition to take care of herself—he could have taken refuge in to disguise the parting for a definitive period of their lives. This parting between them deserved more than that. He said, Write to me, Aila, you must write to me. She did not speak. She put her arms round her husband and kissed him on the mouth, in front of the warders. He saw that, not to shame him, to strengthen him, she pretended not to see the tears rise in his eyes. He saw that as she walked out she put up a hand to set a stray strand of her hair to rights, as well.

Happy for battle.

Aila wrote every month; about family matters. Five hundred words. That was the limit prison regulations allowed. The letters always ended 'Lots of love from all of us'. One prison day that was just like the last there was a letter in a different kind of envelope, addressed on a typewriter. It was from her, Hannah Plowman. Inside, he saw her handwriting for the first time, that voice which speaks from absence. Just a note to say how relieved everyone was (this he read as referring to the reduced sentence; in the know, she was well aware he was lucky not to get even more than five years). Anything we could do (the inference: her organization) to smooth the way where he found himself, or to assist his family, he had only to tell his lawyer. The last line of the single page abandoned the corporate 'we'. This letter ended: 'I know you'll come out happy for battle'.

He realized the wonderful phrase must be a quotation and he was stirred, intrigued to know from where, from whom. There was a message for him in the three words even beyond their aphoristic meaning, which, in itself, unravelled his whole life—how could she, a stranger, possibly have divined that, in his quiet, schoolmaster's being, joy had come first only when he stepped out and led chanting children across the veld to face the police! The message beyond that extraordinary prescience—that would enlarge upon it, confirm a language of shared reference between himself and the writer of the letter—was obviously something she assumed he would understand. Whoever it was who had said or written those three words must represent something particular not only to his present situation in prison but to a whole context of thought and action in which that situation was contained. The phrase didn't come from Shakespeare. Of that at least he thought he could be pretty sure although he could not reach up to the familiar shelf in the glass-fronted bookcase for verification. There were so many gaps in his education although it had seemed awesomely high to the old people who kept his teacher's training certificate framed in the kitchen where they could always see it.

The phrase filled, for a few days, the hours that were so hard to fill, left over from the disciplined programme he had set himself in his cell—deep-breathing exercises, running on the spot, study, reading. Prisoners were made to keep the bed-time of chickens and children. The cell lights were extinguished early and he had not yet succeeded in being advanced to the grade where he would have permission to keep his on for night study. Happy for battle. He lay on his bed in the dark and sounded over in his mind that phrase, so simple, so loaded, audacious, such a shocking, wild glorious juxtaposition of menace and elation, flowers and blood, people sitting in the sun and bodies dismembered by car bombs; the harmonized singing coming from somewhere in the cells, and the snarl of a police dog leaping at his face, once, in a crowd.

It was Hannah who wrote to him: knew how to say everything in three, let alone five hundred words.

He wrote and asked her to apply to the Commissioner of Prisons for a visit but she answered that she did not want to use up one of the quota of visits his family certainly needed.

Needing Hannah.

Oh Aila, Aila.

Why did Aila never speak? Why did she never say what he wanted her to say?

Family matters. He had never built the tree-house with Will and now the boy would be too old to be interested. Baby was being inducted into women's things; between her and her mother. At least he had been able to provide Baby with a room of her own for the process of becoming a woman.

Oh Aila, Aila.

For I don't know how long we believed my mother didn't know. He and I. We were so clever; he made us such a good team, a comic team. What a buffoon he made of me, his son, backward, stumbling along behind, aping his lies. Poor Tom to his Lear (I should have told him that, sometime, it's the sort of sign he'd appreciate that my education hasn't been wasted). I don't think he ever told direct lies, at least when I was around. When he went off to his woman he never said he was going to be somewhere else; he didn't have to, my mother respected the fact that a man doing underground political work (his full-time clandestine occupation once he came out of prison) cannot reveal his movements without involving and endangering his family.

The walls in what was meant to be a white man's house aren't like those in the house outside Benoni through which we couldn't help hearing the neighbours' quarrels and sexual groans. I don't know what went on—how he managed, without me, when they were alone in their bedroom. Their bedroom with the bed-head that extended at right angles like elbows, on either side of the bed, into two small cabinets, each with a lamp for which she had made a shade, on her side the alarm clock and lemon hand-cream pot, on his an overspill of newspapers, torch, aspirins in an ashtray Baby made him when she was small, book he was currently reading. I can only imagine. Invent from what I knew of her, what I knew of what he'd become. What did he think of to say to her while he was untying the shoelaces he'd tied when he got out of bed with that woman. Perhaps when you've been married a long time it's a shared burrow you scuttle along, every feature of it, for one, known by the other, every comment on the way anticipated by the other. The bedrooms, the nights, are like that. But he came and went by secret passages; he had things to say that he never could say. He must have had to watch every word.

And not only words. Once when I got into the back seat of the car I saw something strange on the floor. Everything; anything, alerted me to danger. My mother was getting into the front seat beside him; I waited until we'd driven off and they were deciding whether or not it was necessary to go to the bank before filling up with petrol, and I was able to pick up the object without them noticing. It was the dried head of a sunflower. Just the hard disc from which the seeds had fallen. Exactly like a round honeycomb. I don't know how it could have got there. Why. I only knew he would not be able to explain it to my mother; he did not need to explain anything to me, since the cinema, when he'd told me what to see and made clear what I was not to have seen.

My mother seemed to me as she always had been. Only, because of what I was in with, with him, and so afraid of—for her—there seemed to be some kind of space around her that kept us off—him and me—and that I held my breath for fear of entering. I didn't want to be in the room alone with her, either. But if I kept out of her way she would know there was something wrong, thinking in her innocence this would be something concerning me. And if I tried to be with her, to cover up that he wasn't—that might set her thinking, and I didn't want her to think, I didn't want my mother to think about him in any other but her gentle, trusting way, changed from the old times on the Reef simply by the special respect and privacy she taught us, by her example, he had earned by the pilgrimage through prison.

It's only since Baby cut her wrists that I've known my mother knew about him all the time. Well, not at the beginning (and even I don't know when exactly that was, whether the cinema was early on), but for a long time. She surely couldn't have known when, some weeks after my father was released, she and the wives of two other men who had been in prison with him decided to give a little New Year party for them and their supporters. When she and my father made up their list of people to invite she suggested Hannah Plowman and he wrote the name without comment, as if that were just another guest. It surely would not have been like my mother to have included that woman out of some sort of guile, a test of my father's reaction, of whether the woman herself would have the nerve to come to our house, now?

What a thought to have about my mother. But when you are lying, in your presence at the table, in every expression on your face, in everything you customarily do, going in and out to school, fooling quite naturally over the telephone with friends, you can't imagine anything that isn't devious, anymore.

The whole world is lying, fornicating and lying.

I was at that party. Baby and I were there, first helping with the preparation of food and rearranging the furniture. Baby, carrying a gift of snacks, went with him to our neighbours to tell them there'd be music until late that night; from the day we moved in, my mother had established good if distant relations with these whites. They didn't know about prison, about his political activities—one look at my mother and their Afrikaner fears that our skin meant dirty habits and noise they'd tolerate only from their own colour, were groundless. Everybody drank a lot—not my father, and my mother doesn't drink at all—and Baby was over-made-up and amazed all those people with her wild dancing. She was good, but showing off to the men. I danced a few times, after a beer, but I could feel myself getting angry every time some *tannie* said I was growing up handsome as my father, and I could see him, his face painted with the sweat of his hospitality, shining pride. I don't remember whether he danced with that woman. I can hardly picture her there at all. The moment when she arrived I was passing with a bottle of wine; it was the first time I'd seen her since the cinema and I'd thought about that face so much I could scarcely recognize it—this pink, scrubbed face, blonde hair springing back into shape like the coat of a wet dog, she must've washed it just before leaving for the party. She was smiling comradely at others' greetings, not at me. A moment when suddenly I didn't believe it: she had materialized, and his woman, that I had—like him, I know—always in my mind, vanished. My mother was signalling to me across the room at the group who were waiting for wine. There was a pretty comb in my mother's tight and shiny crown of hair, she was neat and beautiful, with the special care she took to dress for parties; she so enjoyed feeding people.

Baby cut her wrists when she spent a Saturday night with

a friend. She didn't even do it at home, where she had her own room. You think of details like that—crazy—when you don't have any explanation for what has happened. She didn't die. A mess in somebody else's bathroom and some stitches on the inner side of her wrists where you can see the freeways and bypasses of veins just under the skin. Baby is light-skinned, like my mother, not like my father and me. When she was in bed, repaired and sedated by Dr Jasood, for whom my mother worked, my mother came and sat down in the kitchen where I was reading the newspaper because I did not know what I should be doing; he, my father, had taken his briefcase that morning and said he had to be away that weekend. He had looked heavy-limbed, as if he had to make himself go; she must have believed there was some grave political crisis taking him away. She sat on the edge of her chair and looked at me as if she had known me her whole life, not just the span of mine which had begun in her body. As if I were her son and not her son. She said Dr Jasood had just told her it was evident to him that Baby took drugs, that her great liveliness was deep unhappiness. He had been at that party.

She said to me: —What can we do for her?—

The slight emphasis on 'we' gave away, all at once, that my mother knew about my father. That she knew—without knowing how—I knew. She discounted him—couldn't count on him, couldn't call on Sonny, now, wherever he was, even if he were to be hidden from her only round the corner, he was too far away. I understood. What could we do for my sister: a family that ours had become? And at the same moment it came to both of us: what Baby's 'deep unhappiness' that the doctor diagnosed was about.

So Baby knew, too. It was just that she managed differently what she knew. The hip, hyped style she flaunted on street corners (out of sight of my mother; I saw her), the flip and vulgar way she—brought up in the sound of my mother's quiet voice and the poetry of my father's Shakespeare—talked; the emotional outbursts over trifles, that my mother put down to the strain of having had my father in detention and on trial during the time when her menstrual cycle was being established; her manner of distancing herself from the childhood she and I had in common—all these were her attempts to manage.

When she had said to me, D'you expect him to be moping around like you?—was she trying to defend my father? Did she think, then, I didn't know, and probably would find out? Good god. Had she, all this time, been taking his part against my mother? As I tried to shield my mother against him? Female against female. Male against male. So what could we have done for her. To stop her cutting her wrists when she couldn't manage.

What could my mother have done for her.

What could I, her own brother, have done for her.

What a family he made of us.

Poor Tom's a-cold.

And now joy came often. After prison, where there was nothing to please the senses, where there was not even enough light to read and study by, came this bounty. It flowed from such slight stimulation. They met again for the first time at a house meeting. It was called a debriefing; those who had been inside related their experiences in resisting interrogation, intimidation, solitude, for the benefit of those who might sometime find themselves inside, and for individuals and organizations who sought the best means of supporting those on trial, of which there were many. She sat there with her knees broad apart under one of her long skirts, balancing on her lap the briefcase that served as a table for the notebook. She wrote earnestly. While others spoke, while Sonny spoke. When he paused, her gaze flashed up, narrow-blue, the blonde eyelashes met at the outer corners of her eyes as the lids pleated in a slight smile of encouragement.

Joy.

Hannah met Sonny for coffee, for further discussion. It was

possible—to take one's dark face into a coffee bar. And with a white woman companion; to pull out her chair for her and sit opposite her. It had been possible for some time, although, coming from a small town where such barriers fell more slowly if at all, and after two years in a segregated prison, Sonny still had a strange feeling: that he was not really there, a commonplace meeting of this kind was not happening to him. Then they drank coffee and she smoked and said, through the wraiths that undulated between them, he hadn't changed. In two years.
—You look very well. Fine. I thought that at the meeting.—

Her approval was sun on his face. He closed his eyes a moment as he smiled. —Aila was ready to feed me up. But as you can see. . .I put on weight inside. But not fat, really? I've never exercised so regularly in my life! Never had the time, before.—

—You look so much better than you did when I saw you in prison.—

—Ah well. . .detention is terrible. Much worse than a sentence, where you're sure when the end will come, even if it's years ahead—you know as well as I do.—

—Not as well as you do. Or anyone who's been inside. I know only from the consequences I find, if I get to see people.—

—I never want to live through that again.— It was a confession; both knew he might be detained once more.

—It was still great to find you in such good shape after two years of the other kind of inside. I suppose it wouldn't have been so striking if I'd seen you during that time.—

He suddenly found it easy to say to her, in her warming presence: —The letters were almost like visits, to me. In some ways, better. . .because you can read them over. A visit ends quickly. You and the other person never say what you want to say. Tell me—there's something I never asked you when I wrote back, I wanted to ask you like we are now. . .I mean, actually here. . . When you wrote that first time, you said something. . . you knew I'd come out happy for battle—

—Well you have, haven't you.— It was spoken simply, with admiration, no flattery.

There was a beat of silence.

In it, Sonny looked at her face without a decent reserve, as he had not freed himself to, before. Thick-fleshed, pearly-skinned modelling with slight scuffed redness here and there when her fingernail or some rough cloth had brushed it; the defining presence in the colour of the eyes, as the enamelled eyes brought to life the beige stone of colour plates in his book on the art of ancient Egypt. He was aware that there was saliva in that mouth and that blonde hair would have a scent of its own.

—'Happy for battle'.— He murmured it over. —I've wanted to ask where it comes from—I've wanted to find out who said it.— He laughed, excited at the idea: —To read what goes with it, for myself.— She watched him, enjoying his enthusiasm, her chin drawn back underlined by the flesh of her neck.

—Rosa Luxemburg, writing to Karl Kautsky. I'll bring you the book. Oh there's so much in her letters! I look forward to what you'll have to say—

Joy. That was what went with it. The light of joy that illuminates long talk of ideas, not the 60-watt bulbs that shine on family matters.

A long time had passed since his political activity had been confined to his own kind—the sub-division of blackness decided by law—and the single issue of removals. In prison he learnt more than the correspondence courses in local government Aila had arranged for him. He had been educated by his fellow political prisoners in the many tactics that evolve from principles of liberation, and how they are unceasingly extended, adapted and put into practice as each issue, however big or small, provides the opportunity, wherever and however. Where people lived in wretched conditions in a ghetto he was one who would be sent to help them set up a residents' association; when they understood that a rent boycott was a good way to protest, he would be among those to teach them how to organize the campaign. Where miners or municipal workers or workers in a sweet factory or brickyard were on strike, meetings in their support had to be held, T-shirts and stickers had to be seen on the streets until they provoked a ban, and even after, by those people who were prepared at least for a small defiance displayed bobbing against pectorals or breasts. Days of commemoration were arranged in honour of those who had died in uprisings, strikes, school and rent boycotts, street battles with police and army. And all this had to be done anonymously, clandestinely, hoping to escape the eyes of the police, on days and nights when it was better for no-one to know the whereabouts of an absent member of a family.

Sonny was not a major figure but he was frequently one of the principal speakers where it was possible to hold a public meeting in the semi-legality of some church or university. Hannah was always there. One day of freak cold in April (snow on the Drakensberg too early for winter) the jostle of the group with whom he was coming down from the platform of a city church hall converged with some rows of the audience leaving by a side door, and Sonny and Hannah found themselves drifted together. It was not unexpected, just lucky; he had seen her in the fifth row of seats. They left the hall into the cut of icy wind, into the sights of the police movie crew's cameras which await people who attend such gatherings as in other countries television crews wait after galas to record the emergence of film stars.

They turned the corner in the direction opposite to that being taken by the crowd. His face screwed up against the wind, he smiled at her. —So now we've had our snap taken.—

—D'you think they'll send us a print?—

He was high-shouldered against the cold and laughing; they paused a moment, didn't know where they were headed, along that street. He had on only a shirt and light jacket, but she always had garments to spare, it was her style. She took off her striped knitted scarf. —Please. Put it on, you'll catch pneumonia. Go on.—

It was all matter-of-fact. Comradely. —Thanks.—

He wound that scarf round his neck, tucked the fringed ends under his jacket. The scarf was warm with her warmth. In the gritty cold of the street, the sensation lay upon his nape.

Joy. From something so slight.

They were friends for some time before they were lovers. Before the ultimate joy of making love with someone who, too, is in the battle, for whom the people in the battle are her only family, her life, the happiness she understands—as he now does—is the only possible one. She told him afterwards she knew it would be hard for him to allow himself to become her lover; she was satisfied to be his friend so long as that satisfied him. But once they were lying naked together for the first time she made a solemn condition. —I wanted this. Yet I don't want it at all if it's going to replace our friendship with something else.—

He raised himself on his elbow in her bed to look at her with honesty that doesn't belong in bed. She thought he was about to take the opportunity to tell her right away that he loved his wife, his beautiful wife whom she had seen, visited, shared concern with for his welfare, and to tell her that she herself must know the strict limits of this share of him she was taking. He lay back again. —You are the only friend I've ever had.

That's what I feel. Now. That's what making love with you has told me.—

The immense reassurance sent her venturing deeper into the territory of intimacy. She wore a curio-store filigree ring, and she began cleaning the dried soap from its recesses with her thumbnail. —And when you first knew Aila. . .—

She didn't exclude Aila; it was one of the things he found remarkable about her, moving, that she did not want to oust Aila—from his mind, when they were together. She conceived of Aila as an equal, not an adversary defeated: she didn't refer to her as 'your wife'. He was filled with . . .gratitude, yes. No guilt, no concealment between them, with her; everything that had remained hungry, stunted, half-realized, streamed towards her through opened gates.

—We were so simple. You can hardly imagine. In Benoni's coloured township. Such simple people. And young. I think, you know, our understanding was too easy. The first layer. . . And you believe that's all, that's it. For myself, I'd say I didn't know what I needed.—

Needing Hannah. And now she was there, she had discovered Sonny for himself. She was a euphoria natural as a pulse beat with him wherever he went, in the house with him when he came home after he had left her, making him oblivious to the hostility of the boy (after the business of bumping into him at a cinema), making it possible to perform as a father and husband. A husband! Aila was not an emotionally demanding woman—imagine Aila! But she was accustomed to the quiet occurrence of conjugal love-making, that as the children grew up had become less and less frequent, more peripheral to loving. When a daughter begins to show breasts and a son's voice begins to be mistaken, on the phone, for his father's, there comes a kind of reversal of the clandestinity courting couples have to practise in the house of their parents: the long-married now feel an inhibition about making love in the presence—separated only by the bedroom walls—of children who themselves are now capable of feeling the same sexual desires. Of course, this never would be said openly, between Aila and him; but it must have been there, and it meant she didn't expect—she didn't expect *him* to expect—to make love to her more than occasionally. And this periodicity surely had been extended by the two years in prison. It did not mean there was no physical contact between them. On the contrary, once in the dark, wordless, Aila always moved into his shelter, against his chest or round his back, and neither was roused by the warmth of his genitals against her or the shape of her breasts in his hands. They would fall asleep; fall away from each other only in sleep, as they had done for years, as they cleaned their teeth before bed and she creamed her hands.

The first time he had to make love to his wife after he had begun to make love to Hannah—it was not so much that too much time had gone by, but that he quickly learned, as a novice deceiver, that to avoid this was the surest way to give himself away—he trembled with sorrow and disgust at himself after he withdrew from her body. The caresses were an easy performance, rehearsed in the habit of marriage, without feeling, dutiful to please Aila, but the uncontrollable animal thrill of his orgasm was horrible. He wanted to get up out of that bed and house and go to Hannah. Shut out everything, himself, blotted against the being of Hannah. And every now and then, in the carefully arranged and guarded life he was managing, when he judged it was time to approach Aila again—to pretend to want poor Aila, oh my god—the act drained him, in shame. Sometimes he felt a final spurt of anger, towards Aila, sperm turned to venom.

For months the most precious aspect of his new life with

Hannah was that it was clandestine. Like underground political life, it had nothing to do with the everyday. They owned one another because their times together were shared with no-one. They could not even be in anyone else's thoughts in any way that could reach out and touch them, because no-one knew where they were when they were together. To Sonny, who never before had used the commonplace deceptions—the meetings he was supposed to be attending, the visit to Pretoria she was supposed to be making in the course of her work—these were a kind of magic that made them invisible to the ordinary world he had inhabited all his life. Something he never would have thought possible. When he and she found themselves in the same public company at the same time, it was—to them—part of their wonderful spell of intimacy that there shouldn't be the slightest possibility that anyone else present should know of the secret knowledge of each other only those two, themselves, had. They were so successful that now and then somebody would introduce them: I don't think you've met. . .this is. . .

Sonny and Hannah: presented each to the other, as strangers, by a third person. What secret pleasure, to conceal the desire between them that this titillated! Sonny had revealed to him how part of the need in his life had been of a sense of erotic fun. To leave, separately, a gathering where each had given full attention to serious decisions (for the roused state of an ecstatic love affair, in men and women mutually dedicated to a political ideal and battle, heightens their concentration and application in relation to these) and fifteen minutes later be undressing each other: what an exquisite range of changing responses such an afternoon expanded! How much that he never would have known he was capable of experiencing, never ever. That it needed the secret (secret everywhere) presence of this woman, this ample girl—she was younger than she looked—to make possible for him. For months when they talked after love-making it was of the remote places they would like to go together. Islands off this or that continent. Forests in the mountains. Nothing but gulls or owls. Like all lovers, they did not know they were trying to prolong by transformation into words, into the future tense, the physical illusion of personal freedom that fades as the lulled and sated senses come back and will relay the knowledge of time passing with traffic: work, loss, hunger and pain, pacing out there in the street: other people.

But even if the islands and forests were only post-coital reveries, they had Hannah's cottage, Hannah's bed, which was unlike any other bed Sonny had ever known, not only because of what passed between her and him there but because it was not a bed at all—a very big mattress laid directly on the floor. He thought when he first saw it that it meant she was not properly settled in; or perhaps it was some Japanese idea. There were so many tastes, he, coming from his background, did not know about. Futon? she prompted, and laughed. Ah, no, just that she liked to be close to the wood of the floor, the earth beneath it. And how right she was. How unnecessary to have little bedside cabinets with hand-woven lampshades you had to be careful not to knock over in your sleep. Under the softness of the mattress only the law of gravity itself.

If his need of Hannah was terrible—in a magnificent way—then there was no need of anything or anyone else. She knew a lot of poetry—his Shakespeare was a poor stock, compared with hers. She taught him a love-poem he had never heard of, didn't know it was something done to death everyone who had taken a university first-year course in English literature could reel off. It described perfectly those months when Hannah's one room, for them, was 'an everywhere'.

This perfect isolation existed while Sonny and Hannah

seemed to themselves to be getting away with the impossible. Its very intensity was granted on the condition that it could not last. Everything outside was ready to rupture it. Circumstance, conscience—there was a rictus of dire fear, to admit it—might take her from him, him from her, any day. But months went by. Their concealment of each other from the world continued to be successful. And now they passed into the second stage of the syndrome that Sonny, never having had the experience before, did not recognize. The fascination in living something totally removed from domestic love with its social dimensions of ordinary shared pleasures among other people gave way to dissatisfaction that they could not do these ordinary things together. For these belonged to Aila, Aila and the children. He could visit friends with Aila, and have her sitting there talking trivialities in the usual corner with the women while he was in a discussion at the other end of the room, a discussion Hannah would have been taking part in, they would have been contributing to together, complementing each other's ideas. He could go to a play (since they had moved to the city he had encouraged his family to take the opportunity to enjoy black theatre) with Aila and his son and daughter but there would not come from them the kind of comment, challenging his own thoughts, he would have had if Hannah had been with him. And there grew in him, in her—he knew it was against all sense and reason—a defiant desire *to be seen to belong together*. To show each other off. They didn't admit it, but knew it was there, as they knew everything about one another while in their chosen isolation.

Once they were taken by an obstinate, irresistible hankering to see a film together. An ordinary thing like that, which any other couple could do. Instead of spending the afternoon making love, they went across the city to a cinema complex in a suburb where neither knew anyone, a suburb of rich white people who never attended protest meetings or knew, had seen in flesh and blood, anyone who had been a political prisoner. And there, of course—they might have known it. The one encounter they never could have envisaged, something utterly against all probability. They walked out of the dark cinema straight into the afternoon glare and his son. They showed themselves off; to his son.

The instinct was to go to her cottage and hide. Sonny was silent, his eyes concealed from Hannah, as he could do, drawing his thick eyebrows down around their deep darkness. She was afraid. But he did not leave her, he did not say you have destroyed my family. She saw how he had changed; how she had changed him without knowing. They talked of the Italian film and not about the boy. He embraced her passionately before he left her in the early evening and went back to his family; he must already have made up his mind, calmly, how he would deal with his son. He said only: —Don't worry. Not about Will, either.—

And however it was that he managed, it was clear, later, that the boy never said anything—to his mother, to anyone.

—He didn't mention it to you?—

—No. It's as if it never happened.—

All Hannah said was: —That can't be.—

The room was not an everywhere because it could not contain the commonplaces of being together, the boring humdrum pleasures, the very state of daily deadened life their relationship escaped and was superior to, the state—of marriage?

From the surety of having everything, they had changed to wanting everything. Even that. They began to make more little excursions outside her bed and the cottage. She had a friend who was an absentee farmer. They went to picnic on the farm.

At the beginning of the drive the freeway took them past the Reef town in whose area for his kind he had grown up, taught school, shopped trailing his children on Saturday mornings. . .as he turned his head to watch glint past the lake made of pumped water from the mines, the buff yellow slopes of abandoned dumps, he had the tingling feeling of the unaccountable familiarity of a foreign country. She promised him fields of sunflowers because he liked so much the Van Gogh reproduction that was stuck up in her tiny kitchen among the drawings made by black children. But she had mistaken the season. The sunflower fields were a vast company of the dead, with black faces bowed. She swung against him in contrition as they walked through the veld; they laughed and kissed. He got splinters of fibre in his hands as he picked a dead flower for her, a souvenir.

He had such good alibis. Like all lovers, they longed to sleep together for a whole night, nights. Sonny could be absent from home without explanation, and the old restrictions of colour were abolished in most hotels and resorts. So they were free; once they spent two days of this kind of freedom somewhere in the Eastern Transvaal, and even stood among white Sunday families with grannies and squealing children, watching the young hatch on a crocodile farm. After intervals imposed by Sonny's political obligations—and neither he nor she ever neglected their work—and when another kind of absence from home could be justified by these demands, they went away together, even if sometimes only for a night. He had promised her a whole weekend again, and he managed it, not without some embarrassing lying to be done, to his comrades—a pretence, to them as well, that he would be incommunicado because of some contacts to be made about which he couldn't talk. When he left his home on Saturday morning he had, for the first time, instead of euphoria inside him, a surly unease; there was a moment, as his son stood back as he passed him in the passage, when he almost turned and put down that briefcase (briefcase!) and didn't leave. But the moment was forgotten as soon as he left the house. In a rondavel resort among orange blossom near Rustenburg Sonny and Hannah were unspeakably happy. People say one could die for such happiness, but one also could kill for it, kill all other claims on oneself by people who have failed to bring it about. The scent of orange blossom was air itself, night and day, every drawn breath like the manifest emanation of private happiness, the wafting secretion of their one body, joined in love-making.

When Sonny came back on Sunday night he found his daughter had cut her wrists.

That didn't put an end to it. What Baby did that time.

We were sitting in the kitchen, my mother and I—as if we were back in the old place at Benoni—when we heard him come home. We heard the briefcase put down and the creak of his soles, we were so quiet because Baby was asleep down the passage with her bandaged wrists laid outside the sheet. My mother stood up and went to stop him coming into the kitchen where I was. I heard her soft voice telling him—and then suddenly, high:—Don't!—as his tread broke out hard and fast along the passage.

He came back slowly, and into the kitchen. He had seen my sister but not wakened her. My mother was sitting there again. I was with her, I had been with her ever since it happened, he had to face me. And I to face him. He wandered to the fridge and poured himself his glass of water. I wanted to laugh and knock it out of his hand. He stood there drinking and his head moved, he was not exactly shaking it, it moved vaguely like the involuntary movement of an old man. But it's no good putting on a performance for me, he was not a poor distraught old father, he was only too strong and healthy, a fucker. What could my father say? If Baby had died on Saturday he wouldn't have been there. Couldn't be reached. He made sure of that. Nobody knew where he was. My mother was the one who saw the blood. And I.

—Will there be scars.—

That was all he could dare to say.

And it didn't stop him, it didn't stop them. It only made me cruel. That Sunday night. I wanted to go to my room and take out from behind my old soccer boots and roller skates—kid's things you never throw away—the dead head of a sunflower, and fling it at him.

He never tried to explain anything. He no longer cared enough for us to feel the need—to try and make us understand what had happened to him. Oh he was shattered that night and there was no-one to help him. The three of us were in the kitchen together, and he was alone. I had thought—had I?—he would break down and confess, we would weep, it would be all over, he would take my mother in his arms, she would take him in her arms. 'Will there be scars': that's all. Our presence, my mother's and mine, drove him away alone to the sitting-room, that he and my mother had been so proud of, a decent place for her, at last. He sat there alone in the dark. She put milk on the stove to heat and I watched her make cocoa and take it in there, to him. I don't know if he said anything to her. She seemed to know he wouldn't eat. Still so considerate of him, my mother; still so respectful of this husband and father who had gone to prison for the future of our kind.

Baby was his favourite child—I always knew that—his daughter was his darling, his beauty, even though he quoted Shakespeare to me and wanted me to bring him glory by growing up to be a writer just to please *him*. But although the child he used to be so in love with had now wanted, even if only for a mad moment, to die, and no-one dared get her to say why, he couldn't come back to her. He couldn't stay in the house with us. When my sister was 'better'—what she had done to herself became an illness or accident that had happened to her, that was the only way we could deal with it in our house—she and my mother and father discussed what she wanted to *do*. All was resolved as a matter of the right occupation. And he was the one to know all about guidance, career guidance, he was once a schoolteacher. Her whole future before her etc.; the usual parents' stuff, as if they were the usual parents. My sister fell in with the spirit of the performance. I heard her say it, Oh she was sick of studying. She wanted to take a job. For a while; she'd study again later. (This thrown in, I know, for darling daddy and his old ambitions for his children to be useful, therefore educated, citizens.) She knew my mother wouldn't believe her, my mother knew she would find some other life, unplanned for her. He knew, surely, that something had driven her out; he didn't stay to find out why. He fled the house again with that briefcase—did my father keep a toothbrush in it or was he so thick with that woman that he used hers?

And what I couldn't get over was how my sister made it easy for him. Perhaps she did it for my mother's sake, too, but the fact is it had the effect of letting him off the misery he was sentenced to those first few days; she made it possible for that to be shed with her bandages. She appeared with brightly-painted wooden bracelets on each wrist—African artifacts. He didn't have to see the scars. She has beautiful straight shiny hair, like my mother's, and she had it frizzed; in her 'convalescence' she went about the house, one of my old shirts tied under her naked breasts, midriff showing, her Walkman hooked to a wide belt and plugged into her ears, moving her hips and head to a beat no-one else could hear. It was tacitly accepted that these were signs of a natural girlish independence; she wanted to earn her own living, she had offered.

She talked to *me* about that Saturday night as if it were some particularly daring party escapade to boast about. I couldn't see how she'd want to; she should have talked to *him*, really, it was his affair just like his other affair. She was determined to bring it up with me. —You never open your mouth, but I suppose you wonder why anyone'd do such a stupid thing.—

—Like what?— But she knew I was stalling; and she didn't want to come right out with it, either—'trying to kill myself'.

—I'd had a bust-up with Marcia, she's always so nosy, like into everything, sticky fingers getting in my hair. I don't know why I let her pester me to spend the night, anyway. And the crowd that turned up at her place because they knew her folks were away, Jimmy and Alvin and that lot. I can't stand them, really. She said Jackie and Dawn and them (how many years had my father spent trying to get his Baby to drop her peers' bad grammar) were coming but she's a liar, she did it to persuade me to stay with her, because they never came. What was there to do but smoke. So I was rather stoned, and on top of it, when I wanted to get away from them and their lousy yakking and yelling and dancing like a pack of drunk wildebeest, there was a couple busy on the bed. They hadn't even shut the door.—

I nodded and kept my head turned away. She saw I didn't want to be presented with this version, this performance—another one, in our house.

—The bathroom was the only place to get away.—

The packet of Gillette Sword, the dagga and the self-pity. I wish I didn't have so much imagination, I wish that other people's lives were closed to me.

—They just made me sick. Sick of them.—

Now I knew what Baby was really telling me. I knew who 'they' were; known to us both, not the crowd at Marcia's place on a Saturday night who were not my crowd.

She wanted some response to help her inveigle me—her innocent dumb brother—into an attitude she wanted me to adopt. She was trying buddy-buddy with me.

I only listened; she had to say herself what she hoped I would. —I suppose I could have gone home. It's not far. But you can imagine the fuss, with Ma, me arriving at two in the morning when she thinks I'm tucked up giggling in bed with a bosom friend. That's the problem with not having your own place. Living with the family. Parents, okay. Even the best parents in the world, we're different, not like them. Once you're grown up you've got to forget about their life. Let them have it, it's their business and you've got your own life to live. You have to have a place.— She looked at me to see if she was succeeding. —Can't go running to them, they've got a life of their own.—

Now she chattered away from what she had got said, gabbling about the flat in another grey area she and Jackie and Dawn and two Indian fellows, probably, were going to share, they'd take her in as soon as she got a job, and I understood what she'd been telling me when she was supposed to be confessing why she wanted to die on a Saturday night among strangers. Baby was covering up for him, again. My father. She was warning me off: his life. Poor Baby. His Baby, still.

He was able to forget so quickly.

She encouraged him—she's just like him, after all, although she looks like my mother, she's devious and lying as he is. She found a job with an insurance agent (I think one of the fellows who were sharing the flat and perhaps she was sleeping with him) and she would come flying into the house when it suited her, bringing flowers or a ripped hem for my mother to mend, hooking an arm round my father's neck and kissing his ear, if he happened to be there, and calling, if he was not—as she left, her mouth full of some of my mother's goodies she was carrying away: —Don't forget to give Pa my love!— She was pretty and talkative and amusing, mimicking and laughing and begging for gossip about family and friends she never saw, any more.

I don't know whether my mother ever told him what Dr Jasood said about her animation. Her vulgarity splashed all over my mother. Yet she said to me more than once —As long as Baby's busy and happy— My mother, too, was saying something else: that since nothing could be done about Dr Jasood's diagnosis of my sister's state, my mother was thankful she was proving resilient enough to divert it to some purpose of her own.

You would have thought nothing had happened. We settled into an uncanny sort of normality, an acceptance of the rearrangement of our lives to *his* convenience. I know for a fact that several times he took my mother to gatherings at the house of some white people where that woman of his was also present. My mother had to sit down and eat with her.

And I have been to where she lives. Where he goes to her. He sent me. Could you believe it?

There was someone who always knew where Sonny was.

The Security Police. He knew that, Hannah knew that. It did not count as witness, as intrusion. The Security Police work secretly as any love affair.

A man who has been convicted of a crime against the State will continue to be watched as long as his life or the State that convicted him lasts; whichever endures the longer. A woman who associates with such a man will be watched. The third presence in the lovers' privacy is the Security Police; anonymous, unseen: a condition of the intimacy of political activists. The men who had taken Sonny away and locked him up in detention, knew. Knew about him. Were in it with him. It was not in their interest to blow this kind of cover. If he had been an important revolutionary figure they (easily) might have arranged with a country hotel to bug the rondavel, and leaked tapes to the Sunday press to smear his character. They could have got the Minister to place a ban on his movements. But they did not, because while he was without restriction, running to the rendezvous of his lady-love, he might also lead them to those of his underground associates still unknown to them.

After what nearly happened that Saturday night (this was the only way he could allow himself to formulate it) Sonny realized that someone else ought to know where he could be found. In case something actually happened. There in the house. But to whom could he go? Whom could he tell, if my daughter is bleeding to death in the bathroom, fetch me from this address? If Aila collapses in that kitchen, if he—Will—gets electrocuted fixing a light-plug, call me from Hannah's bed, close to the earth. He would be driving alone—once it was to the ghettos of the Vaal Triangle, where the community organizations' rent boycott was becoming a major campaign, he was thinking how best to respond to their problems of spontaneous violence against corrupt councillors—and, suddenly, he would have an impulse to lift his hands from the steering-wheel. Let go. The car skidding, careering, turning over and over, taking him. He would gain control of himself in a sweat. Had not let go; had not let his mind swerve back to what might have happened that Saturday night.

Hannah did not know about these moments—it was perhaps the first thing ever he kept from her—but she had the instinct, for her own protection, that he ought to be encouraged to talk about his daughter—Baby. The very name of the girl came awkwardly from him: Hannah saw he was hearing it now as he imagined she must—silly, sugary, cheap lower-class sentimentality of the ignorant poor in the ghetto of a small town where you couldn't even use the library. It embarrassed him to realize, indeed, how stupidly, crassly, the substitute for a name was stuck upon the grown girl. The woman; a woman, now, like Aila and like Hannah. —D'you remember her at all, dancing, the night you were at my house for a party?—

—Of course.— How could she not remember every detail of that party, the second time only that she had seen in their own home the family to which he belonged by right, and when he was still, just out of prison, a materialization she couldn't take her eyes off.

—The party the women arranged, music and so on.—

—Yes, you invited me. . .—

—I saw the fellows looking at her, you know. . .the way men look at women, and I looked too and saw her little round backsides, the cheeks, riding up and down in that skirt or dress, whatever it was, and nipples showing under thin stuff as she moved—

—And how fantastically she moved!— Hannah wanted to coax him to laugh with her and accept lightly what he was innocently confessing, that he had been sexually stirred by his daughter.

—That little girl who used to make me ashtrays out of backyard mud although I never smoked. She was a lovely young woman. Even though I say it, she was beautiful, hey, and a lovely expression, too. So full of spirit.—

—But you're talking about her as if she's dead!— Hannah was distressed, strangely laughing. —Sonny, she's alive. It's not 'was'! She is, she is!—

What would I do if I did not have you, Sonny said to Hannah when he was safe, still inside her after love-making—she liked to keep him there, held by her broad thighs that trembled when she walked naked about the room. And tranquilly, because it was all one, in them, they turned from caresses to worried discussion about the action of police *agents provocateurs* among church groups in the rent boycotts.

There was Will. What would he have done if there hadn't been Will. Only to Will could he find some way of indicating where he could be found if something happened. Like the Security Police, Will would be in on it; Will already was in on the mystery of his absences. Will could not evade being drawn further in.

Sonny had no choice. *Needing Hannah.*

I went on the motorbike. I had it by then. They gave it to me for my birthday. He said to me with that smile of a loving parent concealing a fine surprise, you can get a licence at sixteen now, can't you. So I knew he was going to buy me a bike. I never asked for it but they gave it to me. With the latest, most expensive helmet for my safety; he must have had to promise my mother that.

I went with the helmet and chin-guard and goggles hiding my face. You can't see the place from the street, where he goes. Dogs at the gate, and a black gardener had to come to let me in; I suppose they wag their tails for someone who comes often, is well known to them by his own scent. There was a big house but that's not where he goes. She lives in a cottage behind trees at the end of the garden. Maybe there's even a private entrance from there I didn't know about, he didn't like to tell me. All open and above-board through the front entrance.

He must have told her, she was expecting me. Oh it's Will, isn't it—as if the helmet and stuff prevented her from recognizing me, from remembering the cinema that time. It also playfully implied, determined to be friendly, that I was rude, not taking the helmet off. So I did. So she could see it was me, Will, yes. I gave her whatever it was he'd sent me with. It was a package, books or something, he told me 'Miss Plowman' needed urgently. —You're the family Mercury now, with that wonderful machine of yours—off you go, son, but don't tear along like a Hell's Angel, hey.— A perfect performance in front of my mother.

This was where he came. It must be familiar as our house to him, where we live now and where we lived when we were in Benoni, because our house is where we are, our furniture, our things, his complete Shakespeare, the smells of my mother's cooking and the flowers she puts on the table. But this isn't like a house at all; well, all right, a cottage, but not even any kind of place where you'd expect a white would live. The screen door full of holes. Bare floor and a huge picture like spilt paint that dazzles your eyes, a word-processor, hi-fi going with organ music, twisted stubs in ashtrays, fruit, packets of bran and wheatgerm, crumpled strings of women's underthings drying on a radiator—and a bed, on the floor. There was the bed, just a very big wide mattress on the floor, covered with some cloth with embroidered elephants and flowers and bits of mirror in the design—the bed, just like that, right there in the room where anybody can walk in, the room where I was standing with my helmet in my hand.

So now I know.

Who is Hannah Plowman?

Not only his father's blonde. Not the woman cast by the adolescent son as an excuse for sulky defensiveness, disdain—and jealousy. Not the fancy-woman fellow-traveller of a coloured with a subversive record, known to the Security Police. The dossier of an individual's conscious origins is really all that is sure, and it goes back only so far as the individual's own living memory. Hers begins with her maternal grandfather, and she knew, at least, that she was named for his Quaker mother although he was an Anglican—a missionary in one of the British Protectorates on the borders of the country. After some minor members of British royalty had come to see the Union Jack lowered and the flag of independence raised, the missionary stayed on in his retirement among the old black *baputi** whose souls he was convinced he had saved and whose language had become the one he most used. He did a little translating of

*Clergymen.

religious works for the local Sunday schools and he reminisced with old Chiefs. His brother had gone to South Africa and become chairman of a finance corporation, with directorships in mining, maize products and the packaging industry. The brother paid for Hannah's education in England when she outgrew the village mission school she attended with the local black children; for her mother had studied nursing in what was then Rhodesia, and come back to the mission pregnant with what turned out to be a girl child. Hannah was told her father had been a soldier, and since she knew soldiers got killed in wars, presumed he was dead. Later she found out he was a Bulawayo policeman who already had a wife. Hannah's mother married a Jewish doctor she met when she was theatre sister at the mission hospital taken over by the independent government, and went to live in Cape Town. Until her mother emigrated with him to Australia, Hannah spent part of her school holidays in the grandfather's mud-brick and thatch house at the mission, and part in the Cape Town suburb among her step-father's collection of modern paintings.

An individual life, Hannah's, but one that has followed the shifts in power of the communities into which she was born. So that what she really is, is a matter of 'at that time' and 'then'; qualifications and uncertainties. Her step-father would have paid to send her to the Michaelis School of Art, since she showed such intelligent ignorance when studying his pictures, but she hankered after her late-afternoon wanderings in the mission village that had become the outskirts of a town, talking with the young men she had always known, now wearing T-shirts distributed by the brewery, the girls she had played with, now coming back from shift as cleaners at the Holiday Inn. And when she was with her grandfather and he suggested she would be happy qualifying to teach at what had been her old school, founded by him, the idea settled over her in dismay. In Cape Town she had met young people, university students, sons and daughters of comfortable, cultivated white households like her step-father's, who were working with trade unions, legal aid bureaux, community arts programmes, human rights projects in squatter camps—while she would be teaching children just enough to fit them to bottle beer and clean the dirt rims off tourists' bath-tubs. She was not a dilettante but not socially programmed, so to speak; had to choose where to place herself more realistically than in her childish broad sense that all Southern Africa was home: there were boundaries, treaties, barbed wire, heavily-armed border posts.

South Africa is a centripetal force that draws people, in the region, not only out of economic necessity, but also out of the fascination of commitment to political struggle. The fascination came to her in the mud-brick and thatch of the mission, the dust that had reddened her Nordic hair and pink ears: from her grandfather's commitment to struggle against evil in men, for God. For her the drive was to struggle against it for man—for humans. (She was a feminist, careful of genders. But she wouldn't have thought of it as 'evil'—too pretentious, too sanctimonious for her, though not in her grandfather.) She worked to that end in a number of organizations around South Africa. Some were banned, and she would have to move on to a similar socially-committed job elsewhere. She was married for a while to a young lawyer who became clinically depressed by the government's abrogations of the rule of law and persuaded her to emigrate; he went ahead to London but there recovered and fell in love with someone else, she never joined him. The hi-fi equipment, records and books were shipped to him. She took only the mattress from the king-size bed (because with that you could live anywhere) and a painting by a follower of Jackson

Pollock her step-father had given her when he packed up for Australia. The trusts and foundations that employed her paid very little, out of a dependency on charitable grants from abroad. Yet you cannot be called poor if you are poor by choice—if she had wanted to, she could have been set up in a boutique or public relations career by the branch of her grandfather's family who had 'made good' not in the way he had shown her.

The nature of work she did develops high emotions. It arises from crises. It deals only with disruption, disjunction—circumstances in people's lives that cannot be met with the responses that serve for continuity. To monitor trials is to 'monitor' the soaring and plunging graph of feelings that move men and women to act, endangering themselves; the curves and drops of bravery, loss of nerve, betrayal; cunning learnt by courage, courage learnt by discipline—and others which exceed the competence of any graph to record, would melt its needle in the heat of intensity: the record of people who, receiving a long jail sentence, tell the court they regret nothing; of those who, offered amnesty on condition that they accept this as 'freedom' in place of the concept for which they went to prison, choose to live out their lives there. Such inconceivable decisions are beyond the capacity of anyone who does not make one. The spirit's shouldering of the world, as Atlas's muscles took on the physical weight of the world. Such people cannot be monitored. But knowing them and their families, who have this abnormal—Hannah, speaking of it once with Sonny, corrects herself—no, not abnormal, can't use that word for it—that divine strength expands the emotional resources of an ordinary individual (like Hannah) even in grasping that it *does exist*.

Association with prisoners of conscience is a special climate in which this heightening infloresces. Listening in courts while the sacrifice of their individual lives for man against evil slowly is distorted by the law in volumes of recorded words, police videos, in the mouths of State witnesses, into an indictment for having committed evil; touching the hands of the accused across the barrier while they joke about their jailers; visiting the wives, husbands, parents, children, the partners in many kinds of alliances broken by imprisonment—all this extended Hannah's feelings in a way she would not have known possible for anyone. In love. She was in love. Not as the term is understood, as she had been in love, at twenty-three, with her lawyer, and they had ceased to love. *In* love, a temperature and atmospheric pressure of shared tension, response, the glancing contact of trust in place of caresses, and the important, proud responsibility of doing anything asked, even the humblest tasks, in place of passionate private avowals. A loving state of being.

It was in this state that she developed the persistence, the bold lies, the lack of scruple in threatening international action to pressure prison authorities to allow her to see detainees. And it was in this state she understood her mission to visit their families.

She drove a Volkswagen Beetle through the battleground streets of Soweto to find old people who didn't know whether to trust her, she was received in the neat segregated suburbia of Bosmont and Lenasia by women who didn't know how they were going to keep up payments on the glossy furniture, she lost herself in the squatter camps where addresses didn't exist and the only routes marked in the summer muck of mud and rot were those rutted by the wheelbarrows of people fetching their supplies of beer from the liquor store on the main road. The house in the lower-class white suburb into which one of the detainees had moved his family illegally had a twirly wrought-iron gate and a plaster pelican, no doubt left behind by the white owners as the shed cast of any creature exactly reveals itself. The wife was beautiful and correct, composed, stockings and high heels—it had the effect of making Hannah feel not intrusive but unnecessary, and talking away to cover this up. The wife kept listening sympathetically, making Hannah's confusion worse. This quiet woman apparently was accustomed to being obeyed. There was tea ordered to be brought in by a daughter in whom the mother's beauty was reproduced as pert prettiness. A schoolgirl who worked at weekends; and the wife had a good job, she politely made it perfectly clear they wanted no-one to enter the arrangements they themselves had made to manage without the father of the family. The mother, with her fine, slow smile (what perfect teeth for a middle-aged woman; Hannah's were much repaired at only thirty) put a hand on the shoulder of an overgrown-looking boy who had kept Hannah standing a moment, in suspicion, before letting her in. —My son's the man of the house now.—

A house that smelled of stale spiced cooking. On the wall a travelling salesman's Kahlil Gibran texts. But in the glass-fronted bookcase a surprising little library, not only the imitation-leather-bound mail-order classics usually to be found as a sign of hunger for knowledge, and not only the Marx, Lenin, Fanon, Gandhi and Nkrumah, Mandela and Biko always to be found as a sign of political self-education, but Kafka and D. H. Lawrence, she noticed in glimpses aside, while talking, talking, talking like that.

She had been there once again. But that was after. It was when the house was invaded by laughter and music, all that it had been the first time thrust aside, as the furniture was for dancing. The loving state of being in which she had sat with the beautiful wife, the daughter, the son, was also thrust away, terrifyingly transformed into something else: passionate awareness of the ex-prisoner host. The first time he and she made love she had felt a strange threat of loss in the midst of joy, and had tried to explain it to herself by attempting to put it, in another way, to him. He didn't really understand; but sexual love has the matchless advantage of the flesh as reassurance for anything, everything, for the moment. The body speaks and all is silenced.

So everything in that house she remembered from that first day was cherished because it was part of him. It was all she had of that part of him she could not really know, which she had transformed into a lover. It was what both he and she discounted between them, in her room.

She would have liked to be the older confidante of the girl (looked as if she needed someone) and the adult-who-is-not-a-parent, so useful to an adolescent, in the life of the boy, his son. Even the pseudo-philosophy of the cheap framed texts became tender evidence of the qualities of the man who had left behind him fake consolations of uplift taken by the powerless and poor. She put away for safe-keeping her first day's vision of his house like a lock of hair from the head of the child that has become the man.

It's part of the commonplace strategy of adultery to appear in company where both wife and mistress are present. It's accepted as merely a way of hiding, by displaying there's nothing to hide. But Sonny was so inexperienced, he did not know how to suppress, in himself, the real urge discovered to underlie such confrontations. He learned they were not brought about by any social inevitability it would look suspicious to avoid; they were not arranged to reassure and protect Aila or to ensure that if he and Hannah were by chance to be seen in public together it would appear an innocent encounter within a mutual political circle. Giving his view on how to get the boycotting youth back into school without compromising their political clout, he had the attention of a lawyer and two educationists, comrades on the National Education Crisis Committee, when somewhere behind him he heard mingled in group conversation the two voices he knew best in the world. Two birds singing in his emotion: he did not hear the chatter of the other women, the cheeping of sparrows. He became eloquent, his nostrils round with conviction, he had never expressed himself more forcefully than while, the first time, instead of keeping the two women fastidiously apart within him, he possessed both at once. The exaltation was the reverse of his fear of Aila finding out.

Later, alone, desolated, shamed, he understood. He sought, even contrived, ways of appearing with his wife in houses where his other woman would be a guest.

The sexual excitement of bringing the two women together entered him as a tincture, curling cloudy in a glass of water.

She reminds me of pig. Our ancestors didn't eat pig.

A few bright hairs look like filaments of glass embedded in the pink flesh round her mouth.

I have terrible thoughts. About her. About my father with her. I imagine them. . .could I ever think of my mother like that! I'm sick with myself. What he's made me think about.

What'd he send me there for? I keep going over the place. What I saw, what he made me see. Her pants and bras on the radiator. The bed, right there where you walk in. Don't they know about privacy? People like her, so dedicated to our freedom, worming their way to get to see our prisoners, standing on our doorsteps. I should never have let her pass. Stupid kid that I was. The man of the house. They bring you up to be polite and then put you in situations they didn't tell you could ever happen.

What did he send me there for? I keep thinking about it and as I change, get older—every month makes a difference when you're young and finding out about yourself—my answers change. Forbidden pig. Pink pig. I've thought what he wanted was to mix me up in it. What men feel. It suits him, now, to think of me as a man like himself. Who wants to fuck. Who feels guilty about it; he *counts* on me, a kid like me, being guilty of having these mad wild feelings. When I was really a kid he told me just the opposite: I tried to hide the signs of masturbation on my underpants and he told me, son, there's nothing to feel guilty about—what I did to myself was natural. Now he wants me to see her, see what he enjoys and be guilty with him of what he feels because I understand it in myself. A bond. *Tied.* Father and son more like good buddies.

That's what I've thought.

And then again—I've come to understand something else. I think I have. It's come to me from my body, yes. (If he believed I'd learn from my own body, he's right, there.) I think what he wants is to show off his virility. To me. The proof of his virility. That clumsy blonde. The bed where *he* does it, the highbrow music *he's* doing it to, the show-off picture on the wall *he* sees while he's doing it, the underwear she takes off those places where *he* can touch her—he, not me, not me. (Not I—he would correct me.) He sent me to her to show me it's not my turn yet. He's not moving aside, off women's bodies, for me. I needn't think, because I'm tall as he is and I've got the same things between my legs he's got, and (the *tannies* don't let me forget it) I'm growing up 'handsome as he is', I haven't even been let off those bloody thick eyebrows that make his eyes so sexy—I shouldn't think he needs to give over to me. The old bull still owns the cows, he's still capable of serving his harem, my mother and his blonde.

I don't think my father knows any of these things about himself. Only I know, only I.

When the schoolteacher led the children across the veld he did so on his own impulse and responsibility. That naïvety was no longer possible. —There's no freedom in working for freedom.— He could say it to Hannah, and they both laughed. There was pride and scepticism in the laughter. You couldn't say such things to Aila; between Aila and him was the old habit of simple reverence for living useful lives. He had to keep it up, as other things had to be kept up, before her. Why, when he was in prison she evidently had not disturbed her habits, somehow carried on as if nothing had happened; now she treated his way of life—its structures clandestine, its activities directed by Committees and Desks, its dangers constant—as if he had been still the schoolmaster and received a posting to a new school. An enemy of the State: and when he told her the few things about his work he could tell her (he had to talk to her about something, had to find something to drive away the silence between Aila and him) she listened consideringly as she had to the tales of those petty problems he used to have teaching school, when they lived in the ghetto outside Benoni-son-of-sorrow, first married.

He took part in policy decisions somewhere below the highest level and thereafter, in a group where he himself participated in allocation of the activities of others, was in turn given his orders. How much any one should be exposed was always a worried calculation based on the current number of comrades detained or serving prison sentences—how many, outside, could be spared. There were agonized decisions about who should appear where, when public occasions demanded a presence if the movement were to retain its popular power. He was no Tutu or Boesak or Chikane, and he could have been blacker, but as one of the best speakers, bloodied by prison, he had to be used only where he would be most effective with least risk. But who could calculate risk? Something to smile over, again, with Hannah. The black ghettos were army encampments and police dogs with their gun-carrying handlers replaced white ladies with poodles in the shopping malls. The headquarters of trade unions and militant church organizations were tramped through regularly by raiding police. Some were mysteriously blown up or burned. At road-blocks around the city armoured cars stood and every black driver was flagged down and searched. As the schools boycott combined with rent boycotts proved exceptionally effective, taking whole communities out of government control, Sonny was used mostly on occasions when someone from the blacks' National Education Crisis Committee was needed to attack the State education system. At university campuses and ghetto congresses his endearing middle name no longer appeared on posters—he was billed anonymously as 'a prominent educationist'. At least the police would not have previous knowledge of his arrival on a public platform, if they were planning to pick him up.

But there were times when an event often—and best—cohered hastily, before the proposed gathering could be banned. The call for a speaker would come when there was no choice but to send whoever was available in the area.

Sonny told them both. Aila and Hannah.

He mentioned the black township graveyard ceremony at home, and when he told his wife, his daughter was there—she didn't appear for weeks and then suddenly would come in through the kitchen door at some odd hour. She sat eating her cornflakes, the good little girl. The boy avoided meals with him; Sunday breakfast was one of them.

He was confusedly distracted at the sight of his Baby, where she used to be, in her place. As if in sudden disjuncture everything was back where once it was. But his girl was wearing a black satin blouse creased under the arms and the unnecessary paint round her eyes (they were striking enough already) darkened sleep-crumbs at the corners—she had more likely been out all night rather than have got up early to drop in for breakfast at her old home. A bile of distress rose and was swallowed. No time to deal with that; no right time ever, now.

—Where's that place, Daddy?—

Before he could say, Aila turned her head from the gush of water filling the kettle. —The other side of Pretoria. North.—

—Oh there. But you'll never get in. The army's all round.—

He saw that Aila was making fresh tea. She always filled the kettle with cold water when making tea, she would never boil up what was already hot. —I'll have what's in the pot. I've no time.—

—Since when are you a priest, my dear pa-pa.— Coquetry was inborn, for his Baby, even—and since she *was* a baby—when addressing her father. —Anyway, you're unique, they'll recognize you in your disguise of cassock and whatnot. Your eyebrows! Shall I pluck your eyebrows? Daddy? Yes!— She jumped up and rushed over to him with fingers extended like pincers.

—Don't be silly, I'm not going to be disguised as anything.—

The girl's playful threat turned into an embrace, her arm hooked round her father's neck. They were laughing, protesting to each other, and then abruptly stopped; she kissed him fiercely on his cheek. He felt her jaw jar against the bone.

—It's the 'cleansing of the graves' of the nine youngsters who were shot by the police last week outside Jubilee Hall. They were buried yesterday. The street committees have asked for some kind of oration. The kids were comrades.—

As he said 'oration' the boy came in, after all. In the glance of greeting he gave his son he felt a tic of embarrassment, as if he had been caught out quoting Shakespeare as he used to do to give the boy the freedom, at least, of great art.

They sat together round the table in the breakfast nook Sonny had built with Will's help, as they had made things together back in Benoni; Saturday shopping, the love of a schoolteacher for a virgin, the happiness of the first Baby and then the son named for genius—all this was pressing hard against their thighs. Aila rose and slid into her place again with the grace that did not brush against cup or cloth, fetching yogurt and replenishing margarine. Baby was recounting the highly embellished story of the driving test she had just taken, and tried to rile her brother into the old exchange of sibling insults. —Oh I'm perfectly confident. I even drove a truck while I was still on my learner's. You know that? The only thing that bugs me is the behaviour of you barbarians on your souped-up bikes, rushing out of nowhere. You think just by keeping your lights on everyone's got to pull out of your way as if you were the fire engine—I don't know why Dad ever gave in to your nagging for one of these things, honestly, Will.—

He hesitated, choosing an apple. —I never asked for it.—

There was warning in her big, kohl-smeared eyes as he looked up fully at her, though she quickly laughed: —Oh no, I'll bet you never! Never dreamt of asking! Never entered your curly head, brother of mine!—

Jars and cups passed warm from hand to hand, a headline was read out by someone, the mother arranged with the son to do an errand for her, the chitter of china, crunch of knives through toast and splutter of poured tea linked the ellipses of breakfast remarks. All had been rehearsed countless times. It was not really happening; an echo, a formula being followed. The inconsequential talk was contained in the silence between them that all gathered there heard.

Sonny had said he was in a hurry, in order to get away before the boy appeared. He had to bear out the lie. He rose from the table but Aila got up when he did and left the kitchen before him.

—Ciao, Will.—

Goodbye, he said. The boy always took care to make Sonny feel his son wanted him to be imprisoned again: something to put a stop to him. Farewell. Never come back.

The lovely girl had wiped her eyes clean with her mother's dishcloth, and now was quite unblemished by whatever her night had been. —Be careful, Daddy. Here—put this down for me.— She took a rose, grown in Aila's garden, out of the vase on the breakfast table.

He had Baby's flower in his hand when Aila met him in the passage with a zipped carryall. He knew what was in it. Toothbrush and paste, towel, soap, pyjamas, change of socks and underpants, sweater. The essentials you were allowed to pack up if you were lucky enough to be taken into detention from home and not while speaking at the cleansing of the graves. She had been gone from the kitchen less than a minute. —How did you do that?—

—I keep it ready.— She was smiling. She shrugged as if to discount herself, excuse some interference.

—It's not necessary. I'll be all right.—

She stood there. She licked her lips. Stood there.

He picked up the bag in the hand in which he held the flower. —Baby's, to put on the graves.— He looked about, out of habit, for the briefcase, took it in the other hand, and she opened the front door for him.

Not *ciao*, no *goodbye*. —Don't worry, Aila.—

—I'll be there. I'll hear you. I was going with the DPSC* and Black Sash,** anyway.—

He had time for breakfast, with Hannah. A cup of coffee and half a slice of her toast spread with fish-paste—Because I taste of it already.— She was still in the outsize T-shirt in which she slept, and the slight hollow that trembled along the underside of her soft-fleshed arm from armpit to elbow, as she lifted it about the objects on the table, drew his eye and made him lean over and taste her mouth for himself. Her breasts and belly were so near under the cotton rag that the flesh warmed his hand as if it were held before a sleepy fire.

—Couldn't you come with me?—

She took deep, smiling breaths to regain control of herself. —Better not, don't you think?—

—Of course. Maybe I can give you a lift back. You'll find some excuse.—

The treat of spending the short journey together was tempting; she smiled and played with his hand, which recently she had swabbed with cerise water-colour and imprinted on a sheet

*Detainees' Parents Support Committee.

**A women's anti-apartheid organization.

of paper now pinned to the wall. —No. Unless I get them to drop me off in Pretoria, that I could do—and we'd meet somewhere?—

—Outside the Palace of Justice?— It was at that rendezvous that he had stood trial. His dark, cocky grin that came from prison, happy for battle, delighted her. —Unfortunately I'm going to have to hurry back. There's a meeting around five.— I imagine the ceremony should be over by four-thirty. . .if the police don't shut it down long before. Hadn't you better get dressed? What time's your bus leaving?—

—Oh it doesn't take me ten minutes. . .is that for me?— He had thrown the carryall in the boot but absently brought in the rose with his briefcase.

—For the graves.—

—What a lovely thing to do.—

He could not lie to her. —My daughter gave it. She came in this morning.—

—Good for her. I must pick up some flowers, too, on the way.—

The face of a woman who uses no make-up has unity with her body. Seeing Hannah's fair eyelashes catching the morning sun and the shine of the few little cat's whiskers that were revealed, in this innocent early clarity, at the upper corners of her mouth, he was seeing the whole of her; he understood why, in the reproductions of paintings he had puzzled over in the days of his self-education, Picasso represented frontally all the features of a woman—head, breasts, eyes, vagina, nose, buttocks, mouth—as if all were always present even to the casual glance. What would he have known, without Hannah!

She had picked up his hand and buried her big soft face in it, kissing the palm. When she lifted her head her cheeks were stinging pink, slapped by pride. —I'm so glad you're the one chosen to speak.—

Sunday peace.

The combis that, sending gusts of taped reggae and *mbaqanga* into the traffic, transport blacks back and forth between township and city, now carry a strange cargo of whites. The street committees in the township have advised that this is the way to bring them in, the nature of the vehicles in themselves giving the signal to the people that these envoys from outside the siege are approved.

Through the white suburbs. Past bowling greens where figures like aged schoolboys and girls in banded hats genuflect over balls; past the Robin Hood fantasy of an archery club, the whoops of regular Sunday tennis partners in private gardens, the nylon frills and black suits of the congregation leaving a Nederduitse Gereformeerde Kerk, and the young girls with cupboards full of clothes who choose to stroll barefoot in jeans slashed off at the thigh. Past electronically-operated gates pinnacled with plaster eagles, spike- and razorwire-topped walls behind which peacock-tails of water open over flowers and birds sing. Sunday peace. If it were not for the combi owners' township names and addresses painted on the vehicles, the convoy might be some sort of charity outing on its way to a picnic. Now and then it is paced by joggers who drop back without noticing it.

Mechanical knights—vehicles visored in steel-plating and chain-mailed in thick mesh—barred the turnoff to the township. Before them were mounted police and soldiers with automatic shotguns and R4 rifles, standing legs planted apart.

To most of the white people in the combis the yellow armoured vans, the clumsy brown armoured cars the blacks dub zoomorphically 'Hippos', the stolid figures with the power of death in their hands were ranged like the toys of war children set up. Or it was as if someone suddenly flipped the switch of a TV programme selector and a scene from some mini-series flashed on. Violence was so thin an appearance in the living-room that the shadow of someone's head, moving across the room, was enough to blot it out. Now, why, you could see the hair on a policeman's forearm. No matter if the person in the next seat stood up; when he shifted again, armoured cars, police guns were there. The steel whips of aerials swung in the sun. Alsatian dogs—once desirable and beautiful pets, now tails down in the cowed and coiled bearing of readiness to attack—were weapons leashed in the fists of police handlers.

Everyone had been briefed about how to behave: each combi had its marshal. Accept police provocation calmly, leave the talking to those appointed to do it. Some people climbed out to stretch their legs, proving they were not afraid, and were sent back to their seats. Lawyers and civil rights leaders among the groups were conferring with the comrades from within the township who had arrived to meet the convoy in an old American car lumbering low on its suspension. Others were negotiating with the police. The group broke up and re-formed, gesticulating individuals shouldered their way in upon it, left to approach others, ran back. The group moved, as they argued, from one side of the blockade to the other, pulled this way and that in the arena of their contention; a process in dumb show people encapsulated in the combis craned their necks to interpret. Look at that! That policeman shaking his fist! Can't you see? Next to that Hippo. He hit him, he's hit him! Oh my god. . . No no no nobody's been hurt! Just look at those brutal clots, that one could press the trigger easily as he's scratching himself. . . Oh don't you worry, they'd think twice before firing at us—we're white. . . The major or whatever-he-is—he's walking away—What's happening? No he isn't, he's just giving some instruction. They're arresting someone! Who? Can't see—oh my god, it's Dave! Dave Seaton. No that's not Dave. . .

Alarm and excitement died away into impatience and a new kind of boredom: was it possible to be bored while in an extraordinary situation? In one of the combis a lay nun in ankle socks offered round a plastic bottle of water, and there was the rustle of rolls of peppermints being peeled. The difference is, if we were black we'd at least be singing. Well, come on then! We were told to keep out of it. . . Singing! Not to sing! Well, freedom songs could be provocation. . . Who knows the words. . . Some students did, they belonged to the new generation who learned from blacks; but freedom songs need volume, and the older people from the church and civil rights movements could participate only by smiling solidarity.

A young marshal raced up and down with her walkie-talkie.

Everything about her was in movement, long hair, breasts and rubber-thong sandals bobbing, swirling in contrast with the police planted with guns at their posts. Harassed and grinning, she pulled herself up to the windows of each combi. —They say we can't enter. But Allan and Dave have shown them the statute, it's not against the law, they can't stop us!— She dropped and was off before questions could reach her. People gabbled suppositions; in the silence of others was concealed disappointment—or relief. Who could tell from their faces? In a few minutes the girl was back again, running her open-fingered hand to lift her hair high off her forehead. —They say we'll be killed. We go in at our own risk— She was fighting her own elation. She burst into laughter. People in the combi rose from their seats—but she was gone. Some climbed out of the combis and grouped in an exchange of rumours and opinions, bravado and caution. Marshals ran like sheepdogs between them, getting them back into the combis. No-one sat where they had before, everyone competed for attention, I think, I said, I told. . . And then the lawyers did the rounds. There was silence. —We've decided to go in. The comrades from the street committees are going to escort us—they have many more of their ranks inside and they'll be with us all the way. But anyone who feels, because of family or any other circumstances, he or she should not ignore the police warning, should feel free to leave us now. There's transport for those who wish to return to town. Please. And no stigma whatever attached to this choice. . . I assure you. None of us will draw any wrong conclusions. So. . .—

But it was not possible for anyone to find the courage to get up and leave; no fear equal to that. There was a moment like a breath held. And then all faces were turned to him: —You're coming?— And the company applauded; applauded each other, themselves. If they never were to meet again, each would have this moment of self-respect ratified between them. The Hippos, the police, soldiers, horses and dogs, guns, opened a way. The black drivers who had been chatting and smoking with the detachment of hired onlookers accustomed to dealing with the police every day, jumped into their vehicles and drove their passengers where many had never been before.

Across the veld.

Hannah was in one of the combis. Of course, she had crossed the veld from many cities, towns and dorps, many times before. She sat quietly in the illusion sunglasses give that one is behind them in some kind of hide, able to think of what was most concealed, surely, among all the secret thoughts of the people around her—her anxiety whether Sonny had evaded the police by choosing some other way into the township, and—most unimaginable of all, by those whose shoulders were touching hers—what the man who would speak to them at the graves was to her. So the experience for her surely was unlike what it could be for anyone else. She had met with police interference often before, she was one of their film stars. . .if a policeman recognized her (she took off the sunglasses) among the collection of whites in the convoy, he would know that the ex-political prisoner who was to speak at the graves was her lover. It sometimes happened that there was this crazy bond of confirmation in their eyes when hers met those of some plain-clothes man.

The combis plunged into the township—into the valley where the township had proliferated over three generations, and into the thick-layered human presence of Sunday, when all the life that is dispersed across the veld in the industrial areas and the city during the week has crammed back. Everyone home: 'home' the streets; a habitation without barriers, the houses' breached walls spilling inmates, the tottering fences one with the components—tin, hubcaps, rotting board—of totemic rubbish mounds. Workers' dungarees were the flags hung out, drying spread cruciform with the logos of construction companies and soft-drink plants stitched across them. Drumming at yard church meetings thumped across the gibber of radio commercials and ragged singing from beer-drinks. The convoy pitched and tossed over the gullies that were the streets and also the children's sandpits, the fecal streams, the fodder-ground of pigs, chickens and dogs. If the way was not demarcated by cambering and sidewalk gutters as the whites were accustomed to, it was defined by people who ran towards the combis and gathered ahead on either side of the route. An avenue of black faces looked into the windows, pressing close, so that the combis had to slow to these people's walking pace in order not to crush them under the wheels. No picnic party; the whites found themselves at once surrounded by, gazed at, gazing into the faces of these blacks who had stoned white drivers on the main road, who had taken control of this place out of the hands of white authority, who refused to pay for the right to exist in the decaying ruins of the war of attrition against their presence too close across the veld; these people who killed police collaborators, in their impotence to stop the police killing their children. One thing to read about them in the papers, to empathize with them, across the veld; Hannah felt the fear in her companions like a rise in temperature inside the vehicle. She slid open the window beside her. Instead of stones, black hands reached in, met and touched first hers and then those of all inside who reached out to them. The windows were opened. Passengers jostled one another for the blessing of the hands, the healing touch. Some never saw the faces of those whose fingers they held for a moment before the combi's progress broke the grasp. In the crush outside faces gleaming in welcome bobbed up. There were the cries,

Amandla! Viva! and joy when these were taken up by the whites, and there were the deep dreamy intonations of the old-time greetings, '*nkos*' from people too ancient to grasp that this, granted to whites, now represents shameful servility. In the smiling haze of weekend-drunks the procession of white people was part of the illusions that softened the realities of the week's labour, and made the improbable appear possible. The crowd began to sing, of course, and *toyi-toyi*, the half-dance, half-procession alongside the convoy bringing, among the raised fists of most in the combis, a kind of embarrassed papal or royal weighing-of-air-in-the-hand as a gracious response from others.

At the graveyard Hannah saw him. Sonny, the detainee in his cell, the political personality, the gentle lover—all these personae were present to her in the sight of him. He stood with his friend Father Mayekiso and some young white people from the End Conscription Campaign. As she watched his curly black hair rise away from his head in the dusty wind, moving over forgotten graves with the party from the combis she stumbled on a broken plastic dome of paper flowers and was quickly caught and put on her feet by a black man in torn and dirty clothes: *sorry, sorry*. They were all around, those who had followed the convoy, and those who were streaming down from all parts of the township to the graveyard. Smoke from the night's cooking fires hung its acrid incense over them. The old graves and leaning crosses were disappearing under the feet of the living. They stopped at nine fresh mounds. Hannah wanted to say—but only to him, over there with Father Mayekiso—these aren't graves yet, not yet, it's too soon, they are beds, the shape of sleeping bodies with a soft cover of this red, woolly earth drawn over the heads. She knew that the young men down there were between fifteen and twenty-six years old; she did not know what to do with her emotion. She pulled some irises from the bunch she had bought and gave them out to people around her.

The blacks were accustomed to closeness. In queues for transport, for work permits, for housing allocation, for all the stamped paper that authorized their lives; loaded into over-crowded trains and buses to take them back and forth across the veld, fitting a family into one room, they cannot keep the outline of space—another, invisible skin—whites project around themselves, distanced from each other in everything but sexual and parental intimacy. But now in the graveyard the people from the combis were dispersed from one another and the spatial aura they instinctively kept, and pressed into a single, vast, stirring being with the people of the township. The nun was close against the breast of a man. A black child with his little naked penis waggling under a shirt clung to the leg of a professor. A woman's French perfume and the sweat of a drunk merged as if one breath came from them. And yet it was not alarming for the whites; in fact, an old fear of closeness, of the odours and heat of other flesh, was gone. One ultimate body of bodies was inhaling and exhaling in the single diastole and systole, and above was the freedom of the great open afternoon sky.

At a gesture from someone, whites turned heads; on the rise on the side of the graveyard opposed to that of the township the whole force of police and soldiers had reassembled. The yellow vans and brown Hippos made an horizon, the mounted men before them, and, in front, the line on foot. But these were no longer standing stolidly as they did at the road-block. They were half-crouched, their rifles and shotguns pointing down straight at this body, the body of the gathering. Blacks didn't bother to look. The police, mingled with army conscripts from whom they were indistinguishable most of the time, because they often wore the same camouflage outfit, had been camped on the township soccer fields for weeks. There was no getting away from them. They were life; and death. They had shot the nine young men lying in the graves where the earth had not yet settled.

The priest led prayers in Twsana and Pedi, and hymns, banners of sound, were borne away into the sky, over to the battle-lines on the hill. One of the young white men who had refused conscription to join those up there, and were ready to go to prison for this decision, told the gathering why the white people had come to the people of the township. *We're here to show you that whites don't have to come to kill. We come to share your anger and sorrow at the killing of these, our brothers. We come to tell you that we'll take no part in the army or the police who do these things to you.* The interpreter's translation into one of their own languages set off freedom songs among the people but the street committee comrades skilfully led a transition to hymns; the armed onlookers on the hill must not be provided with any pretext that this was a subversive gathering.

Hannah knew Sonny's speech. That is, she knew his thinking, his way of expressing a political line in a manner, as far as feasible, his own way, part of which had been developed in his long dialogue with her, another part of which came from some source in him as the sea is in human blood from the time when humans were creatures of some other element. She did not know him there in his old element, nor could he make himself known to her. He was perhaps even ashamed of this base as too uninformed and simple; could not know that she observed it in him as a quality that drew her to him more than anything they shared. She kept for herself something she would never speak, not to anyone, certainly not to him—his mystery: *He's a good man.*

Sonny was wearing the hand-dyed aubergine shirt she had

given him and the rich colour accentuated his darkness—no-one could say Sonny wasn't black enough to be a spokesman of the people, either in terms of his skin or his actions! When he spoke now of detentions and imprisonment, he had been there; when he spoke now of the deaths of the nine young men by police brutality, he himself had risked such a death in his own life. His existence gave her the surety: that was what authority meant, it was not the authority of the weapons on the hill. If he used the vocabulary of politics because certain words and phrases were codes everybody understood—no interpreter necessary, even in the English in which they were formulated they expanded in each individual's hearing to carry the meaning of his own frustrations, demands and desire—Sonny did not adopt the usual mannerisms the vocabulary produces. He did not have a calculated way of standing or using his hands, when the eyes of a crowd were on him. When he posed some rhetorical question, his eyes, all pupil in their intensity, would come, as if in ordinary conversation, to some individual for the response that would influence his own reflections. When he paused before explaining a point, he was unembarrassed by the moment he created, confident there would be acceptance of it, and he would use a gesture, more of an aid to clarity of thought, used in private discussion—maybe turning up his palm and looking down to trace in it a circular movement with the thumb of the other hand. He also had the gift of spontaneity, drawing into his own discourse his response to previous speakers, so that what he said never seemed prepared in advance, but to have come to him from his colleagues and the vitality of the crowd before him. Watching Sonny, listening to Sonny, she felt at last she could define sincerity, also—it was never speaking from *an idea of oneself*. And frankness: frankness, something dangerous and beautiful. The subterfuges of an illicit love made the frankness of its emotions possible; the subterfuges of resistance made frankness in a lying society possible. Sonny once said, what the oppressors call subversion is the exposure of the rot in the State.

What is the meaning of the death of nine comrades we honour today? Nine young people who were hardly yet grown to be men but who were men in their resistance to the people who have surrounded and terrorized you in your homes. These young comrades and thousands of others who have been killed by apartheid's agents, the police, the army, the witdoeke, *have given to the struggle their share of the future the struggle is going to win for us. They will never share with all our people in the country's wealth, instead of working to provide thirteen percent of the population with the highest standard of living in the world, while the majority of the people cannot feed their children. They will never know what it is to get out of ghettos like this one and live where there is electricity and clean running water in decent houses. They will never know the time when our sick will no longer lie on the floor in apartheid hospitals while there are wards full of empty beds in hospitals for whites; when our old fathers and mothers will no longer have to starve on pensions a fraction of those whites get. They will never know the single and open education for all, never mind colour or race, our democratic education will establish, and they will not know that the migratory labour system, which now divides husbands and wives, parents and children, and has created the prostitutes, the homeless children of the streets, and the spread of the terrible disease called AIDS, will be a horror of the past. They will never walk on our land, our land restored to the people, instead of being sent away after the day's work to urban rubbish heaps like this and to rural resettlement slums in areas of our country given tribal names and called 'foreign states'. They will never live in the unitary, non-racial, democratic country our struggle is going to create. They have died without freedom; but they have died for freedom. Our freedom. We have heard from a young comrade who is not up there on the hill pointing a gun at us, although he is white. The presence of our white comrades from the city here today is surely proof that the nine died also for* their *freedom. They died for the freedom of all the people of this country who want to see oppression destroyed and are ready to join the people's struggle to achieve this. That is the meaning of the death of the nine, for us.*

When such young men die it's usual to speak of a senseless death. There's anger that a life should be so short and brutally ended. Well, for those who shot and killed these nine young comrades last week these really are senseless deaths, because this killing, and all the other killings of our people in the ghettos and in the prisons, will not stop us from winning our freedom. That, for this government, is the meaning of the deaths of the nine young comrades who lie buried here. That is the message. They are *senseless deaths, because no amount of killing will mean that the oppression of our people can continue to survive. No violence against us can shoot down the struggle for peace and justice.*

How much of this blew over in the wind to the formation on the hill is not known, but the litany of freedom cries that interrupted Sonny at expected points (he knew when to pause for them) certainly must have. Father Mayekiso's closing prayer did not, for a minute or two, quiet calls that still came from here and there. The Amen stirred deeply through the crowd, seemed to sway them towards the graves. The comrades held them back; there was silence. Gusts of wind sculpted the soft earth mounds. The silence came from there, down there outside time, so that Hannah did not know if it lasted seconds or minutes, only that for its kind of duration she had no awareness of him, Sonny, he did not exist in it. And then the nun came forward and knelt on the earth, laying a flower. A thick straggling queue shuffled past the nine mounds with their new bright tin numbers. The township people stretched out everywhere for flowers. Small children took them to be gifts for themselves. Hannah's irises were laid by many hands. Soon the mounds were transformed by a disguise of the lovely temporal; colours and fragrance and petals that would not last. She saw Sonny again. He was delivering his daughter's rose to the dead. In a sideways glance with only a few feet between them they acknowledged each other across the graves like people who cannot put a name to a face.

The crowd began to thin at the edges, slowly turned away from the graves. The small children were running with the treasure of their single flowers. The young people were singing, We greet you, Mandela, call us, Mandela. . .in the rhythm of a walking song, gently harmonizing rather than rousing, parting from the dead with respect. Hannah and the other whites took their pace, flowing with people, people flowing past, life draining out of the graveyard. Somewhere behind, Sonny, Father Mayekiso—the official group—were waylaid by members of the street committees and crones and drunks who wanted to take their hands to receive the vague benediction believed to emanate from important people. Then a kind of seismic tremor went through the trooping crowd. There was no shout, but everybody began to bump into everybody else; some had stopped abruptly: up there, from the hill, the men with pointing guns were racing down upon them. The broad swathe of people broke into a hobbling run from which the young surged out ahead. As people ran they pulled rags from somewhere in their clothing, doeks from their heads, and tied them across noses and mouths. The whites trotted embarrassedly: they were not used to having to flee anything or anyone. Some foolish idea of dignity, some armchair idea of courage, inhibited them. Even Hannah had never before experienced what the blacks, with their rags kept on their persons as protection against tear-gas as white people carry credit cards, were ready for every day. Canisters were exploding at the tail of the crowd; the foul cloud pursued them and a shot—in the air, perhaps only triggered by the scramble of the police and soldiers through trash and bushes—cracked a whip over them.

Hannah was young and her strong freckled legs could carry her fast, but an agonizing brake of resistance fought against the instinct. She wanted to stop her legs; she stopped and ran, stopped and ran, crashing into the path of others, looking back, looking everywhere. Now there was a scream; the police had plunged down into the crowd, long wails of terror were cut through by the dry syllables of shots, a sound hard as the steel that flies and pierces flesh and bone, goes to the heart that is bursting with the effort to run away and to the throat where the yell rises. She was running back, sideways, thrust aside, sometimes clutched by someone determinedly making a way, she caught a whiff of the gas, the wind had blown it back to the hill, her eyes were streaming and there he was, there was Sonny, his shiny black curls, the bar of his eyebrows above desperate eyes like black holes in his head. He clutched her arm so that it was almost wrenched out of its socket; she thought she was weeping at the sight of Sonny, the tear-gas tears were something else. —Get to the combi! Get to the combi! *Go!*— She pulled against leaving him, he pushed her away; and then amid shots and screams he began to run with her, run as if he were chained to her. The people were racing and flying into their street-burrows in the township. From there came the stare of hundreds of others gathered on walls, on roof-tops, afar, their murmur a tumultuous lament. Mayekiso appeared level with Sonny and Hannah. His arms were raised, he was shouting. intoning in his own language; but the people tore past the crucified one's representative in their midst, nothing could cast out their fear. There was a shot like all the other shots: this time a young man fell face-down in the path of Sonny, Hannah and Father Mayekiso. People shrieked and backed off, struggling to get away from what had become a target; a single woman dropped to her knees at his side, calling out, tugging to turn him over. Blood came glistening through the black fibrous mat of his hair and, as she moved him, ran, obliterating the slogan on his trade-union T-shirt *An Injury To One Is An Injury To All*.

Buffetted on all sides, Sonny and Hannah were dragged on, managed to resist, turned to fight their way back to where the boy lay. Mayekiso was with him, the woman was hysterically beating the ground. They saw this one second and the next it was obliterated by the press of fleeing people, appeared again, disappeared. They were forcing their way back against shoulders, backsides, flailing arms, and now there were shots smashing right past their heads. Sonny suddenly was looking at her as if he were making a terrible discovery. His face was distorted by anguish and incoherence. He pressed down her head with his raised arm and they ran, ran away with the crowd.

In Sonny's car, Hannah sat gasping, saliva at the corners of her open mouth. —The others will look for me. . .combi won't go without me.—

—The drivers saw us. They'll tell them you left with someone else.—

—I'm afraid they'll think something happened to me.—

He did not answer for a moment. He dropped his head on his hands, on the steering wheel. Then recovered himself. —Nothing's happened to you, Hannah.—

Her hand was squeezed bloodless where it had been in his clutch. She was sure, as lovers imagine at such times, that she would relive the sensation of that grasp to the end of her life.

What was she slipping out to do for him, now? What were they saying in the passage? They have nothing private, from me, now. She has no right to talk to him behind my back.

I went to the kitchen window and then I saw—ah, she's given him the carryall, that was what it was all about. I saw him throw the carryall into the boot before he got into the car.

My sister shoved my plate away from under my nose as I came back to the table. —What're you spying on him for? What d'you think you're trying to do, man, hinting. . . 'I never asked for it'—

—Oh I know you're quite happy to take bribes—him letting you go off and live away from home. Leaving Ma. Leaving me with them.—

—If you're so pure why did you take it, then!— The motorbike again.

—Leave me alone. You don't live here. Coming to kiss him all over and bringing your bloody dresses for her to sew like a servant.—

—Listen, man. The trouble with you, you don't grow up. Oh a big hulk with hair on your chin, but a case of—of arrested development. Voluntary.—

Now I couldn't help laughing at my sister, how could I give her the satisfaction of taking her seriously. —My, where did you pick that up? Got some new boyfriend studying psychology? Or would it be medicine? Is that the sort of stuff you rap among your disco pals? My, my.—

—You have no friends, that's your problem. Hang around the house glowering. Obsessed.— She paused, threatening, eyes staring insolently wide at me, to say with what. —There's more than a family.—

—Yes, smoking pot and sleeping around and bumming off anybody. I don't believe you even work, half the time. We don't know what you're doing.—

Her aggression dropped like a weapon laid down. —That's right.—

I wondered what was the matter with her. She sat breaking the crusts she had left; my mother always had made her eat her crusts. The thought came startlingly, reasonably to me: —You're not pregnant, are you, Baby?—

She laughed in the affected way she has adopted since she was about fourteen, throwing her hair and head back for men—including even me. —Of course what else could you imagine could happen to me! Oh little Will!— And I laughed, too, in relief; for my mother.

But when my mother came in fresh from whatever the discussion had been with my father before he departed on one of his important missions (there are so many funerals, so many 'cleansings of the graves' among blacks, he had a good chance of getting away with this Sunday's alibi) I didn't look at her, so that she might not see my disgust. She knows—we know—that if I withdraw she is without support—it's not that I can guide my mother, I'm too young and ignorant for that, but that my attention is a bit like an ordinary old pocket torch that I hold, walking backwards before her as she manages to keep to her way in its light. That Sunday morning I couldn't do it. I know what's in the carryall. When she's out of the house—and he's nearly always out of the house—I look in their things. It's a strong compulsion; has to be strong because one of the rules of respect he taught Baby and me was never to open drawers or read letters belonging to others. (As a result, we used to tell on each other when we filched each other's toys or books, giving occasion for another contradictory lesson in ethics, eh—one doesn't betray. The only thing he left me to find out for myself was his own contradictions.)

She keeps the carryall in the cabinet on her side of their bed—poor thing, must have it right there beside her so that she can lay her hands on it at once if he's taken in the middle of the night. On the shelf at the top are the creams with which she takes care of her skin—for him. I used to smell the scent on her hands if she came into our room—Baby's and mine, the Benoni house—when one of us had a nightmare. In the carryall she keeps toothpaste and a new toothbrush still in its plastic film, towel and soap, clean underpants, socks, pyjamas, a pull-over. The list is a code of her fears that he might be taken away next time as he was the first, without the means to keep himself clean—the means of self-respect so important to him—and warm: the pullover is her means of love, whether that's important to him or not. And she gives the carryall to him to take along with that briefcase! How could I look at her.

I could feel her dismay at my rejection, hear her timidly determined efforts to put together, for her daughter and son and herself, a leisurely Sunday lingering at breakfast, pouring her-

self tea, murmuring whether anyone would like another slice of bread toasted. But Baby was staring at her, I saw Baby take breath to begin to speak, twice, flicking her long eyelashes, before she actually did. And as she did, I quickly looked to my mother, at least I was with my mother when Baby spoke.
—Ma, I want to tell you. I don't want to give you a fright again. . .—

Aila found the carryall in the boot of the car when she wanted to load a bag of potatoes she had bought. She unpacked the new toothbrush, the toothpaste, the towel, soap and clothing and put them where they would be in daily use: the toilet articles in the family bathroom cupboard, her husband's clothes in the wardrobe acquired on hire purchase in Benoni—on the first Saturday of each month it had been part of the family outing to make the regular payment from the schoolteacher's salary.

He watched what Aila was doing, going back and forth, emptying the carryall.

—It's surprising she told you when I wasn't there.—

Aila couldn't get a full drawer to take the thickness of the pullover. She was refolding it slowly and carefully.

—After I'd gone out, I mean.—

Aila pressed the pullover into the drawer and shut it.

—Didn't you know.— A statement. She looked at him unchallengingly.

—If I'd known, wouldn't I have told you!—

What a thing to have let slip his lips—as if he told her anything, now. —How could I have known? What do you mean? You don't think I had something to do with it! Do you? Is that it?—

Aila stood in the middle of their bedroom. It was ridiculous—Aila, so quiet and dignified and harmless—but he felt he couldn't get past her, if he tried to walk away she would step in front of him. —It's the kind of thing I thought you'd know about.—

—Well I wouldn't. The less each group knows of the activities of the others, the better. But you're perfectly aware of that—you are. Particularly in the matter of recruitment to proceed outside. The people I work with don't deal with that. There are others. She must have been with them—perhaps all these months, and we didn't know it. She's been well schooled, that's clear. Didn't want to involve you—us— Paused, yearningly; but there was nothing to be shared with Aila, standing there. —Clever little girl, after all.—

—Perhaps you can still see her. We won't know when she's going.—

—You want me to persuade her. . .—

Aila was slowly moving her head, dipped to one side, not in denial but in doubt at his success.

He had an urge to take the risk of talking to Aila, really talking to her, he felt everything pressing up against his diaphragm: speak, speak. —I don't know what to feel about it, the whole thing.—

—It's not what you have to feel about it, it's how you feel.—

—I suppose I can't believe it. Baby. So I don't feel. She's been out of the house, I miss her because of that, I've missed her all the time, it's not the same. . .without her. . . And now she won't be here, for another reason.— But everything he was saying seemed to be something else; he stopped with a loss of breath like a groan. He felt himself in great danger; one move from Aila, Aila—

She picked up the empty carryall and pressed it flat under her right arm. She waited; but was it only her politeness, that had never been neglected, even in the days of their intimacy? Aila, Aila. A terrible temptation to tear off her clothes, burst into tears, enter her, *destroy himself* as surely as his Baby could have done when she cut her wrists. —You're not too upset, Aila? What I could do. . .I could try to arrange that she doesn't have to get into anything too risky. . . But you seem to be taking it pretty well. . .?—

She looked at him with great sorrow in her face. He had never seen that face before, although he knew he had deserved it. And now there was the pain that he could not be sure it was for him.

—It's not so bad as the other time.—

Aila, Aila, what has she said. The other time, he was not making a speech at a graveside, he was in bed with his woman. He remembered the only thing he had found to say to Aila: *Will there be scars.* Now she believes, she does, she does, he has made his daughter into a revolutionary, sent her into exile, to live in a camp, never to come home, perhaps to die even if she didn't bleed to death that other time. He has done this although it is the truth that he did not even know she had joined the military wing of the movement. That truth is not all the truth.

The danger drained from him. His heart hesitated from beat to beat. Aila went out with the carryall under her arm and he left behind her. She put the bag into the hall cupboard where they kept old newspapers, cleaning utensils, and the cheap luggage in which they had moved their possessions to the city. He took his briefcase and went to Hannah, needing Hannah.

A storm raided the sky. Flashed its beams on them in the darkened afternoon and tramped away, rolling tanks of thunder.

So they had fallen asleep: his gaze came into focus on lilies.

Flowers he had bought for her from a street vendor the day before it happened—the cleansing of the graves. Last week it was roses. Red roses, furled like umbrellas; roses have the scent of sex, she said, lilies the shape: he discovered all these delights while with her. They came up close, under magnified senses.

Neither was asleep any longer, but not yet on the waking level of speech. When he arrived at her cottage his mood transformed: the loss of his daughter—her totally unexpected commitment to revolution—became a matter for pride and even excitement. —On her own! She made the big decision on her own! That little girl of mine!— This realization cleared suddenly from where it had been obscured, with Aila; by Aila's very existence.

Hannah was moved—and proud, for him, too. Hannah's emotions were those of the world of commitment he and she shared, emotions changed, by harsh circumstance, to enable one to deal with a whole order of situations not accounted for in family affairs. Hannah had comforted that same girl, now on her way to a Freedom Fighters' training camp, when she was a tearful child at her father's trial; comforted her not 'like a mother', no, but as a comrade who is never a stranger to another's (Sonny's) distress. There was a filament of continuity from that day to this. With Hannah he felt what he ought to feel. His Baby was not the dainty little daughter of a schoolteacher, now. Aila must realize they were not living humbly in their designated place outside Benoni. . .

His high emotion over Baby naturally flooded into desire between Hannah and him and there was no conflict to taint it because in her—needing Hannah—sexual happiness and political commitment were one. They made love half-clothed and fell asleep.

His awakening linked disconnected impressions and recall

as he gazed at the lilies. Baby's rose. The brilliance of petals and leaves on graves. Hannah. . .her voice, one day when they were talking, criticizing someone in the movement. . . —But perhaps all action springs from self-preservation—paradoxically? If someone's drowning, and I jump in to save him, what's behind my compassion (which—all right—fires my courage, because I'm scared)? Isn't it the fear that if *I* were drowning someone might walk away and ignore me?— With a contraction round the heart he suddenly was flung awake (the glare of the bulb that watched him in prison) to what had been completely avoided by preoccupation with Baby. Not come up, in speech or silences, before they loved and slept. The shot man fell again before them, and Sonny's own body, obedient to instilled principles, the old Benoni ghetto avowals, turned to drive him somehow back through the crowd to lift up the fallen and then a bullet missed her head by not more than an inch of her blonde hair and he disobeyed and ran with her. Mayekiso was beside the man; the bony structures of Mayekiso's forehead gleamed under sweat, the persistence of that irrelevant image was testimony to how it really happened. The man was probably dead, anyway. And Mayekiso stopped dead, as the saying goes, no-one thinks of the meaning it can have, he could have been shot dead while he bent there over the dead man. By luck (God's will, Mayekiso with his dangling cross would believe) the bullets missed Mayekiso, too, although he didn't turn.

The old Benoni ghetto avowals. Not living for oneself, etc. etc. Not living *only* for oneself, that was the qualification. She was not oneself; neither she nor the man who fell. The other—the other life, outside self—was either of them. To run or to stop: a choice between them. Who was to say which was the most valuable? But this woman whose hand was curled against his neck, wasn't she oneself, his need?

Saved himself.

Now he had something he would never speak, not to anyone, certainly not to her.

For what if she took it smugly as a proof of love? A female triumph. What would that do to him? To his judgment of himself. To his belief that she was not like any other woman and their relationship was formed in a special and different morality: the excruciating recasting of the meaning of love in the struggle, that made him celebrate a particular kind of parting from his own child.

But her mind surfaced on the periphery of his, maybe through the contact of their bodies, not divining what he was experiencing there beside her but instinctively circling the danger of its context. —When people make violence the ultimate test of who's right and who's wrong, here—you know the argument I mean—'the struggle is no better than the oppression because violence on the part of the oppressed can never be justified', it reduces them to the level of the oppressor and so on. . .people like that are so naïve. . . I'd almost say innocent. I don't mean that excuses them. But they babble like toddlers who don't know what they're saying because they haven't lived enough to connect words with the reality of acts. Most white people here haven't lived—not lived what life really is here. . . if you define the life of a country by the most general experience. If they could have been there the other day, just once, seen the police come down on us, no reason, we were all leaving the place, anyway. . .just shooting, and three people dead. . . That man, dead. If they could be there when it happens, only once, and it happens somewhere every day. They'd understand why people murder informers with whatever weapons they can lay their hands on.—

She had given him safe passage to the open waters of generality.

—Yes, but it's more than that. If you define *when* violence is a necessity, then you're accepting it can't be done without in this world. And that's hard to take, even here, even now.—

—Oh Sonny, at least we know one thing when we're forced, in ourselves, to accept it. We know the spit and polish of armies is to conceal the truth that war is blood, agony, rot and shit. That's all it's ever been. The high technology of ARMSCOR Magnus Malan boasts about. The marvellous sophistication of the latest killer, what's-it, the Rooikat, the tank they say out-ranges and outfires anything the Russians or Americans have made. Napoleon's grand army crawling back from Moscow on frozen feet. The Japanese skinned alive by the thing that was dropped on Hiroshima. That's the famous military tradition. Our wars—guerrilla wars with their ragged improvisation have put an end to the lie. No more going off to fight with a brass-band send-off. If you blow yourself up with the bomb you're placing, only the police are going to pick up the pieces. Take even the hijackers and hostage-takers: they shoot their victims or they get shot themselves when they're overcome; or both. It's nothing but suffering. Any kind of war, any kind. So at least if we have to accept violence, we know what we're doing, we're not dolling it up. I find that helps.—

—Not for me. I never thought I ever would accept violence, even if I didn't have to do it myself. . . Even if others were to do it for me. I sit in meetings, I take part in decisions where it's taken for granted counter-violence. . .our violence. . .has its absolutely necessary role. That's what it's called, a role; it's what I call it. Like in a play; and I'm not playing that particular role but I'm in the cast.—

—Could you do it yourself?—

But it was a mystery; Sonny could not even say he did not know. A mystery the schoolteacher had not taken into account, dreamt of, during the period when, remote from induction, he was philosophically puzzling over the extra-religious mystery of power: the power of life and death. He might have said only: all I have had was the courage to be a victim. Until now.

A watery after-light of the storm glossed the everted lips of each lily's single fold. They seemed to be of wet white marble, the pistils rising from carved shadow.

—No scent.— She was remembering his daughter's rose, in comparison.

He stroked her now. —How would you know, you smoke so much.—

A long moment of peace between them.

—Could you get me to stop?—

—How? If you'd tell me how.—

She turned on her elbow, in her familiar way, propped up to see again the dark smile, the bold features scrolled about by black curls, the eyes looking out from some forest of her imagination that she had found for the first time across the visitors' barrier in a prison.

For him, the flesh of her face fell forward a little, plumping her cheeks. Her eyes—living all his life among soft dark eyes, he never ceased to see the curiousness of blue as the perception trained on him. —Tell me.—

—I don't know. Only you could find out.—

Where to find out? In her lolling breasts that hung and swung against him, on her pale swollen lips, in the seaweed-coloured hair under her arms and the quiff, like the tuft brushed up on a fair baby's head, over the place he entered her? Nowhere there. Somewhere else, in himself.

Although they talked together often of his family, she seldom mentioned her ex-husband; this was because, and he understood, she seldom thought of him. He drifted to the surface of her mind, now. —Derek used to drink. . .a lot. He wanted to write something, he always wanted to, and then when he was fed up with law, he tried. It was interesting to watch. Just enough to drink, and it would—seem to—I don't know—dilate his sensibilities. He would say marvellous things. He'd tell me what he was going to write. But next day it was gone. Apparently if you drink you have to write down what you've got hold of, right away. It's a brief flare in the brain. It's gone once the alcohol burns out. He couldn't remember, next day. He never wrote it. I saw how drink wipes out memory; opens a door and then closes it. It was scary.—

—You couldn't stop the drinking.—

By itself, out of habit, her hand took the packet of cigarettes from the floor beside her, shook one free and put it in her mouth, then, in a second of bewilderment, took it out and put it down awkwardly on the pillow. —No. We were finished. I couldn't find out how. I couldn't do anything for him.—

Sonny sank into dread; and from that cold, sucking clay the only escape was unwelcome resentment—women, these two women with their capacity to wound, to threaten. And this one's innocent capacity simply to be needed, resting her healing mouth on his, now, so that he squirmed in a wild tangle of bedclothes to lie over her.

They're more proud of Baby than of me. Even my mother. She cried when we got a message from Lusaka so we knew Baby'd gone, Baby was there, and I didn't know what to do except what you see on television: I put my arm round her and patted her shoulder. The message came through him, one of his contacts, but she cried only when he was out of the house. And I haven't seen her cry again.

I gained three distinctions and a university pass and he's going to get me a bursary through his white fellow-traveller friends. What shall I study (once you've left school, adults ask you that, they don't ask patronizingly what are you going to be, any more); he doesn't say anything, I know he's hoping I'll make use of his old complete works, but I've applied for entry to the faculty of commerce. I'll be an educated shopkeeper with a business-school degree, how's that, a shopkeeper, in the tradition of some of my mother's relatives who run fruit and vegetable stalls and palm off to the blacks produce that's gone bad. What's the difference? It's merchandising, same as the wholesaler who once gave him a job out of charity, and the great supporter of the cause who comes sometimes to our house—the one who's made his fortune out of work clothing sold to the exploited masses he and my father are going to free—he supplies those maroon jerseys you see stretched over the bosoms of black nurses.

My parents wanted to give a party to celebrate my success. And did they think they would invite—his blonde woman?

We still have my mother's occasional big teas for the aunties and cousins and the two grannies from our old place outside Benoni—my grandfathers are both dead, now. If nothing else exists between my mother and him, for some reason I can't understand they co-operate in this keeping up of appearances. He makes a great effort to be there on the day. I wonder what he tells his comrades if they need him, I wonder what he tells her when she expects him in that room where her grubby bras and pants lie about. (My mother irons our shirts, his and mine, and folds them so beautifully you'd think they'd just come from a shop.)

I have to be around on that kind of Saturday afternoon, too. I tell her I think I'm going to be out somewhere, just to see her lovely face giving me full attention, confirming, for me, that without me she's deserted—but of course I don't go. I won't do what her daughter did, leave her to weep.

The conversation of relatives over sweet cakes and fancy biscuits rolled in coconut is all questions and answers—*how old is this one now, is that one married, has so and so had a baby, where is so and so living*—which reach standard conclusions: *that nice oh really what a blessing oh shame ay. And where's Baby, Aila? Aren't we going to see Baby my, last time we see her she's growing really pretty now glamorous, né, I'm telling you, I said to Ma, we was watching a fillum, isn't that actress the dead spit of Aila's Baby. . .*

My mother has her answer. Baby is far away. Overseas.

Overseas! Oh that's nice. And the old ones, out of pride in our superiorly educated branch of the family and a dim notion that the places of learning are designated once and for all, as the Mount is for the Sermon, Mecca for the Black Stone (according to their religious beliefs) think they must have heard Baby is in London or even America—for if there follows another question, *and what's she doing*, my father answers: furthering her education.

And so it is my mother who's told the lie, not he. He was telling the truth, Baby's learning what's necessary, in our time and for our place in the world. He's a teacher—although they know he's been to prison for his political activities most no doubt believe he still practises the profession they respect as the height of intellectual achievement—and his remark opens up before them, sightseers at the gates, the broad receding avenues of the grand vista they will never enter, while he and his children disappear freely down distant perspectives.

They don't speak the way we do (how could they, they haven't had a teacher in the house to correct their grammar) and, on my father's side of the family, expect to drink too much beer—that's their way of enjoying themselves. Our house wakes up for one afternoon to the tramping back and forth to the lavatory, the coarse harmless laughter, the happy shrills and mournful wails of children, the giggling of hand-holding sweethearts, the loud partisanships of soccer and the exchange of recipes. They are our people, they are what we might have been: our parents who bettered themselves; Baby and I. How could you compare my father with Uncle Gavin debonairly wearing, even in the house, his straw hat with its paisley band, that honey-coloured, wily, quick-eyed man laughing kindly on an expanse of empty gums, who has done time for his traffic in sending stolen cars over the border to Swaziland and made enough profit to set himself up in his transport business? 'Doing time' isn't just their euphemism for 'serving a prison sentence', which my father did: it's the hazard of an entirely different attitude to the meaning of living. I see that, when the relatives are among us—or rather when we're among them. My father went to prison for them—these aunties and uncles and cousins and kids who live back in the ghetto we come from. And I see that my father really loves them—more, he respects them, he hasn't left them behind out of any ambition for himself. He has no GAVIN'S TRUCK AND CAR HIRE to show for the time he's done. What am I to do? When I see my father like this, just as when I've sat, without his ever knowing, at the back of a hall when he was making a speech, I love him—again; forget everything. My mother, myself; that woman.

The relatives are warily impressed by this house we live in illegally in a street among white people. Cousin Vyvian (our people often give their children fancy names, a distinction those who count for nothing among whites may nevertheless claim) who was brought up in the same house with my father, harangues the men on his fill of beer, using an imagined movie gangster manner although he is a shelf-packer in a supermarket. —Listen, my baby, let me tell you—Sonny's going to do a good thing for us, ek sé. . . A good thing.— He gazes jerkily round the colonial-pillared archway in the entrance to our sitting-room, but the imperial pretensions of some white owner who lived here, long before the neighbourhood went down enough for us to risk moving in, don't represent the aims he's stumbling to draw from a fuddle of frustrations. —No shit, my baby. I'm not going to take it for ever, ay. Me neither. *Hotnot* do this do that. Things is going to be very different. They not going to sit on their arses while I break mine for a hundred and fifty bucks a week. Ye-suss! No ways, my baby, and I'm telling you. . . .a good thing. Let them go where they like, we coming right on and push them out. Ay, Sonny, no shit, ay? A good thing for us.—

Forget it man Vyv Ag, come on, such a big mouth Lay off old Vyv he's all right

But my father steadies the arm of the ignorant and bewildered man he shared a bed with (he's told us many times) as a child, and thanks him; it's not a sober man holding up a drunk one, it's an exchange of support. I don't understand.

I snap back the rings on the beer cans bought for the occasion, I hand round the tea and cakes for her. When they ask me what I'm doing I say I'm going to study at the university. Among whites: of course. It's what they expect of Sonny's boy. Sonny was always the clever one, the one who would go far. And my mother shows the women her kitchen; they're full of admiring envy, they can see how lucky she is, always was, so refined, a real lady, and deserving, chosen by Sonny, marked out to go far with him.

They've all left, the performance is over. He came out of the cinema into bright daylight; and me.

Imagine the prestige he gets out of it among his comrades—his daughter, skipped the country to join the Freedom Fighters. Dedicated in the tradition of her father, who 'recently narrowly escaped death', so the papers said, when the police charged a cleansing-of-the-graves gathering where he was speaking. 'Sonny' the popular figure in resistance politics, whereabouts often unknown since sometimes he's obliged to go underground. During the boycott campaign against yet another of the elections where we can vote to put people of our colour onto councils whose decisions can be reversed by whites, he didn't sleep at home at night because that's the place and time the police would come for him; suits him fine—oh but then I suppose the police know as well as I do where to find that big bed right there in the room as you enter. So he wouldn't have been able to use his perfect alibi to spend nights with her. I suppose she wouldn't let him, anyway. She's what the comrades would call 'a good girl', and they don't mean she's not easy with men. They mean she can be relied upon to know the priorities. My mother's not in the struggle so my mother is no priority. When he looks at me as he sometimes does I'm supposed to remember that.

If his woman were not a good girl it would be all right for me to loathe her.

I got my parents to pay me to go away for a week as the celebration of my success in matric. I went down to Durban on the motorbike and picked up a girl on the beach the first day. It was easy. Some of the beaches are open to all of us now. So I've lived with a woman for six days, fucked her and slept in the same bed with her, and don't want ever to see her again.

Sonny realized only too well he had the advantage. Aila being Aila, she couldn't be expected to take the sacrifice of her daughter (that was how she would see it) as he did. Aila did not have access to his kind of acceptance of Baby's choice to begin her life, the resource discovered in himself from which his responses came, now: his political commitment. He could quite see it: for Aila, all was loss. There was no gain. Although her eyes had changed—he noticed her dark-grained lids were slightly lowered, she no longer looked out with the ready gaze of the young Aila—she still saw 'not living for yourself' in terms of a schoolteacher's extra-curricular activities of social uplift in a little community across the veld somewhere. He had left her behind, there.

Poor Aila.

But nobody loved Baby more than he did, nobody! The boy was 'her' child; Baby was 'his'; these things were never admitted in the virtuous convention of an obscure little schoolteacher's family in a dorp ghetto. But it always had been so; even then, he knew he was not the socially impotent male whose only positive contribution to his outcast people is to beget another male to carry on a family name. What had Aila done to assuage his anguish at Baby's attempt to end her life before it had begun? Nothing. Silence. Silence upon the other silence. Comfort and understanding he had had to find elsewhere. 'I could do nothing for him. We were finished.' Hannah's flash of perception suddenly passed from the ominous focus it had had for him at the time and picked out of his darkness, Aila. Lit upon her. Aila could do nothing for him. He could do nothing for Aila. Thank god she had the boy. Such a disappointment in other ways, at least there was this to be said for him.

First there had been Sonny's discovery that the individual decision to lead a protest party of children is only an amateur's beginning, a half-conscious sign of readiness to learn disciplined political action. Then, in the process (and he retained a pedagogue's faith in the learning process as a never-ending one) there came the inspiring satisfaction of action arising from the decisions of like minds. Then the bonding of prison, a brotherhood those in the safe world can only mimic with their play-play ordeals of ordination or initiation, taking the habit and vows of chastity or getting vomit-drunk. In solitary confinement there is no choice but chastity and abstention. No sacrifice or celebration. The secret signs between initiates are messages tapped with a knuckle to be received by an ear pressed to the other side of a wall. The blood brotherhood is exchanged when hymns are taken up from cell to cell to accompany an unknown to the hangman. Sonny had heard this dread choir. He had told

Hannah about those dark mornings, while he and she were waking to the song of birds. Confessed everything about them. —How is it for a man when those hymns don't mean anything to him? What would happen to me, if I were going off to die like that, with no prayers and no god. . .I lay there while it got light. . .—

—I'm told they sing freedom songs.—

—Then the warders come and kick the cell doors and swear. I'm not talking about fear. . . Normally, people like us never think what it must be like because as far as we're concerned criminals, murderers, hang. We don't. But here, where politicals are hanged, when you're inside and you hear the singing, you think of things that didn't ever have to enter your mind before.—

The learning process continues.

Although a liberation movement strives to act rather than react, because its existence is a phenomenon of opposition to power it is constantly forced to respond to what those in power do, to move in the foreshadow of what the power is planning to do, and to predict what it might or might not be led to do by any pre-emptive action. 'Taking into account changing circumstances' is a tenet like that of a farmer taking into account the weather, and it covers as many factors as there are signs in the heavens, variables in the four winds. Sonny's late development of political sense, grown slowly out of a priggish and subservient morality, ensured that his judgment never lost touch with principle, while his unhesitating return to the struggle after detainment and imprisonment ensured that he was capable of bold pragmatism. With these credentials added to his intelligence and gifts as a speaker, he had emerged from among others to the company of decision-makers. There, the combination in his personality was reflected in his position: considered as one of the radicals, he was yet reassuring to the cautious; he could be used to press decisions in a form acceptable to them. There was an exhilarating war-time will to consensus on the strategy and tactics of attacking the government and its supports, military and economic, throughout the world, as well as in the country itself. Comrades who were arrested were immediately replaced by others ready to do their work; the interchangeability of leadership again and again defeated bans and imprisonments. Under the endless disruption of a hounding State—files seized, offices burned down, comrades become political nomads sleeping when and where they could—the huge problems of mass organization continued to be debated and tackled. How to emphasize a constituency among hoes and factory overalls without losing the chance to draw in the people the government were co-opting with the penny sweetmeats of middle class instead of rights? How to get rid of corrupt, government-protected councillors without the people taking the decision into the hands of their own anger and killing them? How to keep proper contact with the youth and street committees who wear the T-shirts and carry the colours but go beyond the approved methods of struggle and give the State the opportunity to charge leadership with incitement to murder? What issues—population removals, strikes, stay-at-homes, boycotts—would be most effective, pursued where, at what period?

There were also internal problems. Sonny brought them all home—to Hannah, that is. Hannah understood the inferences behind the positions various individuals took; he and she argued over and unravelled them together. Comrades who were united in a line of thought sometimes apparently unaccountably diverged. Someone whom Sonny had been sure of: —He didn't back down, he just sidled away.— The question was of alliances; he and Hannah were sitting outside her cottage in the garden, which they had to themselves because the people who lived in the main house were overseas. —I can't agree we should 'take each case on its merits' until we've decided exactly what are the minimum areas of policy agreement necessary before a group should be accepted.— Sonny's distended nostrils were his familiar sign of tension. —Only when we confront these people with that can we judge whether they're coming in with a genuine commitment or with the intention of influencing our objectives in some way. All smiles, and the next thing you've got a palace revolution. That's the problem with a broad alliance—which we want, which we pursue, we must have—each organization has the right to work in its own way, but that doesn't mean a licence to creep in and subvert. It's been used for that before, it'll be tried again. We can't have it. Can't risk it.—

Her soft breasts rose and fell in the low-necked dress she wore to enjoy the sun, a water-colour wash coloured her blonde skin, but he was staring for her response and did not see her. —I think that may be an exaggeration. It's not as if this lot represents any great constituency. To attempt anything like that, they'd have to have strong support on the executive, they'd have to have people with influence—people among you—

—But that's exactly what worries me. Why does someone on the executive with whom I've discussed the whole matter in principle, again and again, before the actual situation came up—and we had exactly the same point of view—why today does he say nothing?—

—He's changed his mind. Doesn't necessarily mean someone's changed it for him.—

—Yes it does. Because we've always been so open—you know—between us, it would be natural for him to tell me he'd changed his mind. Say why, discuss it.—

She sat up straight and picked ants off his sleeve. —Who was it he was along with?—

—A couple of people he hasn't been particularly enthusiastic about before. If you can call it 'with'; as I say, he gave himself away by saying nothing. I suppose it amounted to being with them.—

—You'd better take off your shirt. Ants all over you; look.—He held up his arms and she helped him out of the sleeves. While she shook and slapped at the shirt he ran his hand back and forth in the hair on his breast, turned in upon himself.

—Here, my love.— But he did not take the shirt from her and she sat down with it in her lap. —You don't want to say what you're thinking.—

—No I don't. But he's ambitious. . .I've told you that before. Oh in the right way, I meant; he believes he could be used more effectively, he thinks he knows better how to deal with some of the forces against us. He feels he's the one who understands big business. And he knows the mentality of the Afrikaners. . . But he'd like to be in the papers more often . . . You know?— She laughed at his reluctant realization of this. —If he could gather supporters, a faction around him, he might just feel justified in pushing somebody else out, at the top—

She continued for him: —And maybe there's a way to do it.—

—But what a way! This is the crowd who wanted to put up candidates for the regional council elections, eh. We had to work to persuade them to call it off.—

—Are you going to talk to him?—

—I don't want to before I've talked to others. . .if there are others. . .flush them out.—

—Be careful. No palace revolution, but no witch-hunt. Certainly not led by you.—

On these days when they talked like this in a garden, there not by right but by calculation of someone else's absence, as if theirs was a clandestine meeting of the other kind he so often attended, there was no love-making. Now while Hannah went on, speaking his thoughts as well as her own, in her private, perceptive way, his sense of where he was underwent a strange intensity. It was physical. He became aware on the very surface of his skin, his bare breast and arms, as well as through sight and smell, of this that was called 'the garden' hovering and pressing in upon him. The shadowless mauve of the jacaranda full-blown, ectoplasmic, near his face, tree ferns airing green wings spread over the pond tiled with lily leaves, the mist of live warmth from cut grass. A tingling peace on his nerve-endings, in his ears, murmured over by some sort of birds with grey tails rustling in a fig tree. As he sat with Hannah, the blurred rush of the chronology of living was halted for a while. The absolute of existence: an alpine pine hatched against failing light above the darkening earth, the bright tiny moths of the first stars flitting out of the hazy radiance of the sky. Clouds obscuring like shadows; the northern tree shivering at the tips of feathered branches as the heat waves of the day rose. The red-polished stoep and the rotting wooden windows, the room there, with the bed, the chaotic, disintegrated forms of the painting—all was stayed, as before a hand held up. Over the moment he sees the foreign tree, the element like himself that doesn't belong, fall majestically, following its giant shadow that is falling across the man and woman in this garden, now. Where the saw has razed through its stout trunk the rings of its years are revealed under a powdering of sawdust.

What was sensuously close drew suddenly away; he was

removed from it and the isolation of his presence offered its meaning. A rich white man's domain of quiet and beauty screened by green from screams of fear and chants of rage, from the filth of scrap-heap settlements and the smashed symmetry of shot bodies; he had no part in it. He did not know what he was doing there.

He pulled himself out of the chair and went into the cottage; to that one room.

Now there are things *he* doesn't know. I wasn't snooping, this time. I was alone in the house and I heard one of the women who come from the farms hawking mealies in the street. Her call hollowed my stomach; as kids, mealies were one of our favourite treats, my sister and I loved any hand-held food you could eat while you played. I heard that old cry GRE—EE—NN MEA-LIES right through the reggae beat of UB-40 on my cassette player, and I ran out to catch the woman before the cry became too distant. She swung the sack down from her head; everything about her was stockily foreshortened to carry weight —bare chunky feet, thick body, pediment neck, face and skull broadened for burdens. How black they always were, these women; black blackened by labour in the sun, it's as if nature, which supplied our founding parents with the right degree of pigment to inhabit this continent, also supplies them with the camouflage under which to appear to submit to slavery. If you're mixed you don't have the protection. She strips the green leaves and spills the floss back from the cobs, digging her earth-rimmed nail to spurt milk from a row of nubs, because I ask her for young mealies, and her black face has no recognition for me, my half-blackness and this half-white man's street we live in as one of my father's political acts. She doesn't know I have anything to do with her. So much for his solidarity with the people.

And then I found I didn't have enough money in my pocket to pay her. She smells the same, of the grease smeared on her red-black cheeks and the smoke of wood-fires in her clothes, but mealies have gone up in price since the days in Benoni-son-of-sorrow. One of our Afrikaans neighbours had come out to buy, as well, and she intervened to pay for me—Ag now, don't worry, you can give me back later, it's nothing—once you get one of them round to making an exception of you, there's no limit to their neighbourliness. My mother's dignity and beauty make our family an exception, although my father says exceptions change nothing, they merely confirm mob racism. For him, we are in this street to challenge the general.

I ran back to the house to look for my mother's store of small change, as my sister and I used to do. But there was no jam-jar on the kitchen shelf. She was at work and would have her handbag with her; I thought there might be another purse or loose money in her dressing-table drawers. I know my mother; her sort of innocent, easily-found 'safe places' for things. Under the plastic tray where her cosmetics are ranged was a five-rand note and an envelope printed with the logo of a passport-photograph vending machine.

I ran, again, to the black woman seated with indifferent patience under the blanket-skirt and the young Afrikaner wife, legs strutted wide on high heels, arms crossed under her breasts, smiling at me as if I were an athlete racing for the tape. She was another pink-and-yellow one. But not emancipated, like the other, not a prison visitor or a lover. She greeted me with a little sharp twist of the smile in the direction of the mealie vendor. —They just charging whatever they think you'll pay. I've told her, not fifty cents each, forty cents. So no, wait, that's too much—you only owe one-twenty.—

My father's passport (he went overseas to a conference in Germany before he was detained) has been withdrawn, Baby left illegally, I've never had one. Neither has my mother. I went back into their bedroom to find what she had placed under her cosmetic tray. Photographs are not like letters, anyone may look at them. There were six. There she was, her neck held as you do when seated upright in the booth as the flash comes. The slightly defiant embarrassment with which exposure is met, because you never know for whom, in the world, your image is meant. Hair smoothed a moment before; wearing her seed pearls.

Where is she going? Is she going to leave him? Wild idea . . .my mother! Where is there for her to go. There's an accountant cousin who emigrated to Toronto a few years ago, at the Saturday tea-parties there's news of him doing well.

So I know nothing about her. Like him, I don't know the invasion of unhappiness in her; the devastation left by him and his daughter.

I don't have a photograph of my mother. If I took one of these, would she miss it?

Aila has her passport. She told her husband only after it had been granted and issued.

He had the curious impression that she must have mentioned, indicated, her intention. A torn-off strip of paper buried in a pile of problems documented in his mind; the new series of bans imposed on his comrades had brought a crisis and reshuffle of responsibilities.

There was a moment's pause. His wife evidently decided—they both decided without a glance—to accept the lapse as genuine. Her taking the necessary steps for application with the absolute minimum of reference to him was what he would have advised; it was as if she had acted upon this. Aila was in the clear, innocent. She had done nothing beyond visiting him in prison as his wife and keeping a carryall packed with toiletries against his re-detention. But of course there was guilt by association, by loyalty. Aila had to show she was not involved; a stay-at-home wife. The affectionate diminutive by which she knew her only girlhood sweetheart, the chummy appellation by which crowds knew him—the police files' *alias Sonny*—did not have to be filled in between first and surname on forms requiring name of husband. Aila's best chance of getting a passport was to distance herself from him, his record, his activities, his life.

A stay-at-home wife—and mother. There was the question of Baby, as well. The Security Police surely knew about Baby; but maybe not, the illegal movements of young people presumed to be erratic and adventurous could pass unnoticed until and unless someone was picked up and gave out names under interrogation.

Sonny knew where Aila would go. —And a visa?— He spoke almost humbly.

She had one; everything was arranged through a lawyer both knew well. Lawyers have the habit of discretion sometimes to the point of absurdity or unintentional slight; he saw the man frequently, he was a close adviser to the trade unions, and there had been no mention of a passport for Aila. Well, the lawyer, too, had other things on his mind. Anyway, it was necessary to feel assured Aila had been in good hands.

As Baby's mother and father, they discussed money. —I thought I'd take some clothes. I'm making warm things—they say it gets quite chilly there in winter.— Yes, lately the sewing-machine had to be put aside when the table was used for meals, he'd noticed, without attaching any significance to Aila's preoccupation. —She'll always need money. Wherever you are— (he stopped himself from citing his prison experience, the inference would be alarming to Aila). —You don't know the value of money until you're in certain situations— He laughed, as an explanation, confession: he and Aila had begun their child's life in a situation where money was associated with greed.

He knew best in political matters; they had some small savings she would withdraw from the bank and take with her.

—How much is there, exactly?—

She fetched the savings booklet and they stood heads together reading the figures. —Oh, it's more than I thought. I'd forgotten about the interest.— Aila was smiling almost as she used to.

—You can't take all that. It'll exceed the exchange-control allowance, I'm sure. The allowance is smaller for neighbouring countries than for overseas.—

—How will they know? I'll take the notes in cash.—

—Aila. . .— He had gone back to excising articles from a newspaper, running a blade along columns.

—Somehow. I could.—

Impatience was something new in him; like the moustache he had grown to show he was someone else, now. This person still had responsibility for her, nevertheless. —Aila, for god's sake, you can't do things like that. D'you know what'll happen if you're caught out? Can you imagine yourself in prison? Go and see Baby and enjoy it. Forget what I said about money. Take the dresses and whatever. Those kinds of games are not for you.—

He turned pages of the paper without seeing them, then forced himself to read and began pressing the blade cleanly along a margin. His hand fumbled for a pen to mark the date;

she was still in the room, he knew it in spite of the silence—he thought of the special quality of her presence he used to sense when he would come into the house calling out her name. —You're so lucky you're going to see Baby.—

What was she doing—looking at him? Turned away? He would not lift his head and the blade sliced dryly through the fibres of newsprint, a faint domestic echo of the electric saws that destroyed the trees from which it was made; the pine tree. . . But his words were as feeble an echo of the surging envy he felt—of her option of distancing herself from the struggle, of the passport, of the right to go to the girl as the one who had been there to bandage her wrists.

—I know.—

Was that all? All to be expected of his wife when they were talking of their first child? Who could tolerate Aila's tranquil blamelessness!

He heard her double step, high heels touching the floor before the soles came lightly down, and thought she had left the room. But she had paused: —I wish you could go.—

With her? With Aila? On his own? In place of her? Aila never had much relish for journeys, she didn't know how to deal with officialdom, she had found it difficult even to speak in the presence of his warder.

Or she wished he had not done all he had done, all that she would not reproach him with ever, to the boy, to Baby, to her—so that it would not be only his lack of a passport, his commitment to political action that took away from him the right to be in her place.

Is it because of me?

Since my mother's been away he's been spending time at home. He even brought out the chess board. We've played together a few evenings. But I'm careful. I don't know what he may be trying to get me into, now. I cook supper for us. Once I found the nerve to say something: —Haven't you got a meeting?—

He waited for a moment, showing me he knew, strictly between ourselves, my real question, and he replied to it. —No. No meeting. I'll be at home.—

At once I fetched my helmet and bike keys and put my head round the door. —Well, I'm off.—

He was playing that record he likes so much, some Mozart overture, he thinks he's only got to set up the scene and we'll do something educational together or watch soccer on the tele, dad and his boy. But he also knew I hadn't been going anywhere.

When I came home, late, the lights were still on. I thought he was waiting up for me and I went straight along the passage to my room. But there I became aware that there were voices, men's voices, in the house. They became more audible—their insistence, their cross-talk—as whoever it was must have left the sitting-room and been pausing in the entrance. There was the sound of the front door being closed and bolted by him, and the creaks and subdued clatter of his movements, tidying up, clicking off lights. He knocked at my door. After me again. I didn't say come in, I said, Yes?

He looked slowly round my room; I suppose it must be a year, more, since he's been in it. There was the beginning of a crinkling round his eyes, affirmation rather than recognition, at what I've kept, and he went over and stood a moment, head back, as if he were in an art gallery, not his son's bedroom, before a poster of a desert. That's new. Just space. I don't know what desert, where—I hoped he wasn't going to expect me to say.

He sat on the end of my bed and his weight tightened the

covers over my feet, I felt pinned down. —There was a meeting, after all. Here.—

My father has such a wonderful smile, all the planes of his face are so strongly defined, so encouraging, the open feelings sculptured so deep—no wonder he is attractive to crowds, and to women. My mother and the other. I resemble him but my face is a mask moulded from his and I only look out through it, I don't inhabit it as he does. I suddenly was alarmed that he was going to talk about her, his woman, about the cinema, yes, at last, the whole story, that's what he'd come into my room for, Baby was right, you can't live with them, you ought to get away from them.

I had to speak quickly. —I heard someone leave.—

—I know. It's unfortunate. Something turned up soon after you'd left. I was settling down to read, for once. . .when did I last finish a book. I get halfway through and by the time I can get back to it I've forgotten the first part. D'you get any reading done, Will?—

Everything we say to each other has a meaning other than what comes out. That's what makes it difficult to be in the house with him. Now he was admitting he doesn't know anything much about me except that I know about the woman, who she is, where she lives. He has no hand in enriching my life (as he would think of it) anymore. Although we couldn't be members of the library when we lived across the veld, I mustn't forget he bought children's books and read to us.

I didn't tell him that in the past year I've read almost everything in his bookcase. If he'd been interested enough, if he'd come into my room for any reason other than his own concerns (what was it now, the danger of confession was averted but there must be something else) he might have found his Gramsci or his Kafka among the clutter on my table. I opened my hand towards Dornbusch and Fisher's *Macroeconomics*, on the reading list for my second-year courses.

—Well, that's essential. Of course I did it the other way round. . .you know, the other kind of books first. Poetry and stuff. I had a different idea of what's necessary. When I was your age. The wrong way round— He lifted his hands, seemed about to place one on the mound of my feet, touch me, but did not. —Ignorance.—

I was yawning uncontrollably, I didn't mean to be rude to him. I didn't know whether I was tense to get rid of him or I wanted him to stay.

—Will, you didn't hear anyone here tonight. You didn't hear anyone talking and you didn't hear anyone leave.—

After he'd said what he'd come for he continued to sit with me for—how long—a few moments, it seemed a long quiet time. Then he got up and went out softly, as if I were sleeping.

So that was it. Someone on the run, or an infiltrator from outside. Or there was a meeting with some of his people he doesn't want the rest to know about; since he's been home more, I've seen that he's in some kind of trouble with his crowd: these emotions don't have to be concealed in quite the same way as his love affair. There are long discussions with this one and that one—who come here openly, I don't have to pretend, for my own safety and his, I haven't seen them. There are reports in the newspapers speculating about changes and realignments in the organizations, including his, that make up the movement. That's his business; he doesn't need any complicity with me, beyond warning me to keep my eyes closed and my mouth shut. Which is already what he has taught me to do for other reasons. That's ended up being his only contribution to my further education.

Perhaps my mother said something to him about keeping an

eye on me while she's away, and he feels he ought to do that much for her. So he's sacrificing the nights he could be spending in the big bed on the floor. As if I would ever know what time he crept in, midnight or dawn, I'm young and when I sleep, I sleep. Only older people wait up.

Home every night. Is it possible it's because he wants to be with me? It's for me?

Every third day, at the agreed hour, he waited alone in the room for a call from Lesotho, where she had gone because her grandfather had died. The cottage was locked up. She'd left him the key. Of course she was often alone in that room but he had never been there without her before. He tried to read but could not; the room distracted him, beckoning with this and that. He was a spectator of his own life there; the edge of the table he often bumped against when he went, dazed with after-love sleep, to the kitchen or bathroom; the shape of the word processor seen from a particular eye-level, now viewed from a different perspective; the huge painting with all its running colours that was more familiarly felt than seen, since when he stretched an arm behind his head, on the bed, he came in contact with the lumpy surface of what she had told him was the impasto. An ugly, meaningless painting, to him; there is always something about the beloved—some small habit—some expression of taste—one dislikes and about which one says nothing, or lies. Also she might have taken into account his background—lack of cultural context for the understanding of such work, so he had had to pretend (to protect each's idea of the other) that he thought it fine. Now he was alone with its great stain of incoherence spreading above the bed from which, at least, it had been out of sight. Of course, for her it was something handed down, like the old studio photograph of a bespectacled lady with cropped white hair—probably her grandmother—which stood in a small easel frame on top of the bookshelves. These things belonged to a life not followed, a continuity set aside; somehow he never thought of her in connection with a family. She wasn't placed, as he was, whatever he felt or did, with wife and son and daughter in the Saturday afternoon tea-parties.

Some days the call was delayed. She used a post-office booth for discretion, and they had agreed he should not call her at her grandfather's house, where others were likely to be around to overhear. He saw traverse the empty bed the stripe of sun that used to move like a clock's hand across their afternoons, over their bodies. Once he tidily took off his shoes and lay down on the bedcover's tiny mirrors and embroidered flowers. He must use the time to return to the problems of his relations with his comrades; this was the room, after all, the only room, where such matters could be examined openly; no fear of anyone taking advantage of frankness or admissions. But without her, Hannah, it was a stranger's room, a witness; while the house without Aila was unchanged, as if Aila were simply out of his way in some other part of it—maybe it was because the boy was still there, he and the boy among all Aila's family trappings.

He lay on the bed, a tramp who has broken in. He got up and wandered, looking at the jottings in Hannah's handwriting, but did not read open letters addressed to her. And then, the telephone: and with its croo-croo croo-croo it was their room again he was padding over intimately in his socks, to hear her. Each did not use the other's name (for discretion); there was always a lot of smiling and laughter, and certainly she must hear in his voice that he was at once sexually aroused by the sound of her, but on this day after the initial pleasure there was an urgent break, out of which she told him: —Don't be alarmed . . .not good news. I've been P.I'd*—I think.—

—Oh my god. How d'you know?—

—A letter came yesterday. I'm *duly informed* I must apply for a visa. But I'm sure it'll be all right.—

—Have you told London?—

—I spoke to my director right away. They're already working on it. And several people here. . . By the time I've wound things up I'm sure it'll be fixed. I couldn't come back for another few weeks anyway—I've got to decide what to do with the old house, the books—I'm giving away the furniture, such as it is, but the books. . .and the papers. . .the papers must be preserved. What d'you think? They want them for the little archive here but . . . I'm inclined to believe I ought to look after them—

Agitation was invading his whole body. —Listen. Something must be done at *this* end. I'll find out.—

—Don't, don't. Please don't. I don't want you to get mixed up. . .—

An unexpressed struggle between them hummed across the distance. He severed it for both. —But you must come back, you must come back.—

When he had put the receiver down, it seized him: because of me. Because of this room, it's happened. But she was gone. He was desperate not to be able to pick up the receiver at once and tell her, it's because this place has been an everywhere

*Declared a prohibited immigrant.

and they know it and they think you've been seduced—not to lie in that bed but to run as courier for the jailbird and his cause.

But when they talked again on the next third day he could not tell her; he could say nothing over the telephone. He could not tell her how, playing chess with his son to steady his nerves and enable him to think rationally (thank god Aila wasn't there, thank god he wasn't alone) he examined and discarded different ways to set about getting the order against her re-entry rescinded. He tried out, in his mind, taking one of the comrades into his confidence, a militant, worldly priest whose liberation theology would include an understanding of a man's responsibility for loving, inside or outside conventional morality. Father, I need advice. But no. A prisoner of conscience, you sit in detention, on trial, convicted for the liberty of all your people. That conscience takes precedence over any conscience about a wife and family left to shift for themselves, and over any woman you have need of. The comrades might know about her; probably did. But as an irrelevance. The struggle is what matters; and he and they are at one in dedication to that. Nothing that could be seen to deflect his attention from the struggle should be evidenced in him, who has even given his daughter for liberation. Particularly in the present phase, of factionalism. He thought of the merchant, by colour one of their own, who gave money—as insurance for a future or maybe out of real conviction, a Bakunin—but who also must know high government officials who would woo his support for their policy of privileging a middle class; perhaps he was the man to approach. He thought of the white newspaper editor who was challenging the government, front and editorial pages, over suppression of press freedom, and was too influential among whites to be refused meetings with cabinet ministers. A small favour might be asked of him. . . But newspapermen—they sniff out the perfume of a woman the way certain creatures (the schoolmaster picked up such oddities of information in his reading days) can detect the presence of truffles under the ground. 'Sonny' the platform speaker ex-political prisoner and Hannah Plowman, representative of an international human rights organization. Next thing, there would be a reporter at the door, and if he himself were not there, well, the son would be better than nothing. Will would be asked if he could say anything about the refusal of a visa to this friend of the family who monitored political trials.

As a hypochondriac runs to his doctor with every personal problem transmuted into a diagnosable ache or pain, he went to the lawyer who had represented him during his detention and trial. Metkin looked like a rabbi and listened as his client thought a psychiatrist would listen; in this presence of contemporary and ancient wisdom, divination, surviving between the telephone and intercom on a desk, Sonny felt humiliation as he might have been experiencing some physical urge. He was explaining that he wanted to hand the whole matter over to the lawyer; he himself could do nothing to help anyone in conflict with the authorities. This person had no-one else to speak for her, within the country; she was not in contact with her few relatives, and they were not the sort of people to act in this type of matter. Whatever the government did they would believe was justified.

But he saw in the lawyer's face that he had explained nothing, and he tried once more to evade the complete understanding there. He sat back in the chair on the other side of the desk and looked into eyes black as his own, the eyes of old races. —She's an invaluable person.—

Despite the unwelcome understanding of the lawyer he felt relieved—when you are in a political trial every hidden motive, every vestige of contradiction, every hesitation of purpose must be confided, so that you may be defended even against your own high principles, the dangerous licence of confidence cannot be revoked. The matter was in hand—the lawyer's soothing phrase. For results, one must be patient; and as she said, she could not come back for some weeks, anyway. . .

Right from the first day she had been less alarmed than Sonny; he realized he had discounted the preoccupation of her feelings at the loss of her grandfather, who had been also a father—and mother—to her. She was back there sorting the old missionary's papers and simple possessions, sorting through her childhood, unable even to point it out to him in passing as he had done the place in the veld outside Benoni, to her, when they were driving by. Action on her behalf was being taken at home and in London. He was kept busy planning and running workshops—'resistance education' (the name he coined for it, approved)—in shanties and mud churches, under the guise of local club meetings, since the National Education Crisis Committee was restricted by a ban, and in the spare time he would have been able to spend with her there was the quiet house, thank heaven, with only the boy around. And Will was less hostile, sometimes it seemed even possible to touch him. Ah, without women, what is always subliminally taut between men is relaxed. The boy was a man, almost a man. He could be trusted; hadn't he proved he could be trusted, he would not even meet your eyes to show he remembered. If told to forget he had heard someone visit the house he would do as he must.

The men who had come that night sought to form a cabal (how poor and melodramatic the political vocabulary was) to oust certain leaders. They were 'putting out feelers' to individuals from several organizations to see who was 'like-minded'—sidling euphemisms. They had not succeeded in gaining a recruit; but they read a certain distraction in 'Sonny' as reason to take the chance that he would allow himself to forget they had come, and give no warning to anyone.

There was something on the stoep. A bundle.

As he stopped, coming through the bougainvillea which concealed the side entrance to the garden, he saw an object; suspiciously—explosive booby traps as well as ordure can be placed on the doorsteps of political prisoners' friends. Coming closer, he made out a sleeper—some meths drinker must have found the deserted cottage convenient to camp against—then, seeing that the sleeping bag was new and a man's hand (young, white, with one of those twenty-four-hour military format watches on the wrist) was visible over the hidden head, stopped again.

Who was Sonny to intercept an intruder. How could he account for himself, approaching this cottage, key in his pocket. He had better go away. Come back later. The telephone would ring and not be answered; he called out as if the place belonged to him—What do you think you're doing here! Hey!—

The hand flew away from the head. A young man struggled out of the bag, unembarrassed, with a sleepy glance of recognition, confirmation.

Sonny had never seen him before in his life.

The young man circled his shoulders in their sockets to ease stiffness and breathed deeply. He had pollen-coloured spiky-cut hair too short to be tousled by sleep, a woman's pretty nose and long-lashed grey eyes, and a man's dark strong growth of a few days' beard. He half-smiled, and nodded, as if his man had arrived as summoned, on time.

—This is private property. What do you want here?— This person knew him; must have seen him in newspaper photographs.

Or it could be on video as one of the Security Police's film stars. He believed he had learnt to be alert without becoming paranoid, but the place where this intruder was waiting—waiting for him, clearly—her cottage, their room, to which he would return again and again, unable to keep away, and the move—the entry restriction timed to get rid of her without arresting or deporting her—these circumstances experience entitled him to interpret as put together by the people who knew all about him, the majors and sergeants who had interrogated him in detention, watched him through the Cyclops's eye of his cell door in prison, and were aware, without seeing, when she took him into her body in this cottage. He, like all his kind, educated in political struggle, knew them, too; the majors and sergeants. He knew what could be ready to follow the circumstances: re-detention, blackmail—not with money, between police and revolutionaries there is a higher exchange, the selling of trust. Not a domestic affair, telltattling to the wife that you're playing around (their kind of vocabulary) if you don't answer questions satisfactorily. They know 'Sonny' wouldn't betray his comrades for that; the wife knows about his blonde and she's the submissive type who would forgive him, anyway. Then what? What? His woman in Lesotho; but if they had wanted to strike one of their dread barters with him (we'll detain her for the political confidences you've made to her, unless you give *us* some confidences)—if they wanted to do that, they would have kept her in the country, not shut her out!

The young man was standing there, the jeans, the sneakers, the haircut, like any roadside figure thumbing a lift; but in front of her door. —We'd better go inside.—

Sonny gave an authoritative high laugh. —Look, you take your bag and get out of here. Just go.—

—I've got something to tell you. But inside. From a friend of yours. I was with her the day before yesterday.—

—I'm not expecting any messages from anybody, and I want you out of here. I don't want to know who you are and where you come from.—

The young man listened with assurance and condescending understanding. —All right. I have some sort of fancy credential. 'Sermons in stones, and good in everything'.—

The young man was living in the cottage while he was back at the house with his son, Will. It was what Hannah asked of Sonny, her message: let this person stay in the cottage, give him the key. The key? He stood in a hardware store while a duplicate was cut, and a slow depression sank his gaze to the tools and gadgets that furnished other people's lives—his own, part of Saturday purchases, when he did house-proud repairs in the first, the ghetto home.

The man called himself Nick, since there had to be something to address him by. She must have thought the clandestinity of the cottage was ready-made for another kind, as well; a good place for an infiltrator. As it was known she was away, no-one would have any reason to approach it. And the people in the main house? What about them? Sonny was choked with such questions during the phone calls, unable to ask her anything, unable even to indicate that the guest had arrived and was in the room while the call was made, since he went out only at night. Did she understand it was dangerous for her lover to be in the cottage with this guest even for the duration of the phone call? If the man were discovered to be in the country, were followed and picked up, Sonny would be picked up with him and detained for interrogation about his association with him, charged with aiding and abetting whatever it was he was doing—and what that was Sonny could not ask. The discipline of the struggle prevailed between them; each to his own task. But when the young man was asleep (he slept during the day) Sonny went through the cupboards and likely places in the cottage where guns or explosives might have been stowed away; he would not allow such material to be there to compromise her with some charge that her cottage was in fact a cache for arms. He could not warn her that she might come back and step straight into a Security Police vehicle. He could only say: don't hurry back, take your time. . .

The young man slept in the big bed close to the earth. He did not wake, when being observed. His socks hung on the radiator where her intimate garments had. Sonny left food for him in her kitchen each time and went away for another two days. When he got back home he would call out, Will? But he always knew whether or not the boy was there; like his mother's, his presence could be sensed.

All dogs love me, no problem, the young man had told him when he asked about the dogs raising the alarm when a stranger came and went through the garden. But the people in the main house must nevertheless notice there was someone coming to and fro at the cottage. Someone other than himself, the man they must think of as her man. Perhaps, unlike himself, they expected a woman like her, free-living, alone, doing some kind of leftish good works, content to hire converted servants' quarters, to have men coming and going. Perhaps they had known of some other man before himself.

One afternoon the young man was gone. When Hannah phoned, on time, he couldn't tell her that, either, but the spirit in his voice and the caressing chatter that came from him must have told her for him. He felt strongly sure she would soon be back. He had never cleaned house before—in his kind of family women cooked and cleaned, only his son, wanting to differentiate himself in every way, helped out in the kitchen—but he stripped the bed, swept the room, found the product with which to wash the bath. The man had left behind, shed, his hitchhiker's outfit. Must have changed persona for the next stage of his mission. In the bathroom was an open bottle of hair bleach with a picture of a grinning blonde combing flying tresses. But Sonny's Hannah needed no bleach or paint. He threw out the bottle with the bundle of clothes, it was the day of the week the dustmen came to take away the white suburb's trash and he saw, in the lane as he left the cottage by the hidden gate, one of the black men rummage the bundle out of the mess of newspapers and kitchen debris and consider the usefulness of the garments as other than a disguise. Sonny smiled, felt that it was right. A conclusion that restored balance to something he found distasteful and distorted, a means he did not want for his ends. Sermons in stones, and good in everything; that was not to be used as a password, in the mouth of a third person.

She's cut off her hair.

I had come back from classes to the empty house and parked my motorcycle on the stoep as I always did for safety, and when I opened the door someone was standing there. She'd heard me thumping the bike up the steps and she was waiting, presenting the surprise of her return. I recognized her as you do someone in a photograph taken at a time and in a place when you didn't yet know them, or after they were as you had known them. The shape of her face was changed by the short curls brushed around it, the small flat ears with, always, some little decoration dangling from the lobe, had disappeared, the polished curve of the forehead was hidden by a fluffed-up fringe. She flung her arms round my neck and hugged me. A line drew between her beautiful eyes with the joyful intensity with which she looked at me, took me in. My mother was never demonstrative like that. But they were her eyes.

—What happened?—

She was laughing with pleasure. —Oh everything's fine. Baby is blooming. You wouldn't know her, so grownup, completely in charge. . .—

—What have you done? Why did you do it?—

—You mean this?—she poked her fingers through the curls. —Oh this. All those years. It was enough. Don't you like it? Don't you think it's nice, Will?—

I could only smile and move my shoulders; I'm not her husband, she doesn't have to try to please me.

We went into the kitchen, our old place to talk. She took my mother's chair at the table, she made tea. She was telling me about where Baby lived, what good friends Baby had, responsible people who looked after her, not at all what one thought it would be, considering some of the people she'd mixed with here. —They made me so welcome. She shares the house, of course, but can you imagine, she's planted herbs in the garden—Baby!—

—She didn't leave to go gardening, though. What does she do—or couldn't she say.—

—Well, you don't ask questions, of course, but she was quite open, she seems to be busy with the reception of refugees—not exactly refugees, people like herself, who come out. They have to be investigated. You know.— The big eyes moved over me.

So my mother understands the ambiguities of liberation, now, the screening and interrogation carried out not by the Security Police but by her daughter. Baby has instructed her.

—Was it Baby's idea?— She knows I mean the hair.

—Will! You'd be so pleased to see how she is. . . She was watching me brushing it one day and she said, how old are you now, Ma? She never remembers! She always thinks I'm younger than I am. So I reminded her. She said, and how much of your life have you spent doing that—so next day we went to the hairdresser and I had it off.—

She turned her profile to me as if to let me acknowledge the full effect.

I said nothing.

—I feel so much lighter.— She was looking at me shyly to see if I would not be glad of that. —And has everything been all right?—

We don't mention him by name, not yet. She's thinking of police raids, no doubt; of his safety. Could I tell her something else, that he's been home a lot, even playing chess with me? But I can't because that would be a comment on what we're both not supposed to know, the reality I protect her from. —Oh as usual. Except the yard's a bit of a mess. I did get round to cutting the grass once, but my work-load's quite tough, I've had a lot of reading to do.—

—Did you eat?—

And now we both smile. —I cooked. It seemed to be okay.—

She knows I fed him, she could count on me, now she wants me to like what Baby has done to her, her hair.

—There's more to tell but we'll wait until your father comes in.—

So he's there, spoken out loud between us. —What's it all about? Why not now?—

—Because I'd only have to tell it over again.—

This woman with dull permed curls. She's never put us in the same category before, him and me; since when are our unspoken confidences the same as the sort of silences between them?

She never came back. Cut loose. She was gone for good: my mother.

Aila's mission was the kind to be expected of her; she has brought women's tidings, a mother's news. Baby is married. But for security reasons not even that domestic intelligence could have been transmitted over the telephone or by letter; not to this house. Baby hadn't told her father herself. Couldn't. Sonny was informed along with his son, by his wife. A family matter. There should have been kisses, handclasps, a Saturday tea-party with beer for the uncles, Aila with her shining coil of hair, wearing a new dress home-made for the occasion.

The boy said nothing, as usual. Apparently he had no feeling for his sister. Aila had met the man, Aila thought he was nice, steady, good enough for their—Sonny's—daughter, his Baby; he had not been asked. On the contrary, the fact was accomplished without him and now he was the one humbly to put questions. Aila confirmed that the young man was someone Baby had known before she left: so they left together, then, and that was something else that had not been confided in her father. She went away with a man, she had been living with a man while he was with his woman in the cottage. As discreet, not only politically, as the father himself.

The young man—husband!—was one of their own kind, not some white foreigner (apparently poor Aila had feared that?) his Baby might have been expected to pick up. 'Steady'—as if Benoni standards could apply to the life of a Freedom Fighter . . .poor Aila! He was known by his code name, was something quite important among the younger people in the movement, one didn't ask, he and Baby didn't talk about it, maybe even she does not know exactly. He has been trained in other parts of Africa and overseas. He has a family here at home but thinks it best they should not be contacted to toast the alliance—for security reasons.

—His family aren't involved at all.— Aila is quite self-assured about the whole business, for once she's taken on responsibility for something all by herself, she's the one who's given approval in this matter of his daughter's future.

Out of his hurt, Sonny felt a heavy sense of lack of occasion in all three of them, Aila, Will, himself. He made some effort, before them, for them. —Well, that's good news, let's hope they'll be happy. . .and strong in their work.—

The presence of the boy makes everything he says sound fatuous; the moment the boy's mother is back he withdraws again from any male understanding. And Aila gave instructions: —We won't talk about the marriage to anyone.—

What idea was that? Since when did Aila decide what was politically expedient? Since when did she think she understood such things? Did she really believe the Security Police weren't aware by now where Baby was and what she was doing? —Why not?—

She felt the gibe in her husband's remark and turned her head away from the two men. —I have to be able to go back.—

The day of her return ended as all days do in a marriage, with them alone in their bedroom. Sonny and Aila. No matter what has happened during the day, there is no escaping that dread conclusion. They performed the rituals of preparation for bed that had preceded all kinds of nights, years of nights, for them; drawing curtains, washing, brushing teeth as had been done to be pleasing in the taste of kisses, undressing before each other as they had done in the delightful gaze of desire. His bundle of sex hung like something disowned by his body. She folded her garments one by one over the chair, the stockings holding the form of her legs and feet. She began to unpack toilet things from a floral-printed bag. —I didn't want to say in front of Will— Aila stood there in her nightgown in the middle of the room as if it were somewhere she had entered without knocking. He was setting the hour on his bedside alarm radio, and he looked at her at last. —He's not a child—what's the matter? What is it?— A thrill of fear for Baby flashed through him impatiently.

—She's expecting.—

The genteel euphemism carried over from back-yard gossip in their old life. He laughed, gently correcting: —She's pregnant. I don't think Will is unaware of these possibilities. . . So. So that's the reason for the marriage.—

—Oh no.— She paused to have him acknowledge another possibility. —They would've married anyway. They love each other.—

He pulled back the covers on his side of the bed and sat down. —Family life—babies—it doesn't go too well with activism like theirs. Doesn't really do, anywhere, but particularly in exile.—

—Well, they have permission to live outside the camp.—

—Yes you told us. Her vegetable patch.—

—She's very pleased about the baby. You wouldn't have thought she'd have such strong maternal instincts, would you?—

—When they grow up. . .what can one know about them.—

—And they're even sure what it's going to be—a boy. There's a test you can have, these days, imagine that!—

Yes, Aila has been brought to life—that's how he sees it—by the idea of a birth, a new life coming out of the old one he left her buried in. Aila looks like any other woman, now, with that same hair—do they wear it to make them seem younger. She'll never sit at the dressing-table before bed, brushing that long, straight shining hair, again. He's rid of Aila. Free.

He slowly swung his legs onto the bed and dropped the covers over himself up to the chest. With closed eyes, a moment, he heard her moving about the room, saw Baby dancing, coming to kiss him on the ear, saw her glittering eyes smeared with mascara. Married. Baby. How could she know her own mind, so displaced, far from home. But in the struggle no-one is underage, unprepared for anything, children throw stones and get shot. —She's so young.— He hardly knew he had spoken aloud: Aila heard it as a momentary lapse into intimacy. She said: —So was I.—

He opened his eyes. Much younger. Eighteen-year-old. Aila had taken a long shining black plait from the toilet bag. It was tied with a scrap of ribbon where the hair had been severed. There was the rustle of a sheet of tissue paper Aila smoothed before she folded the plait within it and put it away in a drawer.

The other woman came back the same week. He had longed for her so painfully it seemed at times he couldn't get enough oxygen into his lungs, breathing was constricted by the intensity of the fear she would not be allowed to cross the frontier, and he would never get a passport so that he could go to her. And yet his only relief from tension over the ambiguities and intrigues that were growing in the movement was to turn to this other anguish, his need of Hannah. And from that anguish back to dismay at the position he was being manoeuvred into by certain comrades.

When she told him on the phone that she was cleared, she'd received a visa and was arriving at the weekend he begged, insisted she let him meet her at the airport although that would be an offence against discretion as well as security—that moral code he and she strictly imposed upon themselves.

He wouldn't come into the terminal arrivals hall, he'd be there in the underground car-park, she'd make her way with her suitcase towards him in the echoing daylight dusk of the cement cavern smelling of exhaust fumes. . . The empty cottage where he was holding the telephone receiver was already reinhabited by her. He was wild with anticipation: what Hannah could make him feel! Never in his life before—fifty years, my god—had he been capable of such emotions. He was old when he was young, that was it; a reversal: it was only now he knew what it should have been like to be young. The night before Hannah was to arrive he took a sleeping pill to subdue his excitement; to blot out the presence of Aila beside him in bed.

While he was waiting in half-dark, underground, surrounded by the inert relics vehicles become when they are stationary, by footsteps fading, footsteps approaching and passing on the periphery of his senses, he suddenly felt all life and will leaving him. All at once. It was again the moment when, driving somewhere in the Vaal Triangle, full of purpose directed towards the meeting he was going to address, he had had the awful impulse to let go of the steering-wheel, had seen himself careering in a car out of control, to an end, an abandonment. Now in the garage he got out of the car to master himself; he arranged himself standing to meet her when she would appear. He kept swallowing and his hands felt thick and dull. The place was cold, a vast burial chamber. An old black man slopping a mop from a bucket over a luxury car was a menial entombed along with a Pharaoh. She would appear with her suitcase; nothing would stop that happening. There she was, as she had to be: she had seen him, she was coming towards him slowly, ceremoniously, solemnly after so long and difficult a parting, walking sturdily on her pale freckled legs, her body tilted sideways by the weight of the suitcase, her blondness back-lit by the shaft of light coming from the stairs. He felt nothing. He stood there smiling and managed to open his hands away from his body to make way for her; there was nothing behind these gestures. She took his silence and the hard abrupt embrace as an excess of emotion stifled by prudence in this strange public place where there seemed to be no witness except an old cleaner; but of course she was back here, where one could never be sure to be unobserved. She herself was laughing and in tears. On the way to the cottage she poured out all the details of the visa affair she had had to keep back, over the telephone. Her hand came to rest, spread gently and firmly on his thigh as he drove; a claim upon him.

Once they were again in the bed it was as if what had happened down in that cavern had never been. Close to the earth; Sonny was back to earth, human and struggling, able to touch and feel and scent the wonderful upheaval of life.

—. . .He slept here. I used to come in and see him snoring there on your bed. . .— He shook his head, and she smiled and kissed his neck. —But why did you give him that password, Hannah? Why couldn't you have thought of something else?—

—What else could I have sent that would make you absolutely sure? What else is there that belongs only to us?—

—Well now there's a third person.—

—Oh never. To him it's like anything else that's used. Once the purpose is served, it's over. You know. He's forgotten already. It's only to us. . .for him, there are other things on his mind. He's quite extraordinary. . .what he's brought off. . .in and out, here, several times.—

—Don't tell me. And forget whatever that is, yourself. I don't know how successful he was. Whether he was ever followed, whether they played the old game of letting him lead them to his contacts, including this cottage. How do I know? I couldn't watch the place all the time. . .and he was so cocky and relaxed, didn't give a damn, never said anything. And that telephone was frustrating. I couldn't tell you, ask you anything about the fellow. He could have been picked up and I along with him, and you wouldn't have known.—

She was considering, a moment, whether this was a reproach. But between them, that wasn't possible; you don't live for each other, the loving is contained within the cause, and there would be no love if you were to refuse, because of personal risk, something expected of you by the struggle. She didn't know how to phrase this; did not have to because he was speaking again. —I hope you investigated him thoroughly before you let him use us. You know that, with me, it's not only myself—there's always the risk of the movement being infiltrated through me; any one of us.—

—My dear love, don't you trust me?—

—I've told you before what you are for me.—

She hid her face against him, muffling her voice. —'You are the only friend I've ever had.'—

He pulled her head away, distorting between his long hands her soft pastel cheeks in pressure against the brilliant blue chips of her eyes, and kissed eyes, nose, mouth as if to efface her. They made love again, the kind of love-making that brings the dependent fear that one could never live, again, without it.

When they were lying quiet, she made her usual principled acknowledgement of the limit of her claim. —How are things at home? Is Aila back yet?—

—She arrived a few days ago. Will behaved quite reasonably with me. . .even cooked some meals. . .—

She squeezed his hand. —Of course, he's a good boy, he's just like you, underneath. You'll see how he'll turn out.—

She might have been a wife, reassuring him about his children. What games are played, between lovers! —My daughter's married, you may be surprised to hear. I was.—

Hannah laughed. —No, not surprised at all. She's a very

attractive girl. Not as beautiful as her mother, but still lovely. Who's she married? Someone in Lusaka, of course?—

—But like the rest of us, originally from the ghettos. I've never met him. Aila likes him. So I hope it's not a big mistake.—

—Why should it be a mistake?—

—Marriage, these days. In their circumstances, the instability, exile, no home—what for? Marriage implies certain social structures, and we're busy breaking up the existing ones, we have to, it's the task of our time, our children's time. I don't know why she wants it; she's got a head on her, young as she is. At least I thought she had.—

—You think they should just live together?—

They look at each other: like Baby's father and his lover.

—Yes, while they can. There'll be long separations, each will have to go where they're sent. Marriage is for one place, one way of life. It's a mistake for them. Live together while you can, as long as it's possible, and then, well—

—Aila surely wouldn't want that. Isn't she pleased?—

He put his hands up over his face a moment and breathed out through his fingers. —She's pleased.—

He did not continue with what he was about to say; he did not tell Hannah his daughter was going to have a child.

I wonder how she feels making love with a grandfather. That didn't stop him either. I wonder how he could go on doing it knowing he was so old—what's it? Over fifty—and some other man was also doing the same thing to his darling daughter.

Fucking his pudding-faced blonde (pink blancmange like my mother used to make for us out of a packet when we were kids) while he ought to be dandling his grandchild on his knee. It's disgusting to think like this about him, I know, but he's the one who's brought it about. That's the educational opportunity the progressive schoolteacher arranged for me.

I should have thought—I did think, when my mother told me about my sister's baby—that, at last, would have been the end of it, for him. Even if he hadn't stopped when my sister tried to kill herself because of him, his old obsession with self-respect might have stopped him now. A grandfather, the great lover! My father, who has never looked ridiculous in his whole life. If not his famous self-respect, then self-esteem, vanity, I should have thought—I notice in the bathroom in the mornings he has quite a paunch, there's grey in his chest-hair. When he yawns, his breath is bad. He must have some dignity left, after all.

But no. Everything goes on as it has for—how long is it already? I keep thinking of it as an interlude, something that will be over; but it's our life. When I'm his age and I look back on my youth, that's what it will be.

Of course he's never seen the baby boy. Only the photographs my mother brings back. She tells him the infant looks like him, just as I did when I was born, she says. It already has quite marked eyebrows. But he says babies look like other babies. The lover wants to acknowledge no paternity, neither for me nor his grandchild; unfortunate about the eyebrows . . . and my mother so innocently proud of the proof of succession, something no other woman of his can take away from her. Maybe it's not so much innocence: perhaps women really want men only to supply them with children; when that biological function has been fulfilled down to the second generation, and they themselves can't bear children any more (my mother must be close to that stage now? Like Baby, I always think of her as young) they don't need us. I realize I don't know enough about women. It's not a subject of instruction he's keen to pass on.

My mother goes to visit Baby and the little boy in Lusaka often. Of course—she said 'I need to be able to go back'. Before the birth she was busy knitting and sewing while he was out at his meetings and 'meetings' in the evenings. She pinned the shapes of small garments to the padded ironing board and pressed them under a damp cloth; the smell of warm wool steamed up. Sometimes I was studying in the kitchen to keep her company. There was no-one to collect the pins with the horseshoe magnet.

She went to Lusaka once more before the child was born, and again for the birth. She has no trouble with the authorities; why should they harass the poor woman: they did search her luggage at Jan Smuts airport on that third exit—she was, after all, Sonny's wife—and how foolish they must have felt to have their counter strewn with her beautifully-made baby clothes, emblems of embroidered rabbits instead of subversive documents, white and blue ribbons in place of the colours of a banned political organization. She said they were very nice to her; congratulated her on being about to become an *ouma*. My father remarked, yes, sentimentality is the obverse side of thuggery. He knows that from his prison days. The doctor for whom my mother works is most understanding and accommodating—he doesn't seem to object to her taking frequent absences from the surgery. I suppose it must be unpaid leave; but my mother is used to managing with little money, she doesn't skimp us, in the household, and yet apparently she is able to save enough for the airfares. I suppose that's why she doesn't look like she used to—it's not only that hair, now—she doesn't dress with the care she did, goes off on these trips to my sister in pants and flat shoes, the clothes and toys for the little boy stuffed into my duffel bag. When she comes back she doesn't ask how we—I've managed. And she seems to have made more friends here;

friends of her own, not my father's with whom she was always on the fringe. She's quite often out when I arrive home and her day's work at the surgery is over. The other evening, he came in and I heard him call out from the kitchen as he hasn't done for I don't know how long: Aila? Aila?

But he was mistaken; he's lost the instinct for sensing my mother's presence in some other room. They were empty. She was not there. Not for him, not for me.

As Sonny believed he had found in Hannah the only friend he ever had, so he had believed he had found in the risks of liberation, on public platforms and at clandestine meetings, in prison, the only comrades he had ever had. If that friendship meant for him the blessed reception of sensuality as part of intelligence, then that comradeship meant he and his colleagues in common faith would live or die together. They did not speak each other's names under interrogation. Since they had been equal to that, no other form of betrayal could find a crack to enter between them.

Once a great Shakespearean reader, reverent amateur of the power of words, Sonny must have known that if a term is coined it creates a self-fulfilling possibility and at the same time provides a formulation for dealing with it. 'Disaffected' was coined in political jargon to handle, with prophylactic gloves, the kind of men who came to see him one night when he was alone in the house. He turned them away; as he was certain others would. They were best left to fizzle out through lack of notice taken of them; the acknowledgement of any kind of 'disaffection' in the movement was merely a means of letting the government smell blood. Individuals discussed such visits in confidence, they were known about; the subject was not on the agenda of the executive. But several of those night visitors sat blandly on that executive. Perhaps they were awaiting a more propitious time to act again, rather than affirming contrite submission, a lapse—just once—accepted by the leadership as such. These options in themselves caused conflict. Some thought the men ought to be talked to, privately, by strong personalities; they needed to be dealt with, have it made clear to them, once again, that unity and no other was the condition of resistance—with the underlying message that they didn't stand a chance of getting away with anything they had in mind. Some felt this must be managed with the greatest care, they mustn't feel in danger of expulsion anyway—it would encourage them to pre-empt and make a face-saving announcement of a split. And of course the disaffected cabal scented the sweat of this indecision and moved to take advantage of it. They lobbied (that inappropriate term for a movement that came into being because its entire great constituency was excluded from parliament) among the other executive members where they saw concern for caution might become support. There were leaks interpreted by the press: LEADERSHIP'S BREAKING BRANCH—THE OLD GUARD HANGS ON.

Sonny had read warning signs for a long time; somehow partly misread. Before Lesotho; that man asleep in the bed close to the earth; before the return with news from Lusaka—months ago Sonny had talked over with Hannah the peculiar attitude of a comrade with whom he had always been in close accord. —'All smiles, and the next thing, you've got a palace revolution.'— He had said it without knowing fully what he said. And Hannah, she'd reassured that any potential troublemakers would have to believe they could capture the executive before they could attempt anything. Neither he nor she had thought they already might be convinced of success. However well a human being is known, it is never known what is moving in him towards a decisive act, something 'out of character', it's not to be seen how it is slowly coming about, what is preparing for it: the turning aside, the betrayal. You run away and leave the dying man. Just once.

Sonny had to accept that disaffection wasn't going to fizzle out. The learning process is endless. One of the fellows (as he still, sometimes, in schoolmaster brotherliness, privately thought of his comrades) who had been in detention with him was now part of the palace revolution. It was incredible; a wound in Sonny's side. This was one of the comrades Hannah had visited.

—And he used to write such good letters, so spirited—

—You wrote to him, too?—

—Yes, to everyone, it's our policy, keeping in touch as much as possible. You know that.—

Sermons in stones, and good in everything.

Although Sonny, with his credentials and his articulacy, would have been many people's choice to 'discipline' the disaffected individuals, it was decided that anyone who had been approached by them was ruled out for the task. The candidates must be among those who had not already shown these men the door. The meeting-ground must not be that of assumed hostility. But he was in caucus meetings with trade union leaders and a delegate to secret meetings with other affiliated radical groups, to discuss their support in the matter. Between meetings and travelling from centre to centre around the country for consultation there were the private-within-private obligations to be available to this one or that who must speak to him alone; the rumours to be considered, the reports coming from those on the other side who were in fact acting as informers for the movement; and the suspicion, to be compared, that this one or that was spying on the movement's deliberations for relay to the disaffected. He scarcely had time or mind to fulfil his other responsibilities—the attention owed to what he'd taken on for himself, the two establishments he kept up, the home and the cottage. Fortunately Aila was kept busy either with preparations for her visits to see her grandchild or actually was away on such a visit, and Hannah knew what priorities were. So Aila did not seem to notice when he forgot the date she was to be off again and he looked blank, a moment, when she came into the kitchen with the boy behind her carrying her luggage, to say goodbye.

—What time's your plane? I'll take you to the airport.—

No, there was Will, Will was driving her, he'd bring the car straight back. —You're sure you can manage without it for now?— Aila's usual considerateness made him suddenly remember she must have asked him the previous night if this would inconvenience him; she knew he was hard-pressed although he did not tell her much.

At the cottage, after a few days' absence, he arrived for an hour; at one in the morning Hannah woke instantly to hear the car stop in the lane and flew stumbling to the door. He was in a state of high tension from talk and exhaustion, and the touch of her sleep-hot skin made him start and shudder. His eye-sockets were purple as if from a blow. Don't talk, don't talk any more, Hannah said, although she was the one he talked to, she was the one with whom he shared what there was to live for outside self, she was the one friend he ever had. They quickly made love—no, he fucked her, it was all he had left in him to expend. And then he had to get dressed and go; to put in an appearance for his son, at breakfast, to prepare himself with some rest for the decisions of another day. If he could get to sleep; *But then begins a journey in my head, to work my mind.* The old consolation of fine words become a taunt.

Why was *he* approached that night?

How could he ever have imagined anyone could construe something significant out of that unexpected and insulting visit?

But it actually was remarked to him: Why you?

Said lightly. He could not believe the obvious implication, unsaid: what is there about *you* that made you seem a possibility? There must have been something, why else. . .? The irreproachable comrade, the popular Sonny. . .not such clean hands, after all? Nobody—sometimes not even those who repeated these things, murmur to murmur—knew where they came from; whether from buried malice within themselves, churned up in the mud of uncertainty and suspicion fear of disaffection created, or whether discreetly dropped by the enemy—which was no longer definitively only the government, the police, the army, but also the disaffected; and maybe these last were allied?

Why him?

How was it possible those people should have had the presumption to come to him? What made them think they could? Now it was no longer a simple matter of showing them the door. The idea that he had ever opened it to them filled him with dismayed revulsion. The idea that his comrade prisoners of conscience could expect him to ask himself such a question prised at the wound in his side.

—There are some whose trust I'd have laid my life on, but who don't dismiss these things, raise no objections. . .can you credit it?— He had to find time to talk to Hannah, needed to talk to Hannah.

—The bastards.— Blood showed patchy in her cheeks, bright blue tears stood in her eyes, she was blowzy with anger.

He shook his head at the uselessness. —I'd have put my head on a block for them, they'd never. . .they're the best. . .—

—No, I mean those others—don't you see—*they* want to set you at each other's throats. They want you to discredit each other, make trouble among yourselves. You've got to put a stop to it.—

—'Not such clean hands, after all'—

—You must have it out. Sonny?—

—I suppose so. But to me. . .to have to admit that such things are possible among us—

She wondered whether her touch would humiliate him; whether he needed to close off all his resources to feel intact, unreachable by tenderness as well as assault. But she took his hand and felt the bones, one by one. —No-one who really matters can doubt your integrity for a moment. You know that.—

He had it out with the top leadership; they discussed how best it should be dealt with and chose a method that showed their unquestioned confidence in and value placed on him. For a time they kept him at their side in the most important of discussions and displayed him as privy to critical decisions, even if these had been made without him. He ignored his wound in fervent devotion to see unity restored, purpose made whole again.

I have a little girl of my own. 'Little' not because she's physically small—although she is, she's about the same build as my mother—but in the sense the adjective is often used. She's not important—I don't go in for great loves. She's a nice enough little thing, very fond of me and I'm quite fond of her. I sleep with her at her place, on the couch in the sitting-room when her parents are out, or sometimes in the room a friend of hers lends her.

Just like Dad. My sex life has no home.

It's a sweet and easy experience she takes very seriously. She's intelligent (don't worry, I wouldn't take up with an uneducated girl. . .) and we go to the movies and the progressive theatre I've been brought up to have a taste for, when we can afford to. Her salary as a computer operator would be adequate to support us in a small flat, although I'm still a student and earn only from part-time work, and she keeps suggesting this. Then we can sleep the whole night together, she says, innocently awed. But I can't leave my mother alone, and because my mother counts on me to be there with him when she's away, I can't leave him.

The little girl is proud of being the girl-friend of someone in our family. I know she tells everybody I'm the famous Sonny's son; her parents 'trust me' with her because they are impressed by the high moral standards of a family who live for others; frightened to death to participate in liberation politics themselves, they belong to the people who see 'Sonny' as a kind of hero and I suppose always will; although I notice lately that among his peers he seems to count for less than he used to. The big shots in the movement don't come round for private talks so often. I have the impression he's being eased aside; don't know why, and he wouldn't talk to me about it anyway. He's selective; it's not the sort of secret it suits him to share with me. I suppose in politics as with everything else: you have your day, and then it's over, someone else's turn. And that, again, isn't something he's good at accepting.

I can see my mother's pleased about the little girl. I wouldn't sleep with her in our house even when there's the opportunity, my mother in Lusaka and he in bed on the floor in that love-nest, but I've brought her home for tea. I knew my mother would like that; it's the way things used to be, ought to be, for her. And she was quite like she used to be, before; she had put on stockings and high-heeled shoes. —Oh your mum's beautiful— My girl was enchanted.

—Was. When she still had her long hair.—

The two females at once reached some unspoken accord. The little girl instinctively knows my mother would like to see me—at least one of her children—'settled' with a conventional domestic life, nearby. And hang liberation, eh. Live in the interstices that were once good enough for her and her husband, when they were young; and these are wider, more comfortable, now, no more Benoni-son-of-sorrow ghetto, but illegal occupation of a house in a white area, cinemas open to all. Good enough for me, the stay-at-home, the disappointment (to him) and the mama's boy (to her). She, too, has a role for me: tame Will keeps the home fires burning while noble Sonny and Baby defend the freedom of the people.

I said to her when I brought the results of my first-year studies—distinctions all the way—What am I doing this for? Who's going to employ a business-school graduate in a revolution?— And I laughed. So she took it as a joke. —It's wonderful you've done so well, Will.—

—Oh yes, my father will be proud of me.—

She was looking at me, unguarded for a second, her eyes then quickly lowered, a faint twitch in the left lid. I shouldn't have said it; it was the nearest we've ever come—to what? Betraying him? I don't know what sense there is in this compact, but I see she still wants it observed although the consolation of the grandchild, the visits to Baby—a kind of life of her own— have somehow brought her to terms with what she must feel about her husband.

But I was serious; fed up. —Why should I go on living here as if it's all right to make a nice little corner for yourself— (I didn't say 'with a nice little girl'.)

She was watching my lips as if she couldn't believe what came from them. Her alarm made her shrink and age, just as pleasure at the tea-party with a prospective daughter-in-law had made her soften youthfully. —We're going to need qualified people. Bush fighters won't win the economic war.—

Where does my mother get that kind of jargon? From him, no doubt; or picked up along with the baby-talk in homely visits to Lusaka. It's not her turn of phrase. She and I don't communicate like that.

—You're valuable, Will.—

I know what she's saying: don't leave. Don't leave me. Don't leave us. She won't let me fight. For my people. For my freedom.

I've never thought there was any guile in my mother but I suppose she's a woman, after all, some sort of sister to my father's blonde, since he's fancied them both. And circumstances have brought out the ability in her, as she's been changed in other ways. Perhaps to show me how she depends on me she's taken lately to asking me to drive her around (I've traded in that bike and bought a 'nice little' Japanese car second-hand because the girl's parents wouldn't let her ride clinging to my back). She's going to meet a friend or one of the doctor's patients has invited her to visit—as I remarked, she's become more independent of my father, in her simple way. I drop her at a shopping centre or a street corner convenient for me to turn back. She says she's only a step or two away from her destination, it's not worthwhile to go right up to the entrance. So she doesn't press the dependency too far; it's carefully calculated. She doesn't need me to come and fetch her home again—there's a bus, or the friend will drive her, she assures. Poor woman, I've got the message. Once when my way was blocked by a truck just as I was about to turn the corner, unobserved I saw her walking not up the street on the side she'd said she was going, but round the opposite corner in a different direction. She might have mistaken the address; but it also crossed my mind that the whole outing was a pathetic lie, she had no friend, no planned visit, she just wanted to show me she cannot live with him, without me.

Not all the perfumes of Arabia.

Why him?

The question came back again and again, acid burning in Sonny's breast. It was not quite the same question. New, different, now. Not as if he were to have been the only one. Several comrades were visited that night, or some other night. He knew, because he and they had compared notes privately before taking the matter to the executive. But the suspicion, that had had to be dispelled by a show of leadership, had been set in circulation against him, alone. Why him? Why should it find substance, some confirmation in comrades' minds? There was no suggestion that this could take place in relation to the others who had been approached by the disaffected. *Unreliable.* What shadow had been cast, from where? Behind him, around him; all turned in his mind and burned in that place under his breast-bone. Not even Hannah's soft padded hand on him could still it.

Hannah. They knew about Hannah. They knew what had been going on a long time, now, since prison—they were men, some of them lovers of women—which means they took their chances when these presented themselves. But he was not a lover of women, in that accepted sense—a weekend or a night when a woman looks at you in a certain way in another city, and you come home and forget about her. Revolutionaries, activists, are whole men and women; only human. Such marginal encounters have nothing to do with dedication and dependability.

But Sonny never had been that kind of man. There were no flattering flirtations or one-night peccadillos of manhood to ignore, in his record. He lived in intricate balance an apparently permanent double life. Seriously; he managed it and evidently would not relinquish it. They knew what a good wife for a revolutionary Aila was. And they all knew who the woman was. Useful. She was not afraid of police and prisons, danger by association. One of themselves, in a way. But only in a way; not directly in the movement, certainly not acceptable as party to deliberations, decisions and tactics, and therefore not—most important—subject to discipline. He knew that. Sonny, who had been the most disciplined of men, knew that about her, however close he allowed her to come. And to come close to him was to come close to the movement. He knew he was responsible for that; and of course he was aware they knew it.

He began to discern a shadow cast from Hannah. His needing Hannah. He had not told his peers—who had shown their confidence vested in him—about the man he had found sleeping on her stoep, the man she sent with an intimate password he couldn't refuse to acknowledge, whom he fed and guarded—yes!—not knowing who he was or what he was doing, some piece of adventurism, probably, Hannah had been deceived into.

And they knew about it; that was the explanation. He had lent himself to an action—some sort of mission that his movement had not authorized, about which it had not been informed. Some—the disaffected—knew, and that was why they thought it possible to approach him. And others knew about it, as well as that the approach of the disaffected had taken place.

So why not a triple life? If a man of his old and proven integrity could withhold information from the movement to which total dedication was due, loyalty was the letter of faith, he also might be vulnerable—open, like a wound—to disaffection.

Better to be vile than vile esteemed, when not to be receives reproach of being.

He hated to have coming up at him these tags from an old habit of pedantry; useless, useless to him. In a schoolteacher's safe small life, aphorisms summed up so pleasingly dangers that were never going to have to be lived. There is no elegance in the actuality—the distress of calumny and self-betrayal, difficult to disentangle.

He was reinstated. Yes. But that that term should ever have had to be used in reference to Sonny! Nothing to be proved or disproved against him, no charges, a shadow. Yet reinstated as the others, the disaffected group, were, as if he were in the same category. Perhaps nobody other than himself saw it that way. Leadership held its hand over him; that was enough. Whereas with the disaffected there was a deal. He was present at caucus meetings where the terms to be offered for the sake of unity were discussed. But he contributed nothing. He, who always had had such clear and influential opinions, leaning forward on his hands, his eyes seeming to gather and synthesize the elements of a decision diffused among voices and motives, before he would speak—he was not 'party to' the bargaining under which the disaffected were dealt with. His comrade in the Chair deferred to him with a glance, now and then, taking off his glasses to make the space of a pause seem to be for this trivial purpose. An old friend; they had exercised in a prison yard together. Every time he did feel the urge to intervene with an opinion, an impulse of irrational anger swamped it, but that business was over and done with, nobody wanted to hear accusations, now. Self, self; since when was he obsessed with self. But it was their fault, his comrades sitting where their lives and sometimes deaths were in each other's hands in this abandoned warehouse space, enclosed by eye-level clapboard according to someone's confused idea that all meeting places, however diverse their purposes, were businessmen's offices and boardrooms. The empty water cooler stood as the neglected fish tank did in the Benoni yard when Will and Baby let their pets die. . .the anger was controlled, his attention wandered: self, self. Suspend them now, someone was saying, they can't come and sit here with us!

—Let them go back to the rank and file, man. . .What do they think.— A small black man with the pock-marks of poverty and the scars of warders' punches spat the match from the corner of his mouth.

—Most of them are the rank and file, so?—

—No, no, only three. The other two are exec members.—

—Comrade Chair. . .Comrade Chair. . .can I just. . .—

—Caleb is the only one we see. The other—he hasn't attended a meeting for months.—

—On a mission!—

There was laughter, and private exchanges. —What sort of people are we sending around? Did you hear that?— —Some mission. . .he goes about claiming. . .I'm telling you— —Makes statements supposed to come from us—

They had their break from tension and then were rapped to order. —This is not a circus, comrades.—

One who always could be counted on to hold the floor as if he were eyeing in a mirror his plump handsome face, himself his own appreciative audience, began a prepared speech. —Comrades. . .we are facing a grave crisis whose ultimate consequences we may not foresee. . .the forces of democratic action are threatened from within. . .this Trojan horse, can it be stabled. . .I ask you. . .challenge. . .is it much different from the truck appearing innocently to be carrying its load of cold drinks, that attracted our children into the street and gave the fascists who were hidden with their guns behind the crates a chance to shoot our children down. . .Are we to watch our words and stick out our necks to the knives of potential traitors here in this place where we meet to put our minds and hearts in the struggle. . .are we to sit with Judas in our midst. . .I say, and I dare to speak in the name of our masses, who sacrifice their bread in strike action, who risk the roof over their heads in rent boycotts, our comrade workers who sweat and toil in the dark of the mines. . .let us cast out these betrayers of the people's trust, the unity that is our strength, let them do what they will, but we cannot compromise the struggle that is sacred to us—

Stale, stale. Sonny was unaware that he was slowly weaving his head from side to side, away from the rhetoric and melodrama of this performance given by a man as brave as he was vain—how to explain that someone who had endured without breaking seventeen months in solitary confinement could talk like this; that such conviction should be expressed in this overblown way associated in everyone's ears with cant. He believed the disaffected should be expelled; better a split than a schism within. But now he was filled with distaste at the idea of associating that decision with bombast. He clung desperately to the straw of truth in plain speech, plain words; he did not speak.

But someone had to. A movement cannot be run by fastidious abstention. He should know that. The leadership that had protected him (from nothing! from a shadow!) and who exhibited him at their side, already had arrived in private at a compromise that would be carried by the majority. —Comrades—the chosen spokesman looked round quietly at them all and fingered along the ridge of his jaw-bone a moment while attention gathered—I propose, in the best interests of unity combined with the security of the movement, we do not publicly expel these men from the executive. We suspend them, with their agreement—leave of absence—until the executive is automatically dissolved at our Congress. They will not attend any further meetings, they won't present themselves to speak on our behalf in any capacity. They won't give press interviews. We know they'll agree to this . . .the whole business will become a non-event.—

Everyone waited for another to speak. —They'll remain members—the rank and file as well?—

—Yes. No split. They're being re-educated—if anyone should bother to ask.—

The orator threw back his head and stiffened an heroic profile. —Comrades, I bow to the majority.—

Sonny left with his proper companions, the leaders. A hand took his elbow. —It's the way to deal with it, Sonny.—

—You know what I think.—

Hannah was expecting him to come and report. He drove to the cottage, parked in the lane, pushed through the shrubs where piebald-breasted Cape thrushes flew, whistling, before him. Involuntarily his hands went out to them. There was a pile of cigarette butts beside her, he tasted the smoke of her anxiety dry in her mouth. He told her the decision and then went back to his account to describe how the meeting had gone, leading up to it, paraphrasing even with a little exaggeration for her wry amusement, the speech that, at the time, had embarrassed him. She knew, as he did, the real qualities of that man—what did pomposity matter, despite his sudden yearning to have it otherwise—nothing is simple in a life and a country where conflict breaks up all consistency of character. They'd often talked of that. With particular reference to Baby—his Baby. Her frivolity, the way she manipulated through charm, and the purpose suddenly (who knew?) surfacing in her—the strongest purpose in human society, to change the world.

To change the world. Trumpeting words again.

He leant over and emptied the full ashtray into the garden. —That's enough. No more.—

She pushed the cigarette pack away. —I promise. Not while you're here.— After a pause: —. . .So it's all right. Somehow. Everything's the same again.—

—Not the same.— He tried to answer her smile but his was a strange grin that stayed and stayed with him under the contradiction of those dark thick brows bunched over blackly intense eyes.

—Can you eat with me?—

He couldn't, he'd promised to let Aila have the car that evening—some invitation he'd managed to get out of, pleading paper-work to be done. So he left soon, and that was his second homecoming. Aila didn't expect any report from him, thank god. He was late—but she was accustomed to that. She took the car keys without reproach and hurried off, smelling of perfume. The boy was out, he'd found a girl at last. Sonny could go to bed in blankness, if not peace.

Hannah did not know her lover was a grandfather—and if only he had realized this, nothing would have changed if she had: with his wife and grown son and daughter the news would have belonged to that dimension of his personality which, without her having any place in it, enriched her share. From the first, when she saw him in prison and visited his home, she was fascinated by the complete context of Sonny, half in love with his family as with his political associates.

There was something she hadn't told him, either. The United Nations High Commission for Refugees wanted her to take on a high-level post. She hadn't applied for it—she wouldn't have thought of changing jobs while she was fortunate enough to have one that kept her where he was. One of the observers from the International Commission of Jurists who had made her acquaintance in knots of discussion at Sonny's and other trials, apparently had recommended she be approached. She was gratified at this unexpected estimation of her, surprised and slightly alarmed. It stirred her like a new sense experienced, the touch of something other than a lover. She enjoyed the esteem of the offer as if that were the beginning and end of it; did not think of it as a decision to be made—she was far from even considering that. But she felt this was not a time to tell Sonny anything; anything unexpected. He had just dealt with a conflict he could not have imagined ever would happen. It was not the moment to present him with anything but herself just as she had existed for him since she visited him in prison. Not even the pleasure, as she thought of it, of something to be proud of, in her. Sonny was her farthest horizon. It would take some other sort of courage, one she didn't think she had, to hoist herself up past unease at the prospect; see that, from there, it was no jump off the edge of the world.

Twice lately while I've been alone in the house the phone has rung and when I've answered whoever was on the other end of the line has hung up. I wonder if he's going to be arrested again: Security checking to find out if he's living at home. I supposed I'd better warn him; but he gave a sceptical smile—*Don't worry son.* He doesn't come home so often with that current of—what was it exactly—vigour, excitement, shamelessly, hardly hidden from us when he's been with her, his lips full and that curly black hair combed back to make innocent the tousling in bed he's just left; nor with something of the same fast-flowing blood we used to sense in him for different reasons, when he'd been making one of his speeches and defying the cops. Maybe he and his woman have had a row. Perhaps she's the one who calls, hoping he's alone in the house and he'll answer. But I'm the man who's likely to be around at home in my room because I've begun a project—call it that—that needs solitude. I've found a use for the state, compromised and deserted, he dumped me in when he walked off so calmly with his blonde after an afternoon at the cinema.

Then last week there were two more calls, and this time, after a humming silence (could have meant long distance) someone asked to speak to my mother. A man. What he said was not her name but 'the lady of the house'. The second time—I was irritated at the interruption of my train of thought—I asked if this was a sales pitch, direct marketing (a subject in the curriculum of my business-school courses). The voice said no, apologized politely, but hung up when I thought I'd better be polite, too, and asked if I could take a message. No! It's not possible that now my mother as well—my mother has a lover somewhere. But I find myself snickering, first with embarrassment and then because it's so funny—the joke's on me, and now I can laugh out loud at myself. The clown really is capering for once. Our family in a completely different scenario: one of the sitcoms our State television stations buy from America, where every member of the family is cheating on the other, straight-faced. My mother and I sometimes watch them in the kitchen while she's cooking dinner—it hurts him, after the Shakespeare he used to privilege us with, to see us giggling at such stuff.

My poor mother with her ugly shorn head and her brave show of having a life of her own, knitting baby clothes and trying to make new friends among her employer's patients. I'm old enough, now, almost to wish it were true. I understand the reassurance to be found in a stranger to whom one is something, someone, outside the triangle—father, mother, son; Sonny, Aila, Will—of this house.

A congress had not been called for two years because of Government restrictions on the movement. When this one was held clandestinely the executive council was dissolved as it had been pointed out it would be.

Then the old executive was re-elected en bloc, to applause. The two who had belonged to the cabal of the disaffected had not been phased out; they were there in their seats, the one acknowledging, as his due of honour, the spatter of clapping, the other with mouth drawn down modestly and eyes lowered. This must have been condoned by the leadership, Sonny's peers, because there are ways of preventing these things—blocking candidature with authoritatively-lobbied support for other nominees. Even democratic movements must work like this, for the ends of the struggle. Sonny had been in liberation politics long enough to have been involved in such means himself a number of times.

So those night visitors had been disciplined, brought into line—and obtained their price in the bargain. He had heard nothing further about it. There they sat, his comrades like any others. Just as before. But when the executive council elected among themselves their office bearers, Sonny did not retain his key position. That was arranged, too; he saw this in the eyes of the leader who had taken him by the elbow and said, It's the way to deal with it, Sonny: a look with the disguise of a slightly cocked head so that the blow would be a glancing one, a quick signal of the eyes that Sonny should step down before a stronger nomination—for the good of the struggle. There could be no question in Sonny's mind that his peers, his comrades-in-arms, would not put the struggle above any and all other considerations. Like himself. In spite of what had happened. Therefore there must be good reason; they must be right in giving him some high-sounding but minor responsibility in place of the ones he had fulfilled—unsparingly. His life belonged to them. What had he kept back of it—abandoned a career he loved, given up the forming of minds of a future generation for the bubble reputation (curse learning by rote) of a popular platform demagogue, left the cosy circle of family for the existence under surveillance, the prison cell; broken up—yes, and gladly, for the struggle he'd do it again—the entire containing structure of his emotions so that he was defenceless, anyone could enter him, anyone take up possession there. If he was responsible to the struggle, then the struggle was responsible for him, Sonny become 'Sonny'. He had no existence without it.

And this was being done to him within the purplish brick walls, on the red cement floors, under the tin roof crackling expansion in the heat, of some religious seminary in the veld; exactly the odour and feel of education-department buildings where the schoolteacher had taken petty orders from inspectors and been given his official dismissal for marching children out of the humble and submissive place in society alloted them and him under the sign CARPE DIEM.

There was no complaint to be made by Sonny. It was a principle, application of which to some other comrade he himself had approved whenever it was appropriate, that personality cults should be avoided. If a post is to be well filled, it does not matter who fills it; change is good, the movement must be always in growth, no-one should be in the same position too long. New blood must come from the young cadres. He had used this ready jargon himself. He understood, too—although this did not enable him ever to close the one-man tribunal sitting in his mind—that he would never really know why the wind in his political sails slackened. He could only go on imagining answers that were given behind his back. And these could materialize only out of suspicions he found it possible to have about himself. Things that were forgotten or suppressed, dismissed by him when he was borne and buffeted exhilaratingly at the centre of the movement. He thought of all the criticisms he had made or agreed with, about others. The word goes round that Sonny is too intellectual. Sonny thinks too much. Sonny asks too many questions. Sonny's style of oratory is getting too predictable . . .out of date. Sonny's not a coward, no, no-one could ever say he wouldn't risk his own life, but. . .Sonny has attachments, attachments don't go with revolution, he's said so himself. Sonny's position on violence isn't quite in accordance with policy. And do you remember, that time. . .the business of the cabal . . . And that other time, before, the cleansing of the graves . . .his big speech, and then. . .

When he confronted the only individuals he could, his closest comrades, if they knew the answers they didn't tell him. Not the truth; so that must mean the truth would destroy closeness, he would never forgive them. —That's how it goes, Sonny, a damned shame. . .some people (a shake of the head), *aie!* you can't trust them, they're too ambitious and you're too straight. . .you know what I mean? You don't manoeuvre, it's not your nature, man. You today, me tomorrow—who knows what will happen. . .we just have to hang in there, for the struggle.—

When he confronted Hannah, together with whom, since the first discovery of this possibility between them, every political question had been analysed, she wasn't able to employ the faculty—not this time, not for this. All she could do was comfort him, touch him and enfold him, her soft thighs clamped heavily over his body, her arms tight round his neck, hands thrust into his hair, as if she were gathering him up and putting him together again. In time he grew ashamed of this cosseting, he was her lover, not some victim to be succoured. He made it clear that this did not accord with the discipline of activists; he did so by no longer speaking of what had happened, put it behind him like any stage in the struggle they had dealt with, and continued with good grace to do the work in the movement now allotted to him. He took her in his arms as her man, needing no consolation; and so, unsought, it secretly came to him. He could not resist it, although it was not what he wanted. What he wanted, from her, was what no-one could give him back; his trust in himself.

When she caught sight of herself in the steamy bathroom mirror, she saw the United Nations High Commission for Refugees Regional Representative for Africa there in the familiar pudgy face. (She could not stop smoking, even to please him, because she would get fat.) Hannah never had liked her own face. She had no vanity; and this was one of the qualities, conversely, that attracted Sonny to her. An unsought reward. She would have agreed with Sonny's Will that her kind of looks were too pink-fleshy—though his comparison with the animal by whose name he reviled her to himself certainly would have hurt her cruelly. Particularly coming from him.

She saw the Regional Representative for refugees so often there that she had to tell Sonny. She would have to tell him, anyway, now. The High Commission wanted an answer.

She did not know whether to tell him before love-making or after. Each time she heard his step coming over the cracked cement of the cottage stoep she was taken by an agitation of indecision, moving restlessly about their one room to escape the necessity. It seemed to Hannah a terribly important difference: before or after. A matter of honesty, precious between them. They had never seduced one another. What were known as feminine wiles and male deceptions were denials of equality, an ethic of the wide struggle for human freedom they belonged to. If she brought up the subject after they'd made love, it could seem calculated to catch him in a mood of tenderness, shorn like Samson, not fit to put up resistance. If she told him before, then the love-making (their compact made in the flesh) would seem an attempt to divert him from something on which it was his right to make her concentrate. Yet it was in the end in her disarmed state, love casting out fear or the tranquillizing drug of sex blurring judgment, that she told him. She had put out her hand to feel for the cigarette pack on the floor and he drew his arm from under her head to stop the hand. She smiled with her eyes still shut and curled the hand into the damp nest of hair in his armpit instead. He gave her the childhood kiss on the forehead. She loved him so much she could have told him anything: we're going to die, you'll go to prison again one day, I'm going away—no consequence of words spoken existed.

—An extraordinary thing. . .I've been offered a job.—

He answered sleepily. —That Council of Churches one? You can certainly get it if you want it. . .—

—No. It's really something I can hardly believe—

There was a faint encouraging pressure, his arm and chest against the hollow where her hand was held.

—United Nations. The High Commission for Refugees.— And then it all came from her: —They've actually offered me a post at the level of director—that's just one below the Assistant Secretary General.—

He seemed not to want to move, not to wake fully.

She thought for a moment he would fall asleep again and not remember what she had said. Let him sleep, let him be asleep.

—When did you hear this?—

—A little while ago. I didn't take it seriously.—

—What kind of position. Where.—

—Well, the actual title's the High Commission's Regional Representative for Africa. Based in Addis Ababa. But working all over, of course.—

—Yes, it's a vast continent, Hannah. . .and many wars.—

Sonny disentangled himself gently from her and sat up. —How did all this come about? How do they know about you?—

—Apparently a recommendation from the International Commission of Jurists. I had no idea.—

He nodded slowly; he was rubbing his naked arms, crossed over against himself. —Addis. . .Eritrea, Sudan, Lebanon. God knows where, there are new camps every day, new populations wandering homeless.—

—Mozambique.— She added somewhere nearer by, within reach of him.

He turned and gazed down at her. She kept quite still in her shelter of blonde hair, a straggling wisp sweaty from love-making streaking one cheek. But Sonny only smiled, the smile that lingered and turned into that painful grin of his he couldn't relax. —A wonderful opportunity, my Hannah. An honour to be chosen.—

—Offered.—

—No; chosen.—

—I've just left it. I haven't even replied. . .they've written again. By courier.—

—Of course. They want you. Highly recommended.—

—Lie down, I can't talk to your back. . .please.—

He sank beside her. They were stretched out like two figures on a tomb commemorating a faithful life together. She took his hand. —I don't know what to say to them. I mean, what can I do. . .I'm. . .I've got my work here—

—They know about that, don't they. They know how good at that kind of thing you are; that's why. They know you're capable of something. . .more. . .bigger. . .important.—

—Nothing's more important than what's happening here. For me.—

—You don't know what to say to them.—

—No. I don't. I just don't know.—

—You've thought about it.—

—Yes, in a way. I haven't really. . .it doesn't seem to be something I can take in—

—But you've thought about it.—

—What it would mean—yes.— He had drawn it out of her, he was making her face what she had not, did not want to.

She could not turn to him the fatuous, what do you think?

She got out of bed and padded barefoot into the kitchen, the familiar sight of the Van Gogh sunflowers, to make some coffee. She supposed he would have to go, soon; he always had to go. She did not return to the room while the water was boiling; she left him alone there, god knows what he was thinking—but she knew what it was he was thinking, she did not want to see it. She picked the dead leaves off the pot of oregano growing on the windowsill. There was the whoosh of the lavatory cistern releasing its content; he had used the bathroom, and she found this reassuring—life going on humbly with its small demands of the body.

She brought in two mugs of coffee. He was back in the bed.

—I wish they'd never asked me.—

I was the one to open the door again.

I actually heard them before they hammered on it. I woke and knew immediately what was coming with the screech of the gate and the tramping up the concrete path he laid for my mother so we wouldn't trail mud onto the stoep. It's as if there's a setting in my brain like a wake-up call programmed on a radio clock.

I got up and without even turning on the light went down the passage and unlocked the door with a flourish.

—He's not here.—

Within three silhouettes I made out a pale blur and two dark blanks—a white officer, and the others our kind. One of them shone his torch at my face: *—Dis net die seun, man.—*

—You want to come and search? My father's not here. I don't know where he is, so no good asking.—

One of them pressed the switch of the stoep light, the darkness whisked from them—the officer in uniform and the other two in their kind of drag, dressed in jeans and split running shoes to look like disco-goers instead of fuzz. The white was young but had false teeth, I saw when he smiled at my cockiness to show he was used to the lack of respectful fear you can expect from the families of men like my father. He spoke in Afrikaans. —But you know where your mother is, hey—go and call your mother.—

And he spelled out the full name, maiden and married.

My heart began to thunder up a troop of wild beasts in my chest. —She doesn't know, either.—

The white repeated my mother's names.

I had to believe they didn't believe me, they wanted her only to question her about him, the galloping confusion under my ribs let loose childish impulses to shut the door against them, to yell to her, help me, save me. Me? Him? They had not come for Sonny, they came for her. At my back I heard her approaching from her bedroom and I could see her before I saw her, the flowered dressing-gown with her shiny black plait down her back.

She pushed gently past me as she really is. A short towelling gown and a rough cap of chemically-dulled hair, two stoic lines from nose to mouth that have changed her smile. She answered to her names, the one she had from her family before she married him and the one she took on with everything else that has come from him. I began to shout and she shushed me, pressing my shoulder and signalling her hand towards her mouth as if I could understand only gestures in which I suppose she had communicated with me long before I could understand speech. I followed her back to the entrance hall where—my god, what was she doing, she was taking out of our junk cupboard the carryall she used to keep packed for my father, she took it into the bedroom and started putting her hand-cream hairbrush Kleenex—I shouted, at last, at last: *The bastard! That bastard, what has he done now! What has he done to get you inside! I'll kill him, I tell you when he walks in that kitchen door again I'll kill him!*

She was moving her head, moving her head calmingly at me as she packed her bag, you'd have thought she was about to go on a trip to see Baby and the grandchild. She turned towards me, pleading, modest. —Will. . .I have to get dressed. . .—

God knows what they are going to do to her; but a son cannot look upon his mother's nakedness.

When they had taken her away I thrust myself into a pair of pants and ran from the house that streamed light and drove the fastest I could get out of a beat-up second-hand car to that cottage. The dogs from the main house followed me bounding and snarling across the grass and I tore at shrubs and threw branches at them. I was barefoot and they snapped at my calves as I raced to the steps. Now it's my turn to hammer. I flung back the broken screen door and beat upon the wooden one with both fists. I didn't call on my father; Sonny, I bellowed, Sonny. Sonny. Sonny. Sonny. There was no-one there. I went on beating at the door and was disgusted to find my fists, my face wet. For the second time, first as a youth with a breaking voice, now as a man, I wept.

Lights went on in the main house and there were voices above the howling and barking frenzy of the dogs. I ran shit-scared through the thickest and darkest part of the garden, gleam of a fish-pond, a black intruder pursued by a property owner, tried the fence, fell back, made it a second time and as my head must have become visible against the sky, a bullet cracked past me.

I went to kill him that night.

I was the one who opened the door to her jailers. I was the one who could have died.

It was the weekend of reconciliation.

Sonny and his blonde woman went back to the resort rondavel among the orange blossom. To be away somewhere, once more, to have whole nights together; it was a pause clutched at out of what was pressing them along, breaking in upon them in the timelessness of that one room. Hannah's idea—Hannah's plan; once she sensed he knew she would be the United Nations High Commission's Regional Representative on the vast continent of Africa everything became insidious between them, guilt and fear and regret taught her guile to save her skin from the corrosion of his pain: she could not go, she could not; while she knew she would. She wheedled him into finding a pretext to be away from home for two days. Urgent meetings at national level in some other part of the country? He had somehow always managed to arrange these trips so that his family believed he was with his comrades, and his comrades believed he had some unavoidable domestic obligation meriting a weekend to himself. They had always got away with it. And while she spoke this vulgar phrase she heard in her own ears the cynical deception of any common sexual encounter; not for them. And the 'always' could be construed to refer obliquely to the fact that lately—unlike 'always'—it could not be taken for granted he would be included in important discussions 'at national level'.

Where should they go?

—Rustenburg?—

She suggested this as if at the same time quickly abandoning the possibility. It was where they had experienced their most intense happiness together; but it was also the place from which he had come home to find his daughter had tried to kill herself.

They looked at each other searchingly, awkward. Both, each for their own reasons, were tempted to go back where the scent of orange blossom had been a heady oxygen.

She made it possible with a rational evasion that would not recognize there was an emotional reason of another kind which might make him shudder at returning to that place. —It's nearby.— As if the long drives they had taken were not a particular intimate way of being together, travelling in a contained space, neither here nor there where other ties existed.

So Sonny told the necessary lies. To Aila, who could not have imagined he would lie to her. To his comrades, who seldom had urgent need of him, now, and were unlikely to try to contact him at home. Aila reassured him that Will would lend her his car for her weekend plans. He took the briefcase and left. She had kissed him on the cheek; he put his hand to the place as to a nick made when shaving, while he drove to pick up Hannah.

A gust of gaiety overcame Sonny and Hannah on the drive. Theirs was a splendid day with the sheen of last night's rain on the veld grass and the great glossy caves of wild mahogany trees the road dipped under as they descended to a sub-tropical altitude. She fed him dried apricots and once he pretended to give her fingers a nip. He was reminded, passing a railway siding, that once he took a bunch of kids camping in this area.

—Tell me.— The old desire to have known the conscientious schoolmaster surfaced, only too ready to come to life in her.

—What a disaster. There was a washaway, I herded them together at this siding hoping to get them onto a train. We stood there for hours in torrential rain and when a train came it was for whites and the driver wouldn't let us on.— He laughed at the vision of himself. —The kids were wet as seals. They took it as a great adventure.—

—Well, at least that wouldn't happen now.—

No, the trains on this route were no longer segregated, and there was no law, any longer, against a man of his kind and a woman of her kind sharing a bed. The woman at the reception desk had been trained to make guests feel welcomed with a personal touch. —Weren't you with us here before, sir?—

He was signing the register with her grandfather's surname, their pseudonym as a couple. —No.—

—Funny. . .but so many people come back to us again and again. . .—

Yes, no law against such a couple, now, but by tradition the combination continues to be something of a shock, even if it has to be dismissed for business reasons.

—No— He was aware of Hannah's eyes on his back as he wrote the date in the register; he felt shame (and the wrongness of feeling shame, as if it somehow could be read as an apology for being himself) on behalf of both of them for this lie. Only this lie.

She wanted to tell him to ask for the bungalow they had before but couldn't in view of the denial they had ever been there. The one they were allotted was much the same; she drew back the curtains and flung open the windows to let out the smell of insect repellent. —It's that stuff that made you wheeze in the middle of the night.— He did not let the opportunity of the reference slip. —It was all right. We got up and went for a walk just as we were, the stars were already low and it was so lovely and cool.— What was he going to get her to say: I love you Sonny, I love you so much—but she's like Aila, now, she can't say it. He lay on the bed and closed one eye, his signal that he would take a nap. —Come on. Don't be lazy. Come and swim with me.— They butted and raced each other under water, and it was impossible not to laugh. Later they lay on the bed companionably with the heat of the afternoon shut out, he reading and she with the headphones of her miniature cassette player (your diadem, he called it) buried in her hair tarnished by wet and springing back like grapevine tendrils dried round his absently twirling fingers. Every now and then, without speaking, she would suddenly take off the headphones and put one to his ear, closing her eyes and tightening her soft mouth in ravishment at what she had been listening to. —What is it?— —Concerto for mandolins, Vivaldi. Raindrop music, that slow movement.— She snuggled back into her headphones. But when he laid open on his chest the file of papers, notes and speeches he was reading and she saw he wanted to talk she dropped the headphones like a necklace beneath her chin.

—It worries me more and more.— The back of his hand fell on the dossier. —These young people seem to grind on, doctrinaire in the old style, the old catchwords, while the socialist world—our model—the real socialist world, it's changed so much. People there have *fought and died* to get rid of most of the means the young comrades are still starry-eyed about using after liberation. We have the principle we must be led by the people. . .right, and it's the masses in Eastern Europe who've overthrown the regimes that were supposed to be led by them!

It's the people's choice and will! How can we not recognize that? Not trust them? Do we really want to 'achieve' policies these uprisings prove to have perpetuated misery and poverty? When those who've lived with them are making them obsolete?—

—You're talking about the unemployed, the camp-followers—the school-boycott generation, going on at gatherings. . .? And you owe them so much they must be given the platform . . . Well, and yes, it's true, there're also a few whites, the fossilized Stalinists—

—No, no. Even among us. . .the needle jumps back and you hear the same record. And of course it's still what works best with crowds. We're not innocent of using it. . . particularly with the youth and the workers. It's still what seems to them the answer to their frustrations. The secular promised land. What they want to hear. So. . . And there're still fellows here who, when they're talking about giving the land back to the people, mean some kind of forced collectives. It doesn't matter to them that these have been abandoned everywhere because they don't work—people don't work productively in that structure. It's been proved over seventy hard years! Doesn't that mean anything? And the others, shaking their heads because the Constitutional Guidelines update the Freedom Charter—we've moved on, thirty-five years since Freedom Square, for god's sake—but they sneer sell-out because there's recognition of private property along with land redistribution, a mixed economy with nationalization. So they're outraged that anyone should be allowed to own a family home. Still dreaming our people's democracy will be able through god knows what miracle—you tell me!—to provide state garden suburbs for the workers, when no other regime has succeeded in this, not one, when it's been the great failure of socialism we ought to have the confidence to admit if we want to live as socialists of the twenty-first century.

Because that's what we *already* should be. The twentieth's thinking is the past. Finished. *Viva, viva socialism.* Which one? Which one are we shouting about? The dead one? We'll take the best of it and move on. Must. Don't they see, won't they see? The Soviets, the whole of Eastern Europe, even China—there's a new assessment—yes, that's what comes out of the uprisings, isn't it, Hannah, that's what it really is, quite scientific enough, on the analysis of concrete evidence!—it's a whole new understanding of our human needs and how to go about trying to realize them. And it's not what the capitalist world rubs its hands over, it's not what they think; we're not being taken over. It's not revisionism—but here you get that old parrot accusation.—

She stirred beside him. —Change the way they think . . .again. I don't know. . . It's not so long since you learnt to change the idea you had of yourselves as powerless against whites. The old Left did it, by god! Thank god. Only the old Left. Now new realities to be accepted. . . It's going to be hard for many, looked at from here. It means the loss of absolutes—you know what I mean? I'm a missionary's granddaughter. . . It makes people feel insecure. You can screw up the courage to do what you have to do to get rid of the old structures that hold you down if you can believe there's a paradise on the other side. You die for freedom only if there's the political equivalent of eternal life to come—which is liberation as promised in the old socialist writ, not in some compromise with a mixed economy, people with money—whites, and bourgeois blacks!—still owning property on land the whites stole by conquest! That's how it will seem!—

—But the writ's being *rewritten*! That's the point! People have been willing to die now for *that*. We've got to wake up and realize it, if it's to mean feeding and housing and educating our people in freedom! Giving the generations of uprooted people and refugees somewhere to live instead of somewhere to run from—

There.

The reference lay between them like the name of the recently dead brought up tactlessly before the bereaved. I could have cut my tongue out, the offender says, not meaning it, because reference to the loss is something those concerned will have to accustom themselves to, anyway.

Hannah broke in quickly. —Is this being taken up with the cadres?—

—Not as it should be. No. There's no interest in what's happening outside. Except at the top—leadership—of course. Here and outside, negotiations go on on the basis that the world's changed. How else. But we keep it to ourselves. No-one wants to talk about it except insofar as it affects our allies' attitude towards our struggle. With the cold war melted down, will they still see our enemies, here, as theirs? There's no real open debate on what else the big changes outside mean to our ideological thinking. Nothing! We're afraid to talk about it for fear it weakens our hold on people. Afraid that if we can't offer the old socialist paradise in exchange for the capitalist hell here, we'll have turned traitor to our brothers!—

She sought his hand as a good friend: she had wanted, hadn't she, never to give up their friendship for any other intimacy, and he had confirmed it never would be. *You are the only friend I ever had.* If his opinion did not count for what it should, for some unknown reason, some momentum lost, it was an injustice that did not recognize his worth. A good man.

—This country's always been way ahead in industrial and technological development, considering its history, and way behind in ideas, political culture. British liberalism tottering on with its form of racism long after it was overtaken by Boer nationalism with its form of racism, white power hanging on long after it's been defeated everywhere else; I hope to god we're not going to cling to something that's had its day, when we take over. If the old socialism's dying, let's admit it and make sure we can find our liberation in the new Left that's coming.—

—You sure about that? What's coming also begins to look a lot like the return of old nationalism.— A good man; her paradox was that what she revered in him was a trusting idealism she herself—whom she saw as a lesser being—questioned.

He felt the twinge of her scepticism. —Sure as you and I are in this room. You can't make what you don't believe in. If we don't, what is there. . .—

Talking of change was a danger to the weekend among the orange blossom. That was exactly what Hannah was obeying: the need to change. How would change come, for her, if she stayed on in the cottage, conveniently near for visits from Sonny? How does such a love affair—come about, made inevitable by the law of life between a man and woman—obey the other law of life: moving on? He would never leave Aila; she could never really want him to leave Aila, and Will and his daughter who was an activist, like him, away over the border. He no longer would be Sonny if he did. He always would have to get out of bed and go back home; there would always be an eye on a watch to cut off the long talks, side by side, like this one, the limit of an occasional weekend lies could allow them together. The lies had spread. He knew she lied by omission when she concealed from him under laconic practical references to her future post the excitement working in her at the idea of the vast continent of Africa. The important responsibilities she would have, the visitors' room of the prison where she had sat behind the barrier (a fair caryatid existing as head and shoulders only) opening out for her to a power of ordering life—shelter and food—for starving thousands, thousands upon thousands, the world manufactures an endless wealth of refugees. The important personalities she would meet, the international circles of influence she would move in; the men who would occupy the place made for love in this, as every other way of life—a law of life he had learnt from her.

They walked hand in hand under the trees lit up by pendant oranges, the pale globes of lemons and vivid baubles of naartjies, on a tour of where they had been happy. The variety of citrus cultivated there bloomed and ripened at the same time, even on the same branch; with the perfume of blossom there was a sickly graveyard decay of rotten fruit, fallen and fastened on by flies. It squelched underfoot and she paused on one leg, holding his shoulder for balance, while she scraped her shoe clean against a trunk. He took her head in his hands and began to kiss her cruelly, he pushed hard fingers under her clothes out there where people could have come upon them, like any coarse drunk dragging a woman outside during a party. She had to fight him to stop a mating with her then and there. But back in the rondavel, her head on his arm, looking up together at the thick, smooth-stroked orderliness of thatch, a canopy for them, he was tender Sonny, wondering Sonny at the pleasure of their being. And he made love to Hannah. He would make love to her, this one weekend, make love to her so that she could never forgo it, never leave; needing Sonny.

When he came back there was no thought of killing him.

We went together to the lawyer and then with the lawyer to John Vorster Square to find out where they were holding her. The police wouldn't say.

After they took her away they came back on Sunday morning and searched the house and garage and the room in the yard that must have been a servant's room when white people lived in the house. It was our storeroom. There were garden chairs that needed new canvas and gardening tools and Baby's old bicycle and a broken food-mixer. There was a wooden mushroom I remembered my mother used to use for darning our socks. There was a box of schoolbooks, some off-cuts of material, and wrapped in the material were three hand-grenades, two limpet-mines and two land-mines. The stuff was what was left over from the curtains in my room, she'd made them when we moved in. The hand-grenades looked like small metal pineapples, I recognized them from the charts put up in post offices to alert people to the presence in the city of weapons that might blow them up. I also recognized the tubular limpet-mines. The two other objects looked like air filters from a small car engine. I wouldn't have known them for what they were.

I had followed the search through all our things in the house with smiling rage, enjoying the fruitless and disgusting rummage which discovered, as I knew it would, nothing. My father is too experienced to keep so much as a scrap of compromising paper here in our own house. I said, now you've made your bloody mess, will you go and let me clear it up—but the louts were weaving about our place like dogs who know there's a bone buried somewhere and they started on the yard. They lifted the hood of my car. They emptied the dustbin. And then among the schoolbooks and the bits of cloth left over from the curtains they found what they'd known was somewhere to be found.

He and I worked it out together; in the kitchen grabbing tea and bread to keep us going, in the car driving from police station to police station, determined to find where they were holding her. He had no doubt that it was because of him. A frame-up to trap him. They were after him and couldn't pin a new charge, so they'd come for his wife, hoping that in his anxiety for her he would reveal himself, do something that would give away real involvement with activity like the one they had set up for her. They had planted the explosives and then come back to 'find' them.

—But why take the whole house to pieces first.—

—Because you were there, Will.—

At the reminder of his absence his cheek twitched, I almost felt sorry for him, though where the hell was he. . .he wasn't even where he knows I could find him, when it happened.

He insisted they must have planted the stuff when they came to take her; but I answered the door, I saw them leave with her, nobody went near the storeroom.

—They must have come back after you'd gone to sleep again. You didn't hear anything?—

He was keenly enquiring—I suppose he thinks he might light upon some testimony from me he might use to her advantage; he's accustomed to finding me useful. But he's the one who, once again, wasn't there.

So I stared at him. —I went to look for you.—

—Oh. I see.—

His face closed away, in defence, to an archetype—his big nose carved and dominant, his lips mauvish and curving in a strong dark line. He escaped into an old schoolmasterish gesture, sounding the table with a tapping thumb.

—I left the whole place open, the lights were on. Anyone coming would have thought they'd be bound to be seen.—

No reproach for my carelessness; hardly!

But if we couldn't be father and son in any other way, we had a single purpose in our determination to get my mother out. A new conspiracy. And he was brave, of course—I've always admired his courage—because he constantly showed himself in places and situations where they might have decided to pick him up. They often do this when relatives of a detainee or indicted prisoner are lured to police stations by the presence of one of their own held somewhere behind walls. I was surely in no danger, a 'clean' member of the family, like my mother.

—They even gave her a passport—just like that.— He explained that he was, most unfortunately, away on urgent matters (the lawyer knew that could only mean the movement's affairs) when Aila was arrested but he was taking full responsibility on himself for whatever that innocent woman might be charged with. —Let them arrest me. I'm willing to be involved up to the hilt, so long as they let her go. The whole thing is insane. Aila! Can't you do something, get them to let her out and take me as hostage for her? I'm serious.—

I listened and I saw he was. But the lawyer stretched his legs before his chair and pulled at his lower lip. —Sonny, you're serious about nonsense, then. You know you can't make such deals with them. For god's sake. . .you're not green. . .you know it all well enough. It's the old process; as soon as they charge her we'll keep pegging away for bail, I'll press for the earliest possible appearance for the application.—

I wouldn't let him go alone to police stations when we were looking for her. I don't know why I should have thought that would be any protection for him; but I knew what she'd ask me to do, even when she herself couldn't tell me. We took food and clean clothing. He knows what you need in jail. He also knows how to talk to the police; apparently, once they're aware you've been inside and come out again, not afraid of them no matter what they did to you, you can talk to them and they can't refuse an answer as easily as they do to other people who don't know prisons, familiar ground to both jailers and jailed. Where the lawyer had no success in finding my mother's whereabouts, my father did, acting on a tip, I suppose, from the detainees' support organization. My mother was not at Diepkloof, where we'd thought her to be and he'd argued with the Major who'd refused to accept her change of clothing. They'd taken her to a jail in some dorp. I drove him there. They wouldn't let us see her but they accepted the food and clothes.

—And now?— I waited for him to give the word to start back because he seemed coiled in a daze; he sat hunched beside me as if he might leap out and hammer on the door as I did—the prison doors.

—It's a better place than Sun City.* Better conditions.—

But I'm not an old lag. She's in prison, that's all I know.

The big boys—the leadership—come round to the house

*'Sun City', actually a casino resort, is the name given by political prisoners to Diepkloof Prison, near Johannesburg.

again, the way people who've become too busy or important for old friends arrive to offer condolences. He shuts himself in with them; I suppose there may be something to be gained from their experience in dealing with the ways of Security. But if anything happens to her it's his doing. He knows that, every time he catches me looking at him. The little girl who's attached herself to me burst into tears when I told her what had happened, and she's offered to come and 'look after us'. But it's nobody's business—except his and mine. We eat together and go over the details of that night and anything else of relevance that might be recalled. I've told him of the phone calls; no lead there. One of his comrades suggests someone talked under interrogation—but about what? There had to be something to give away if someone talked. My father said, again, alone with me, what the lawyer had dismissed as nonsense from a man of his experience and intelligence. He carried it further. —What if I walk into the Major's office and tell them I hid the stuff in the yard, the limpet-mines and the hand-grenades planted there are mine?—

No man—no husband—could do more, even if he were to have loved my mother. I don't know the explanation. If she were one of his comrades—maybe they have to do that sort of thing if one individual were to be more valuable to the movement than another. That'd be more like it. But in this case. . .my mother!

If he loves her as much as that, he nevertheless goes off some evenings to that woman. He moves about the kitchen aimlessly with his bent back to me. Says to me at the door, I won't be late, or pauses, not knowing how to say what he really wants to, which is that I'll know where to find him if anything new happens, to assure me that's where he'll be, this time.

He leaves looking as if he's going to hang himself.

What would he do if he came home and found her here, suddenly released?

Before my father could go to the police and claim he was the possessor of the explosives hidden in our yard our lawyer was shown the signed statement in which my mother admitted she had consented to allow the storeroom to be used to store certain persons' property 'for a few nights'.

It was my mother who had talked under interrogation.

I know why she did. It was to be sure neither her husband nor I would be held responsible. She had insisted she didn't know the name or names of whoever was to remove the 'property'; and she refused to reveal the name or names of whoever had entrusted the 'property' to her, or to say why she had co-operated.

She had been briefed on how to deal with interrogators. My father clasped fist in hand as if stunning himself, his knees spread and his head sunk over his sagging body. The lawyer was embarrassed and alarmed. He tamely filled a glass of water; could not offer it to a man who had been through detention and imprisonment himself, a veteran of challenge to jailers of all kinds. My father looked up all round, wanting to know from somewhere—from me, because I was there, I was always there at home, her boy, mother's boy, how it happened? When? Where did my mother learn these things? How, without his having noticed it, had she come to kinds of knowledge that were not for her? And what was it she knew? Whom did she know whose names she couldn't reveal? What was Aila doing, all those months, without him?

I was not stunned; I was elated. It didn't last—she was charged, the case didn't look good, the lawyer admitted—but

(I have my crazy moments, too) I felt a release soar up from somewhere in me, scattering showers of light. She was in prison and she was free, free of him, free of me.

What nonsense.

She was shut in there. She, who had held us close to her, not wanting our clothing to touch the walls of the prison corridors when she had taken us as children to see our father between his jailers on the other side of a dirty glass screen.

It was Hannah who found out where Aila was being held. Hannah's connections. It was Hannah who got a note from Aila's husband smuggled to her. Hannah had helped this family in trouble before. Many families. She had visited the father and husband in prison. The note was a minute tightly-rolled piece of paper—Sonny knew how such things had to be slipped in stuck to the bottom of a tin plate at meal time or under the inner sole of a shoe. Hannah did not read the note before she passed it on for delivery. A note came back in Aila's handwriting. The scrap of paper was the label soaked off an aspirin bottle. There were four words. *Don't contact Baby. Wait.*

Sonny did not tell his son about the notes in case he asked questions. Hannah was, after all, a comrade. Always had been, from the first; and as well. The cause was the lover, the lover the cause.

Hannah's concern about Aila was a comfort; and could not be. It seemed to him she lay beside him now as if in her professional capacity, as she had come to see him when he was in detention, one among others her persistence in devotion to the cause enabled her to get to visit, and to whom, as to him, she wrote morale-building letters. He did not go to her to talk. He could not talk to Hannah as he needed—about how he had let it happen, how Baby and that husband he had never seen had somehow recruited a woman like Aila, poor Aila of all people, exposed her to danger, *used* Aila—and all behind his back. He had let it happen, not seen it, not been told (he sometimes didn't believe the boy hadn't known, didn't know) because of this woman in his arms. She knew that and so it could not be talked about. It was something neither could have foreseen could ever happen, she with her romantic respect for his family, he with his confidence that his capacity for living fully, gained through her, never tapped in the shabby insignificance of a small-town ghetto across the veld, made him equal to everything his birth, country and temperament demanded—dedication to liberation, maintenance of family, private passion. She was the only chance. The source of ecstasy and hubris. She still was, when she made love to him. Aila was in prison, this woman was going away because the common good outside self required this. Yet when he sank into the warmth of her and himself, when the nerves of his tongue passed over the invisible down of her skin, the different, goose-fleshed texture of her buttocks, when her weight was on the pelt of his chest, blinded and choked they were flung together, curved round each other like mythical creatures fixed in a medallion of the zodiac.

A sign. —I'll be able to come back sometimes.— Oh thou weed.

Oh thou weed: who art so lovely faire, and smell'st so sweet that the sense aches at thee, Would thou had'st never been born.

They were going to see her. Father and son went with the lawyer to court to hear him argue application for bail. Sonny knew the procedure: Aila would be produced for formal charges to be laid, the case would be remanded for a later date. They would see her; she would materialize out of all the suppositions and talk and fears of the days since she disappeared—Aila in her new avatar. Disbelieving, Sonny, who himself had been the one to be produced from cells behind courts, did not know how to prepare for this apparition. Without being aware of it, he had dressed as he did when he was the one to be led into the dock.

The hearing was not at the great grey block of the city magistrate's courts in the district of the other great authority, the mining corporations' headquarters, where already an explosion of the kind that could be caused by the objects wrapped in curtain off-cuts had one day taken place. The court allotted was across the veld in Soweto. They travelled in the lawyer's air-conditioned car sealed like a diving bell from the mouthing noise and crowded faces in the combis that nosed past close and fast, and the huge shaking transport vehicles coming and going, crossing to industrial sites rearing up off the highway. In between, a green pile, the remnant of reed-beds, parted under gusts set up by traffic. The lawyer changed cassettes in his console dashboard and there was no conversation. Will sat on the back seat behind his father's head.

In the trampled veld where one area of Soweto ravelled into another the courts enclosed a quadrangle and their only access was from the verandah that ran along all four inner sides; red brick and shrubs, hangover from the old colonial style when the forts of conquest became the administrative oases, ruled into geometrical lawn and flowerbeds that demarcated the gracious standards of the invader from the crude existence of his victims. The lawyer left father and son at once, among people like themselves; drifting, standing, leaning against pillars, clustering around doorways from which they scattered to make way for the purposeful rumps of court officials. Waiting. All, like them, waiting to see a face that had been obliterated by uniforms, armoured vehicles and blind doors to break your fists on.

They were Sonny's constituents. He had taught their children, he had roused them to demand their rights, himself had disappeared into prison for them. But he never before had come, like them, to wait humbly for someone of his own flesh and blood caught up in some incomprehensible disaster. (Wasn't her flesh and blood mingled with his forever in the body of their son, trailing beside him.) These old women drawing snuff through their nostrils, mothers of murderers, these young women, painted and dressed to remind the car thief of the desires they provoked, these others, weary against the wall, swathed about with babies under blankets, and these hawking old men shrunk in baggy cast-off suits—it did not matter if they were waiting to see a common criminal or, like him, to have produced, *habeas corpus*, a prisoner of conscience (Aila! In that role!). He was one of them, now, in a way he had not known. Attending the trials of comrades was no preparation for this; there the solidarity of purpose made one's presence a defiance of the legal process. But to imagine the freedom songs and salutes for poor Aila!

The lawyer had gone to establish formalities and find out in which court she would appear. It was a long wait and at first the father and son walked again and again along the four sides of the verandah, as people do while expecting to be summoned any minute. —Why doesn't he come back?— His father spoke, the son knew, only to break the silence between them in their isolation among other people's voices; he didn't have to answer.

—At least tell us what the delay's about.—

—D'you want me to go and see if I can find him?—

—No point, Will.—

The son jumped down from the verandah. The shadow of one side of the building bisected the quadrangle into shade and sun and he stretched out on the grass among the people who followed warmth there. It was a kind of strange picnic, where patience substituted for holiday relaxation. Some people left the enclave and came back with fat-cakes and oranges, tins of Coke and fresh packets of cigarettes. Children played and fought furtively. Like them, he cupped his hand under a tap and drank. With the unconcern of routine, an employee in government-issue boots and overalls, singing a hymn in Sotho under his breath, unwound a hose and turned the flowerbeds into puddles.

Sonny stood above his son, made as if to prod him with the toe of his shoe. —Isn't it damp? (Smiling faintly.) Do you want something to eat?—

Neither wanted to be the one absent when the unimaginable moment came and she was brought into court. The father paused, with a gesture at the sun, went back to stand on the verandah. Perhaps he thought his son had dropped off, asleep; face up to the sky, eyes closed. But he was on his feet and leaping over the people on the grass before his father beckoned at the sight of the lawyer twisting his shoulders through the crowd on the verandah. —At last!—application's set for two this afternoon, though. The police agreed to bail but the Prosecutor insists on contesting. . .I know that fellow. . .big ego. . .it's absurd, but there you are. And by now no court's available this morning. I'll have to go to chambers and come back, there're urgent matters I have to attend to. But let's not waste time asking questions, just stick with me and say nothing. Will, take my bag. You're my clerk. Come.—

Gabbling in an undertone he hustled them along before him through a corridor and to a walkway enclosed in heavy diamond-mesh wire. —Just hang about. Take no notice of anyone. Point at me if you're asked what you're doing here.—

He strode up to the long counter in the room in which the walkway ended, again using his bulk to push through a confusion of policemen and other people competing for the attention of the officers in charge. A gross tap dance of policemen's boots clipped smartly up and down past the father and son. Whichever way they stood aside, they were in someone's path. Exchanges and orders in the blacks' own languages and the Afrikaans of white officers flew about in the haste and impersonality of individuals dependent, each for his own fingernail hold of authority, on a hierarchy of command. Physical bewilderment made it difficult for the father and son to be self-effacing; both let themselves be buffetted as if they were inanimate obstacles some cleaner or workman had left lying about, while what they were witnessing through the wire mesh and the doorway was some intensely piercing awareness they alone could receive, because Aila belonged to them. Because Aila belonged to them, everything they saw happening to the other victims being escorted across the yard from some cell or Black Maria out of sight could be happening, out of sight, to her. Sonny himself had been brought at that trotting gait of one in handcuffs to register in the anterooms of trials. He had seen wretched, blubbering men dragged by warders, punched, where they bent double, to make them *opstaan jou bliksem*, by white bullies or shaken and shouted at by black bullies, he knew as a commonplace sight a barefoot man hobbled by ankle chains shuffling as a horror risen from the slave past into the memory of computers and the glare of strip lighting in the anteroom. But Aila, Aila, Aila had nothing to do with this! Aila in the neat, sweet-smelling clothes she sewed for herself, the seed-pearl necklace round her throat, her arms drawn to her sides in rightful, subconscious shrinking from the walls that held him—that was as far as Aila had ever been, ever should be, in contact with any of this. And the boy—what must it mean to be the boy, who knew nothing of it, not a particularly manly youngster, protected too much by his mother so that despite his intelligence and his reading (yes, admit it, encouraged in *that* by his father) he knows only at second-hand the ugly, brutal temptation of the power of one being over another, he's been shown only the beauty and nobility of resisting it, father smiling calmly at his adolescent son brought to pay a prison visit. The father could do now what he had not been able to across the glass barriers, then: Sonny put a hand on Will's shoulder. To comfort. To be one with him.

The lawyer was flinging arms wide before the sergeant at the counter, displaying his black robe. —I'm her lawyer—you can't refuse me permission to consult with my client! I demand the officer in charge— He gave a quick imperious lift of the head towards the door, drawing the father and son to him. —My briefcase. Bring me my papers.— A round-bellied policeman blocked the way. But Sonny, like a traveller slipping into the foreign language he hasn't forgotten, argued with him wheedlingly in the idiom of prison Afrikaans. Will sidled by in the confusion and placed himself close to the lawyer. The lawyer signalled Sonny to keep talking and, indeed, the policeman's attention left him at someone's urgent yell to attend to something else. Under the harangue of threats to report the personnel to the Master of the Court, the Prosecutor and the Judge, no-one now questioned the right of the lawyer's entourage to be present.

—Ten minutes, that's all.— The commanding officer retained his self-respect in a sharp edict.

The lawyer gave no sign of accepting the condition and no explanation to the father and son; they followed him to a small partitioned booth at the end of the anteroom, people crossing and recrossing before them, and behind the bubble glass rippling distorted colours of other heads moving. The lawyer opened the door.

She was standing there smiling to greet them, husband, son,

lawyer. The wardress stood back from her, the policeman at a desk was scarcely a presence in contrast to Aila's presence. She wore one of her home-tailored jackets and there were the reassuring touches of her makeup (compact of self-respect made with Sonny, unharmed, thank god) but through the familiar beauty there was a vivid strangeness. Boldly drawn. It was as if some chosen experience had seen in her, as a painter will in his subject, what she was, what was there to be discovered. In Lusaka, in secret, in prison—who knows where—she had sat for her hidden face. They had to recognize her.

This woman hugged them ardently all in turn—Sonny, the lawyer, and then, of course, the one whom she had never let out of her embrace, her son.

Will, put on a tie.

God Bless Africa

I ♡ Kaiser Chiefs

I stared at the back of his head on that drive and everything inside me shut down. I didn't think of anything, I didn't think of her, I was aware only of what was outside me. The stickers on the combis that cowboy lawyer raced and repassed. Sting and The Genuines playing on tape. The thick nap of the sheep-skin-upholstered seat burying my hand. It's all complete, round a vacuum, whenever I want it.

When I saw the man hiding his head between his elbows while a policeman hit him, and everything inside me opened up, loosed—caged fear for her, for myself, fear of life—my father put his hand on my shoulder. He knew. A hand came down on my shoulder. To demand something of me; to be one with him. And after she had come to me, saving me for last as she used to do—a secret between us—when she came to kiss

Baby and me goodnight, I saw her remarking—yes, that's the good old word—taking note: my weight, the softening round the chin and the belt slipped down under the beginnings of belly. No-one in our family's had flesh to spare. Not what she wanted me to be. But on the other hand, Baby has made her what Baby wanted *her* to be.

I didn't know what to say to her. I know that everything he had prepared he saw was wrong. Worse than that: she didn't need it. I could have told him that. I could have told him a lot of things he didn't notice, was always too preoccupied elsewhere to notice, things I understood, now; the visits to 'friends from work' he was pleased to accept as relieving him of responsibility for his neglect, the frequency of her trips over the border—well, he'd already realized they weren't spent sentimentalizing over a grandchild, but he was mistaken in his demeaning decision (typical! of course only his blonde has the intelligence and guts to be a comrade-in-arms) that she was manipulated, beguiled into use by Baby and that husband. He must have seen, the moment the door opened and there she was. He must have seen she was not 'innocent'; epithet that, I've heard him speechify, means denying responsibility towards your people.

He must have seen how she was. She kissed him like a young woman—I've never known my mother could be that way, I suppose now she's on the other side she knows what it's like not to be able to touch—but she didn't need comforting, there were no fears for him to still or tears for him to wipe. A lawyer is more than a husband and son when you are in the hands of those who bellow and beat a man who hides his head. *I* saw that. The lawyer, who had status here among the warders and policemen, he was the power, he was the one she was with. There were quick, voluble questions and answers between them, the ease of two who have established confidence in a matter of survival; he was the only one to have seen her while she was in detention, the only one who knew anything about her as she was now. She didn't have time or thought to ask us how things were at home. My father made several attempts and managed to murmur privately to her—The whole thing's insane, don't worry Aila, nothing will stick.— He meant any charges made against her. She looked at the lawyer, then at me; her dark smooth eyebrows came together in a pleat above the softness of her pausing glance, she's always looked like that when there's something not understood, and which cannot be explained. She touched my father's hand. —My turn, now.— She and the lawyer laughed.

At two o'clock in the afternoon, in Court B, Aila was charged with four offences under the Internal Security Act. —I think of her as 'Aila' since I saw her appear in court, that day, heard her names called out to identify her. The charges included terrorism and furthering the aims of a banned organization. Aila was accused of being a member of something called the Transvaal Implementation Machinery, responsible for acts of terror in the region, and connected to a high command named Amos Sebokeng. She was alleged to have acted as a courier between Umkhonto weSizwe in neighbouring countries and a cell in the Johannesburg area, to have attended meetings where missions for the placing of explosives were planned, and to have concealed terrorist arms on the rented property where she resided illegally.

She came home with us. The lawyer eloquently produced all the good reasons why my mother—that exemplary wife and home-maker whose retiring nature and virtues as a conscientious worker were attested to by the highly-respected medical practitioner by whom she had been employed for years—should be granted bail for Aila. The prosecutor's objections were overruled and ten thousand rands were paid; the lawyer had Dr Jasood's blank cheque ready, as the doctor's bandages had been there, in my father's absence, to bind up Baby's slashed wrists.

I have lived with Aila all the time while he, my father, was living his secret life and I have never heard of this 'Machinery' or this code name for some high command: the secret life she was living. I've been the cover for both of them. That sticks! She didn't even need to confide in me; the silence she kept, for my protection, made me her conspirator, just as I've been his.

Aila happy for battle.

No-one knew better than Sonny that it is always a good thing to let warders and policemen see you laugh. It is difficult for them not to have some respect for one who can laugh while in their hands. But where did she get this from, know how to conduct herself, how to talk to her lawyer, put up a front that gives nothing away—not even to an old political lag who also happened to be her husband. Prison-wise. Aila prison-wise. His Aila; he made the claim to himself. In himself he ignored the crevasse of years he had opened between them and thought of them as Aila-and-Sonny, who together learned how to live, to whom nothing was faced, decided, dealt with that was not conjoined in the little house outside Benoni.

Hannah would sit him down to coffee, now, when he arrived, or offer a glass of wine. They were placed again as they were that first day in a coffee bar, before anything began, where it might never have happened—been rewritten.

—How is Aila? Is she in a state of shock?—

—She's home. They granted bail. Ten thousand.—

Hannah's downy pink face tightened painfully. He and she knew that a high bail price meant the prosecution's confidence that charges would be upheld. —What's she supposed to have done?—

—Internal Security Act. The lot. Missions, a cell, courier.—

Yes, those trips to Lusaka that set him free to spend whole nights in this room, on that bed, behind them now.

—And the storeroom find, of course.—

The silence hung. Suddenly the blue of Hannah's eyes intensified as it did with tears. Whether Aila was a revolutionary or not, whether she had joined the struggle—and who should not rejoice at her choice if she had?—or been naïvely led by the daughter to acts she didn't understand, or was a victim of trumped-up charges and Security Police plants, the quiet, beautiful wife with the curtain material she'd sewn now used to wrap hand-grenades and mines was betrayed, betrayed.

Sonny was amazed; intruded upon. Hannah wept. The tears moved slowly down her broad cheeks and she did not turn from him or cover her face in decency with her hands. She had no right to weep for Aila!

—For god's sake, Hannah.—

But the tears welled and found their way over the contours of that dear face. She tried to speak, had no control of the muscles of her throat, swelling like the throat of a bird. Terrible, terrible, she managed to get out, again and again, flailing her head so that the tears flew. Some fell on his hands. He rose and across the table clasped her in his arms, they clung to each other in wild awkwardness, knocking over cups and sugar bowl.

When they lay on that same bed on the floor, close to the earth as they had liked to be, wakeful, the tides of blood flowing down behind their closed eyelids were washing them apart, the red waters of being widening between them. She did not speak but surely he could hear: this won't happen anymore.

Sonny knew a dire displacement. The wild embrace across

the table belonged to the meeting in the booth of the courts' anteroom.

I wonder when she went away. I didn't take much notice at the time; I suppose the signs were there in him but they passed for something else. The house, our life, was centred round Aila; if he were at home, where else should he be, now? Aila had to report to the police twice a day. Could he let anyone else take her there? One did as much for any comrade, put him first, before personal desires, in any crisis.

Not only the life of our house centred round Aila, the attention of the leadership focused on her now. My father's comrades were frequent visitors again—to see her, to give her reassurance of their support. Arrangements had to be made for her defence in the Supreme Court, from what sources the money would come, what counsel would be best for this case. A woman on trial—there was the question of what judge she might appear before, a punishing misogynist or one likely to be positively influenced by refinement, maturity and beauty, and how best the Defence might take advantage of such a possibility. The women's Federation brought cakes and the trades union Congress sent flowers.

It was through these visitors in the liberation movement that I heard she was gone—my father's woman. Quite by chance. Someone from Cape Town remarked in our living-room, ignorant of any connection between her and Aila's husband, that Amnesty International and other groups concerned with political imprisonment ought to be given more details about Aila. —We shouldn't wait for the trial to begin. Getting people overseas to know the background, telling them what kind of woman we have here, in Aila. . . I tell you who's the best person to do this,

Hannah Plowman, she's great— And someone interrupted: —But she's not here any longer, man. She's got some fancy job with the UN High Commission for Refugees, North Africa somewhere.—

So he was the good husband, the good comrade because that woman was gone. He was alternately business-like and attentive—Aila's side-kick, Aila's entourage, Aila the hero, now—and morose, sitting alone at the kitchen table late at night, not because my mother might go to prison for ten years (I pestered the lawyers to give me an estimate) but because there was no more big bed on the floor, shameless as you walked in, a whore's room.

Aila's mark was awesome on me: the little girl I sleep with treated me like an invalid, when fellow-students saw me, they saw the headlines in the papers: HAND-GRENADES IN GARAGE HOUSEWIFE LIVING ILLEGALLY IN WHITE SUBURB ALLEGED HARBOURED TERROR CACHE. My mother's indictment in the guise of Aila had given me respite. I had stopped thinking about his woman, about him; the stranger's remark suddenly reminded me.

And now I, also, did something shameful. I couldn't resist the compulsion. I don't know why; I went again to the cottage. What did I think I was going to see there? Maybe I just wanted to make sure, sure. Maybe I couldn't believe it; he, she and I have been bound so long. The side gate was padlocked. I climbed over it. The dogs at the main house heard nothing, didn't appear. I went up the steps of the stoep as if to announce myself to her. I stood in front of the sagging screen door but did not touch it because I remembered it squeaked. A carton that had contained wine bottles lay split among dead leaves, holding two rain-swollen telephone directories. A window was broken and the glass had fallen inwards.

No bed. A dirty square on the wall behind where it was; I remembered an ugly picture, hanging there. House-plants dead for lack of water. Two burst cushions spilling their guts in a corner. There was the buzzing silence of desertion. All the movements and syllables that had sounded there, all that had happened there, caught in confusion, eddying without sense, motes drifting within the walls, falling back from them. That's what's over. That's the past, its dust not settled.

I put my head in. The smell of smoke. Her smell. He came home smelling of smoke, he didn't smell of the semen he'd given her. That bed. To paraphrase one of my father's famous quotations (the Bible, this time?), that bed gave up the ghost.

The sensation you expect doesn't come when and where you seek it. I didn't find exorcism then and there.

Aila was applying herself conscientiously to the long lists of questions the lawyers, while planning her defence, gave her, and to the full account required of everything she had thought and done that led to the circumstances of her indictment. She made notes by hand and typed sheet after sheet. He sat across the table from her as they had done when he was the schoolteacher correcting his class papers and she was improving herself by correspondence courses. But if she looked up to ask something of him now, it was seeking the advice of a comrade more experienced in the pitfalls of preparing for a trial. He suppressed a wave of distress and denial that came over him every time, and answered her; she would nod in thanks, and scribble something in a margin. Her image on the other side of the book or newspaper in front of him penetrated the pages. The longer he waited to speak the fewer the opportunities would be; with every line she wrote, every consultation with the Defence, every visit of his comrades in the leadership, the preposterous was becoming the accepted reality, made so not only by the State, but by the lawyers, the movement, taking it as a fact: Aila, Aila a revolutionary responsible for her acts. Preparing Aila for what—he knew, he knew—only a revolutionary with total inner certainty, who has *chosen*, can withstand.

And with a sense of stretching his fingertips at something that was disappearing from his grasp, he suddenly spoke as he handed her a cup of tea he'd brought to sustain her at her task.

—What made you do it?—

Late at night; she looked around the room to make sure they were alone, to see if the boy, Will, was there to give her support or credence—he was often a presence, wearing his headphones so that the music he listened to didn't disturb her.

She took her time. It even could be Aila didn't feel obliged to answer; that, at last, the reproach she had never made would take this form. Sonny had a passing foreboding; but she spoke.

—I understood.—

He gazed at her; she seemed almost to transform into her old laconic gentleness.

—What did you understand that you didn't understand before, here? How could Baby—blatantly!—use her mother like that? I can't believe it. . .I can't forgive her.— With alarm he heard his voice hoarse—if the sphincter of tears failed, Aila would know they were not for her but because he was rejecting Baby. *His* daughter.

—Nothing to forgive. She did nothing.—

—That's not true. All right—so it was the people you met through her. She exposed you. Through her.— (*I'll cast out my daughter for you*, was passing between them in the pause. *See, I'll do that for you.*) —Of course, it's exciting, important, free, there, after the way we are here. Oh I'm sure. The compromises, the pettiness. . .they're gone, it's war, not getting by with your white neighbours to prove a point. But if you wanted more, there's plenty to do here, we could have. . .at least. . .we could have discussed it.—

—I don't know whether I wanted to.—

He waited. —Aila. Be active, or discuss it? Apparently you could discuss it with Baby. If you say she wasn't the one to use you.—

—You were so proud of her. Don't speak badly about her now. Don't spoil something for yourself.—

He experienced a contraction of his stomach muscles in an emotion new to him, inevitable, the nausea of remorse, that always must be experienced entirely alone; he had spoiled so much. Aila drank her tea and he saw her focus, under stiff dark lashes, shift along a line or two of her written testimony, but she turned away from it as if for the moment the words held the wrong meaning. She looked at him and then suddenly began to speak like someone telling a story. —Baby and he take the child with them everywhere, you know. And he's still so little. Meetings, parties—he's up at parties until one in the morning. The first time, I was really shocked, I told them it was wrong, poor little thing. I mean, you and I. . .when we went out while the children were small, someone came to sit in with them, they were at home in their own beds by eight o'clock to get a good night's rest. But one time when I arrived—I don't remember whether that was the fourth visit or the third—they told me that they took the little one with them to a party one night and when they came home they found the house had been bombed. You remember that second South African raid over the border, Baby sent a message after the bombing of a safe house, reassuring us it wasn't where they were living? Well, she did that because she didn't want you—us—to worry; and when she told me, she made me promise not to tell you. But it *was* the house where they'd been living. If they'd left the child at home with a sitter that night—with someone like me. . .—

Isolation is a sensation like cold. It took him up from his hands and feet through to the core of his being. If he had nothing left but to turn against Baby, who had escaped death a second time without his knowing, what place was he in, within himself?

—That was it?—

—I think so.—

—Difficult to follow you, Aila. You leave so much out.—

—I know.—

—You 'understood'.—

—Yes.—

—Can't you explain? Revenge? If you've been getting a political education you should know that's not an acceptable motivation in our struggle. Some mystical experience you've gone through, or what? Understood what?—

—The necessity for what I've done.— She placed the outer edge of each hand, fingers extended and close together, as a frame on either side of the sheets of testimony in front of her. And she placed herself before him, to be judged by him.

If he had been the one with the right to judge her. As her husband? As a comrade? The construction he had skilfully made of his life was uninhabitable, his categories were useless, nothing fitted his need. *Needing Hannah.* His attraction to Hannah belonged to the distorted place and time in which they—all of them—he, Aila, Hannah, lived. With Hannah there was the sexuality of commitment; for commitment implies danger, and the blind primal instinct is to ensure the species survives in circumstances of danger, even when the individual animal dies or the plant has had its season. In this freak displacement, the biological drive of his life, which belonged with his wife and the children he'd begotten, was diverted to his lover. He and Hannah begot no child; the revolutionary movement was to be their survivor. The excitement of their mating was for that.

But Aila was the revolutionary, now.

When they drove together to the police station to report every day, the weird routine performed together seemed to him a possibility of the return to the domestic intimacy they had had, once. A strange return it would have been, but surely something from which they both began must be there, beneath whatever unimaginably changed circumstances between them. He was at home, now, as he used to be, once. The other circumstances made this possible: the cottage was abandoned; he had somehow been eased out of high position in the movement.

He made love to Aila. But then he had never stopped making love to Aila, dutifully calculating the intervals that would not arouse suspicions that he was giving himself to some other woman. The difference was that now he was coming home to her, Aila, his wife, his Aila. She gave no sign of noticing the return of passion; she co-operated well—that was the only way in which he could describe it to himself. And he knew—now with his greater experience of what women can feel, in love—that she faked her pleasure. She was thinking of something else; or she couldn't stop thinking, that was it, and if a man can't drive out everything but consciousness of ecstasy in a woman when he is inside her, he is no man. Sometimes, defying this, urging himself, he was no man, sank from her like dead flesh. She was not embarrassed about him, or for him. She gave him a pat on the hand: —Doesn't matter.—

Doesn't matter. Aila said that and he lay beside her with

his heart beating up in resentment against Hannah. He had listened entranced to the things Hannah said; they seemed to speak from the centre of life, which no-one else he had known had ever mentioned. But the centre of life wasn't there, with her, the centre of life was where the banalities are enacted—the fuss over births, marriages, family affairs with their survival rituals of food and clothing, that were with Aila. Because of Hannah, Aila was gone. Finished off, that self that was Aila. Hannah destroyed it. Aila was gone, too, Yet she lay beside him alive. Something bigger than self saves self; that had been the youthful credo he had taught his shy bride. He listened to Aila breathing, giving a little snore, now and then, and smelt the too-sweet odour of her skin creams warmed by the rise of her body temperature in sleep—the cloying familiarity in marriage, flee from it to the clandestine love wild and free of habit—and he longed unappeasably; nothing, nothing was there to stanch the longing for everything he had fled.

Aila the comrade. Exhibit No. 1 in court was an RPG-7 rocket-launcher, two RPG-7 rockets, three RG-42 hand-grenades, two limpet-mines, two FM-57 land-mines, and a length of flowered curtaining material. It had been bought in the Oriental Plaza by that other Aila, who sewed curtains for her son's bedroom. Aila sat between police officers with her head up, composed, a smile and lift of eyebrows for Sonny and Will in the front row of the public gallery. Sonny had no rational control of his feelings at this period come upon his life. Daylight—the daylight of courtrooms and police footfalls, the huddle of lawyers and the shuffle to rise in court as the judge entered the canopied bench—dazzled his solitary, night mood. But this at least was his place, the unchanging ground of struggle across the veld. With a lance of pain, pride in this woman, Aila, broke through. He scarcely noticed the sudden agitation in the boy.

Will was whispering something in his father's ear; Sonny jerked away his head irritatedly, concentrating on the process in the well of the court. His son was trying to tell him that the RPG-7 launcher and rockets were not in the cache he saw unwrapped from the curtain off-cuts in the storeroom.

There's no air in my life. The polished corridors of police stations and prisons have been the joy-rides I've been taken on with the people I love. Once when I was a schoolboy one of my father's white friends invited me to spend a Saturday with his sons at his farm. *Enkelbos*, it was called; I still remember the sign at the gate one of the sons jumped down to unhitch. They went there every weekend. They had a rubber dinghy on the dam. They had scrambler bikes and we took turns roaring round sending dust up to cloud the pollen scent of the black-trunked wattle trees that were in thick yellow bloom; it was the end of July and winter was melting on your cheeks.

I need air. Again the polished corridors, the company of policemen watching sullenly, the bodies of strangers shifted up for along the boney benches of the public gallery, the eagerness with which we follow the expressions of the lawyers, try to penetrate the distancing that the judge, somewhere a man inside his red robes, keeps between himself and all he sees and hears. People downcast by trouble under the lofty spaces—how many times have I gazed up to the fans in the ceiling, stirring the trouble round and round where no pollen scatters renewal. Staleness. All my life, since we left our old home outside the mining town, I've been breathing the dead breath of these places where life and freedom are supposed to be protected by the law.

Now it's Aila there in the well of the court, and my father sitting beside me as she used to. I felt dulled, I felt like letting myself slump against the stocky old black man asleep sitting at my other side with his hands folded on his stick. Let us sleep together through justice or injustice being done, *baba*, we don't know what they'll decide is just or unjust, we don't know what will come of the judge's measured hand-movements, taking note (of what?), the lawyers exchange of document files, the Clerk of the Court so contemptuous of facing us that he doesn't realize he can be seen picking his nose, the computer operators fingering their fluffy hair-dos, the policemen creaking in and out on the balls of their feet, bobbing heads in obeisance to the judge's bench like people perfunctorily crossing themselves as they leave a church.

The old man beside me began to breathe stertorously. I'm so conditioned to these places that I automatically cow before their authority, and I nudged to wake him before a policeman would come over and reprimand him. I did it to save him fear but he was startled anyway, and his abrupt recovery jolted me alert, too. It was as if I had dropped off during a movie and found myself recognizing, at the point at which my attention returned, a scene that contradicted an earlier one brought to mind. The exhibits were being displayed to the judge by the Prosecutor: the pineapple hand-grenades and the limpet-mines, the land-mines, yes—but here were objects I had never seen before, strange things described as an RPG-7 rocket launcher and two rockets. There was no object like these, no RPG-7 launcher or rocket wrapped in my curtain material in our storeroom. I almost jumped up and shouted to the judge. But my conditioning to prisons and courts kept me down. I tried to whisper to him, my father, but he, too, knows how to behave in these places if you want to get by. He shut me up. I was stifled, stifling with what I knew. I trod between the line of legs on the bench to get out. It was Pretoria, now, the Supreme Court in the Palace of Justice, not the Soweto court for blacks; that was only for her first appearance. I sat in the great entrance hall among majestic pillars with polished brass feet, under lozenges of coloured light that came steeply from stained-glass windows; their churches and their halls of justice are somehow mixed up, they see some divine authority in their laws. Everyone entering had to pass through a metal-detector arch and a body-search; I was confusedly aware of a gun pointed at me—a small black boy, whose female family were slumped, waiting, near me, was running about with a toy automatic rifle. Now a white policeman guarding the door of Court D pretended to be hit. The kid's laughter flew up the vault with the trapped swallows as he scampered round this new playmate, while I sat and saw again, over and over, the lengths of curtaining unfolded, counted the dull-looking objects one by one, the hand-grenades and limpet-mines and land-mines I recognized and I'd heard the Prosecution identify. I felt swollen, immensely important. I don't know what I thought; that I had justice inside me, it would explode among them. Their lies and trickery, *verneukery*, their dirt would fall away from Aila and set her free.

My father didn't come and look for me. Not until the judge took his tea-break. Through the doors of Court D I heard the shout '*Opstaan.* Rise in court' and the stir of feet and clothing and voices as people moved to come out. I felt I would choke. I stood up. Are you ill, he said. He looked as if this would be the last thing he could bear.

I haven't touched him for a long time; I clutched his arms.

—The rockets weren't there. That launcher thing. They were never there. They planted them, like they did the other things earlier. I tell you I saw, and they weren't there.—

He believed me at once but of course the lawyers questioned me. Was I sure? Was I in the storeroom all the time during the search, that morning? Wasn't I in a state of agitation, excitement, anger? Yes, all those and more, believe me, my toes were curled rigid as my fingers in my fists and my shoulders were so tense my neck ached next day as if I'd strained a muscle. But I know what I saw, I could swear to it as many times as any court asked—I wished I'd written down a list of those weapons on a bit of paper and made those bastards sign it, that day, that day!

When the lawyers were satisfied with my reliability and had come to a satisfactory assessment of my ability to stand up to cross-examination without being intimidated by the prosecution, they agreed that mine was an important piece of evidence. It brought into question the whole allegation that Aila had hidden or knowingly allowed to be hidden (you know how they put things) a cache of arms in our storeroom. In her second statement she had said she understood that what was to be stored in the storeroom was 'disused office equipment'. She had not looked into what they left there amid the junk of a family household. On my evidence, if they had stored explosive weapons there, no RPG-7 rocket was among them.

My father surged with elation, he had the grin and strength of gaze he had when Baby and I were children, held high in the air by him, and that he had had when we went to see him shut away in prison. —They not only won't be able to prove she knew what was in the storeroom, it won't be possible for them to prove they didn't plant the lot. Not beyond reasonable doubt—can't, once it's clear they planted the rockets. All their evidence will be totally discredited! If the police have lied on the main charge, how can the case hold up? The judge'll have to throw the whole thing out—there's a good chance of that!—

We were at the lawyers' for consultation. I was at its centre for this, the only time. I was nobody's conspirator, I had found my own point of reference through my own experience. The lawyers were not as certain of the outcome as my father, but I'd become the pivot of their defence, their principal witness. I heard the aside from one of them to my father:—He'll have to be two hundred percent sure he cannot be caught out in uncertainty—not even in tone of voice—on any detail, doesn't matter how small and apparently irrelevant. Because Lombard's going to play on the fact that there's special sentiment involved, a young man naturally will lie, if it's a question of family . . .after all, it's his mother.—

My mother—Aila—listened to everything with her new intentness and did not look at me. I felt strange that she wouldn't look at me. It was as if she wanted to deny this new bond of intimacy between us. I believe I began, then, to think (but I may have known all the time?)—I began to think, very deep within myself, no-one will ever get at it, that Aila knew there were those ugly and deadly things wrapped in the material she had left over when she sewed my curtains. She knew, and she didn't want me to know—I, who've known so much about her that others don't, he—my father—doesn't. When the men had all talked a great deal, the lawyers trying out my answers on one another, and my father, Aila and I had got up to leave, the Senior Counsel told Aila she and I had better come back for briefing with him next day. Aila emanated a stilling atmosphere; the parting jabber stopped. It was as if everyone found he had unnoticingly entered a strange house, and it was hers; she stood there. —I don't want Will to give evidence.—

Preposterous. So shocked, one of the lawyers laughed; they couldn't take her seriously: the lawyers, my father. Naturally the poor woman was confused, they would explain to her, she would come round, they would convince her. No harm would come to the boy. No harm. A woman, after all, she was thinking of her son—

Mama's boy! There was a thrust of rage in me; against myself, against her. Now they were raising their voices, talking over each other, about me. Any moment someone would remember and turn to ask *And what are you going to be when you grow up?*

I drove. She sat beside me and he behind her. I drove fast, with the slamming movements of my mood, and neither cautioned me. For once I felt in charge of them. He was leaning forward, not to be excluded from whatever she and I might say. But he would have missed nothing by being less eager. We did not speak. What I might say to her wouldn't be said before him. On the periphery of my vision I saw him squeeze her shoulder and let his hand lie a moment. *Poor Aila poor Aila.* Was he telling little wifey it's all right, she has her strong clever leader-of-the-people husband, turned up at last to talk her out of her foolish notions?

She asked me to drive by the chemist's. While she was in the shop, he sighed and fidgeted. —It'll be all right. She's upset. It's a bit much for her to take in. Against her nature, Will.—

She came out of the shop and smiled at us, frowning in the sun, it was as if we were expected to take her photograph. He was encouraged to begin again. —It's a matter of the truth, Aila. It's not even just a personal issue, it's not just you involved. Will has to speak the truth. That's a chance to challenge the system itself.—

I had started the engine but I let it stall with a jerk. —Let's leave all this until we get home.—

He ignored me; he was still my father. —Believe me, Aila,

there'll be no action against him just because he's a witness. No question of complicity. No-one's going to arrest Will! Not because of this; not because he's my son or your son. It's the duty of any Defence to subpoena anyone they need. You know that, surely? But I'm not a lawyer, am I, ready to win my case at any cost. . . He's my son. He's my son, too. Would I put him in any danger? Believe me. Would I lie to you?—

And we don't challenge him. Imagine! Neither of us bursts out laughing when he finds the nerve to ask that question. Neither of us affirms, yes, yes, and yes again. Is it all forgotten then, washed up, are the three of us survivors of his shipwreck, under his command to build a new shelter for some dream of family he wants to come back to?

I tilted my head to look at her sidelong. She licked her forefinger and rubbed at a mark on the back of her other hand. She caught me looking at her, dropped the hand and turned her head away. When she knew she had shaken off my glance she spoke to my father and to me. —It's enough. It's enough.—

I don't know what he understood by this but I heard what she was saying. My father the famous Sonny, Baby the revolutionary exile, Aila the accomplice of Umkhonto weSizwe: they are our family's sacrifice for the people, there's no need of me, who needs someone like me? They are the heroes.

Nothing would change her mind. The Defence team appealed to the seasoned activist who was also the person closest to her—her husband—he must be the one to make her see reason and sense. Through the influence of all the years they had lived together; though the lawyers didn't say it: through love.

It's enough, she said. Enough: enough for her to bear without having the boy involved in any way. That was horribly distasteful to her. Frightened her. She was not afraid to act courier for ruthless, shameless Baby in Lusaka and brave enough for god knows what else she had done, but she feared this. Their boy; but it was tacitly accepted, way back, that Will was *her* child, and although Sonny had Lear-like lost his, his Baby—*Best thou had's not been born, than not t'have pleas'd me better*—Aila still claimed a tender unspoken priority in matters concerning the boy.

Through love. Sonny could argue the reason and sense—none better—at his command the simplicity of the schoolmaster who had been her mentor and the wisdom of the veteran of the struggle. Love. Sometimes he thought the way to do it was to tell her everything, to confess Hannah, every night he had spent close to the earth in the cottage, the weekends among the orange blossom, even the perverse pleasure (how could innocent Aila understand that; how awful if she could) he took in seeing her, Aila, his wife, and Hannah in the same company. But then that would have meant telling Aila, too, how he kept Will in the know, how it had started when he bumped into the schoolboy Will when he took his blonde openly out in public, to a cinema. How would Aila forgive him that. What love could convince her after that.

But perhaps Aila could tell him why it all had to happen to him. If he confessed all, exposed all, kept nothing for himself, gave away for ever all that belonged to him in his need of Hannah. Oh Hannah. Oh schoolmaster taunted by the tags of passion he didn't understand when he read them in the little son-of-sorrow house. Oh Hannah.

Beat at this gate that let thy folly in.

She mustn't think she can count forever on the child who used to put himself to sleep stroking his lips with the tail of her long black plait. The plait's cut off, she's shorn, I'm a man. I thrust myself into women as my father does.

I got her out of the house, away from him. She took a walk with me. I wanted air. There wasn't anywhere much to walk to; three blocks down and you come to the discount liquor store, the take-away and the general store the Portuguese calls his supermarket, three blocks the other way and you reach the Dutch Reformed Church where our white neighbours pray on Sundays to their god who doesn't admit people like us in his house. We pass the houses of these neighbours; they've changed several times since my father moved us defiantly into this shabby suburb that seemed so grand to us after our place in the veld. More of our people have moved in as we did, some of the whites have gone because of this and been replaced by poorer ones who can't afford to live anywhere else. Most of our people are like we were—they've fixed up the houses they occupy—paint, tiled stoeps, fancy front door. The whites have the hulks of old cars in the patches that are supposed to be gardens, and cardboard where windowpanes are broken.

The neighbours who used to greet us (my mother such a real lady) seemed not to see us as we walked by; looked away. Perhaps they were different neighbours, I've never taken much notice, all the same to me. Or they had seen the headlines, and the newspaper photographs of Aila, living among them, one and the same woman who'd seemed such a lady you'd greet her just as if she were white.

Aila kept in step beside me. —Ma. You can't decide for me.—

—The whole business is my affair. It's not for the lawyers to defend me in any way they like. It's my right to instruct them, isn't it.—

—That's not what I mean. You must listen to what I mean,

you think you know how things should be for me, but you don't realize. . .—

—I do, I do. I don't want you mixed up in this. I don't want your life decided by mine. It's you who don't realize, Will.—

I stumbled against a stone, she waited for me. I said it aloud at last: —Aila.—

Her black eyes brightened and narrowed, she pursed her mouth wryly and amazedly. But fondly. She—only just—put her hand a moment on my forearm.

—Why do I have to say this again. Why must I be the one excepted, the one left behind, left out, why is it assumed—by you, by him, by Baby, everyone—I haven't any part in the struggle. Why is it just accepted I'm the one who lives the sham normal life you've all rejected, I'm to be happy on the edge of the white man's world of big business, money, going to be smugly settled in a year or two in some big firm or multinational if there're any left here, given loans to build a house just as good as theirs where they say I can, driving a company car, marrying some girl presentable enough by their standards for their annual dinner, producing kids I can afford to send to some private school that takes kids like ours—why? Why is it decided that that's for me? Who decided it? What's wrong with me? Why me? Is there some birthmark or something that says this is what I must be?—

Her shoulders were hunched in distress but I didn't stop. After so long, I couldn't stop. —It's like a curse, I'm supposed to take it as my fate. And now you, you, when I can act like the rest of you, when I can face them in court and tell them they're liars, liars, those thugs who've been let into our house—and I let them in, I'm the one who's let every kind of destruction into our house, I'm always there, handy, Will is going to do it, well-named, he'll do it—now you say, It's enough. Enough! There's nothing for me in the struggle to change our lives. I'm needed at home. I *am* home. It's *enough*! I've had enough of it!—

She was flinching as if I were hitting her; I was hitting her and I stopped only for breath.

—I can't do it. Then you must do it some other way. Not through me. I can't part with you, Will.—

—What's so special about me? So I'm your stake in something, I'm to be something you and he don't really want to give up? Not even for the revolution? The token place in the boardroom you don't really, somewhere in you—you don't want to destroy? Am I your hostage, your middle-class nostalgia for nice things? You don't really want to see your flowered curtains used for a better purpose than dolling up the bedroom in the house meant for a white man.—

We walked on in terrible silence for a while. My heart was thudding with the excitement of my cruelty.

—I don't think it's like that. It won't be like that.—

I gave a snort of rejection,

There was no way out for her, even though she hadn't said as much. She had no way to stop me speaking the truth for myself. We walked quietly down the street where we lived. From some way off we could see something hanging on our gate; in the dusk it looked like a black sweater, perhaps it had been found in the street and displayed there for its owner to reclaim. It was a dead cat, and tied to its strangled neck was a piece of cardboard lettered in red: BLACK COMMUNIST BITCH GET OUT OF HERE. Aila was fumbling desperately to untie the cat. I said, It's dead, Ma, it's no good, it's dead. Leave it. Let's go inside. I'll see to it afterwards.

Somehow our arms went out around each other. Close, we

walked calmly up the cement path and shut the front door behind us. That was all anyone watching the house would have the satisfaction of seeing.

From where did Aila's obstinacy come? Obduracy, rather. That was not in her nature, either; before.

Sonny had to define to himself what he meant by 'before'. Yes, there was a blank in his chronology of her life; he knew little of the changes in her for which, he believed, he was responsible. He had noticed she'd cut her hair, that's about all—women's whims. Meant little to him at the time.

He tried to keep calm and confine himself to reason; he submitted himself to self-criticism as an intelligent man, who had freed his mind through the struggle, should. There must be method. He knew he was having difficulty in accepting Aila as a comrade. He had consciously to rid himself of an outworn perception of Aila. Consciously; that was the problem.

Perhaps if (as he had read, long ago, Jesuit educationists said) character is formed, for life, in the first three years of human existence, the idea of the loved partner remains fixed, arrested at the first few naïve years of a relationship. Reason told him that if he could accept Aila as a comrade like any other, as well as his wife, they might revive and deepen the old Sonny/Aila life together. It would be their life, even if she were to be imprisoned, and he might be, once again, at some time. He knew that to bring this about there were certain requirements. Aila had to be reinstated as his wife. He had done this. He also knew that it was necessary to forgive himself as well as be forgiven by Aila—guilt is self-indulgent and unproductive.

Sonny forgave himself; but this was futile. Aila had never reproached him, so there was nothing for her to forgive. And nothing in her behaviour recognized that anyone but she herself was responsible for it. Even the harm he had done her was no claim on her; he saw that. Perhaps he flattered himself Aila had needed to suffer his love of another woman to change. Perhaps it had nothing to do with that, with him. Perhaps she had freed herself just as he had, through the political struggle. He would never be able to ask her; the question of his woman was irrelevant, now.

The lawyers tacitly understood it was no use depending on Sonny to influence Aila. Consultations, at which he sat in, were becoming more and more difficult. The Defence asked for and was granted an extension of the remand for preparation of fresh evidence. It was to Sonny the Senior Counsel came privately, as a doctor informs a relative, not the patient, of a terminal diagnosis, to say that he was withdrawing from the case. Sonny implored him to reconsider; Aila, when told, merely nodded quietly and cleared her throat, gave no indication of wanting to change the man's decision. Although the advocate had lost patience with her angrily at their last meetings, she thanked him 'for all he had done' and—strange for Aila!—when he shook her hand, suddenly kissed his cheek.

Tuesday the fourteenth of June.

That was the afternoon when I came home and my father was alone. He was standing about at the telephone as if he had just used it or was expecting it to ring. Five o'clock, the time when they went for the second report to the police station every day; one of the routines that order our kind of life. I was so drilled and disciplined to it that I even felt anxious they were going to be late. —You haven't been yet?—

—No.— He stood there.

—Has she gone on her own?—

—I haven't seen her.—

—Did she have to go to town?— 'Town' meant the lawyers' chambers.

—I phoned. She's not there.—

—Oh I suppose she'll come in any minute.—

It was his hands that alarmed me. —The car's in the garage.—

I noticed his hands; the thumbs rubbing against the inner surface of the fingers in the unconscious trembling motion of those old men whose nervous system is deteriorating.

—She must've gone out with someone, then. Weren't you here?—

—Ben gave me a lift—there was a meeting, so I left the car for her. He brought me back an hour ago.—

—There must be a note. I'll look in the kitchen.—

—I've looked.—

We waited for her. The winter cold coming up from the floor and the darkening of the windows to glassy black splintered by streetlights marked the passing of time although he and I avoided being caught, each by the other, looking at a watch. So long as the length of time that had passed was not measured we could believe she would come in soon. —Shouldn't you phone the police station and make some excuse, she's sick or something?—

He looked at me as if what I had just said had the effect of making him recognize what he was avoiding. He held a deep breath. —That's the last thing we ought to do.—

—I can't see why not. They'll withdraw bail if she doesn't report, won't they? We can get a note from Jasood, she was ill.—

—An excuse. . .it's a sign. It alerts them.—

—To what?—

Father-knows-best. Late, late at night, late in our lives and she's not coming back, he somehow knows she's not coming back—what right does he think he has to keep something from me?

I wanted to yell at him to keep his hands still.

—You know what's happened to her. Where is she? Tell me.—

—I don't know, Will, I'm telling you, I don't know where she is. I just don't know.—

Ah yes. The less you know, the better; that's the way we protect one another, I ought to know that, I'd know that if I were one of them. He was telling me the truth.

We went to bed, he and I. He left the door of their bedroom open and so did I mine, I don't know what for. We lay apart in the dark following imaginary passages of Aila through the night, placing her where she might be—both of us, I'm sure. I fell asleep towards dawn because I'm young but I don't suppose he slept at all.

A young girl came early in the morning. She had purple-pink painted lips and nails and she wore white plastic boots, a smart little garment-factory girl on her way to work. Any neighbourly informers watching the house would have thought her one of the girl-friends of the son, she looked exactly the kind of girl they believe the son of our kind of people would be attracted to. Her long nails and her bangles clicked as she scrabbled for the note in her bag and gave it to my father. In the midst of the strain and tension of those moments there was an incongruous aside, in my feelings; pride in the fact of the unguessed-at commitment of our people to the struggle, hidden under this cheap appearance. Whites don't know what they're seeing when they look at us; at her, at the black women from the country knitting jerseys for sale on the city pavements, at the black combi drivers taking over the streets, the miners in their NUM T-shirts; at my sister, Baby, at Aila, my mother. I want to tell them.

The note was from one of my father's comrades in the leadership. It asked him to come to a certain house. I stayed behind to be home when the police came to look for her. Of course; I was the one who opened the door to them. But she wasn't there. Another time, my mother had gone away and never come back. Now Aila is gone, and she won't come back until everything here is changed, there is air, she will not be judged by the laws white men made for us, she will not live across the veld in a ghetto or be an illegal tenant in a white man's street like this one, where the white neighbours have come out to watch—the women with their arms crossed over their breasts, lips drawn back in salacious expectation, the frowning men with their hands dangling—a police van standing at the gate of this house and the police with their guns and dogs on the stoep.

The leadership thought it best not to involve Sonny in the decision that Aila should estreat bail and leave the country.

There was the chance that once her disappearance was discovered he would be detained again, to be questioned about her. This way, at least he could not be proved to have facilitated his wife's escape.

So she did not need him, even for that.

He told his son it was leadership's decision she should go because the case against her was very serious and in the course of evidence important information about the movement might be revealed. There were infiltrators to the movement involved, who would turn State witnesses under indemnity. Aila had performed her missions commendably, but now her cover was blown. Her name would be honoured, from now on, in the movement inside and outside the country—where she could still be active. Dr Jasood regarded the loss of his money as a contribution to the struggle. When Sonny went with his son Will to thank Aila's old employer, he continued to write some report on a patient while he spoke. —She is worth more than ten thousand rands to us. God bless her.—

There was news of Aila after a while. It came through a third or fourth person, probably someone like she had been, who appeared to be moving innocently between countries. Sonny applied for a passport so that he might have a chance to visit her sometime; see Baby, and his grandchild. But the passport was refused, not unexpectedly, although one of his comrades remarked—Can't see why he shouldn't have a good chance of getting one, now.—

The comment stayed with him long after he was resigned to the disappointment over the passport. It was the echo of common acceptance that the keepers of police files would find he no longer counted as particularly representative of the danger of the movement, to them. It is the enemy—the police, the Ministers of Law and Order and Justice—who decides who the leaders of the people are; it is the measure of the attention, the hounding and harassment you receive, that makes you 'Sonny'. Under the States of Emergency in the country the public gatherings at which his speeches had been so successful were banned. The press, fearful of prosecution and shut-down, took a chance on reporting only the words of leaders so prominent, so well known in the outside world that the government hesitated to act when these leaders defied the law. Sonny a backroom boy, useful for writing statements that appeared or were spoken under the names of the venerable, or for tidying up the vocabulary of the rising stars to give them more weight. Again, as he had done once before, in a moment when old comradeship, the special intimacy of the clandestine life, made it seem possible, he embarrassed others with the direct: Aren't I trusted any more? And there were such denials, such protests—what was he thinking of? What had got into his head?

But were they not thinking—had they not thought, what had got into his head, into his life, deflected him from purpose, the only purpose that mattered at the time when they couldn't do without him—what had got into his head was preoccupation with a woman. There is no place for a second obsession in the life of a revolutionary. But he had never neglected the cause, for her! She was enfolded, one with it, she had connected his manhood, his sexual power as a man, with it! She had given commitment the pumping of the heart. He was overcome with distress at this denial of her (in himself); at this injustice to himself.

And then again—in his depression, the absence of Sonny/Aila, his feelings somersaulted violently; he found himself thinking—insanely—that if the law had still forbidden him Hannah, if that Nazi law for the 'purity' of the white race that disgustingly conceived it had still been in force, he would never have risked himself. For Hannah. Could not have. Because needing Hannah, taking the risk of going to prison for that white woman would have put at risk his only freedom, the only freedom of his kind, the freedom to go to prison again and again, if need be, for the struggle. Only for the struggle. Nothing else was worthwhile, recognized, nothing. That filthy law would have saved him.

Out of the shot and danger of desire

And then he feared himself, come to such perverse conjecture. If it should somehow show in his face, if anyone should somehow sense the shame of it passing through his mind, one of their interrogators jeering in glee, one of his comrades: staring, appalled.

He turned fifty-two. The day was not remarked in any way. His son did not remember the birthday but, a few days after, a card came. Pasted on it was the photograph of a laughing small child in a cap with Mickey Mouse ears. Loving wishes (the formula of the card), and hand-written X-ed kisses, signatures—Baby, Aila, the husband he had never met.

A tide wearing away a coastline, little by little, falling into the ocean of time. They fall away, one by one, lovers, the clinging arms of children, the memory of when life was unthinkable without them. Fifty-two. And all the while he was triumphant in his vitality and virility, apparently unaffected by his forty-something years, this decay was taking place. . . His gums (the dentist insisted it was a long-term process) were already shrinking, his prostate (Jasood said he might have to operate) was becoming enlarged. Close to the earth and happy for battle as he had felt himself, age was there, working within him.

Yet what had been the political ideal now became realized in his daily life under circumstances never sought. Living with his son in a house emptied of its life—two silent men, unable to sustain it—he was stripped of every obligation, every preoccupation, left for the cause alone. And unfettered, even, by any ambition, from the seduction of being the crowds' 'Sonny', which perhaps at one time muddied the clear commitment that had evolved in the schoolmaster, he continued to work for the cause now, all his days and half the nights whenever he was needed. He lived like so many others of his kind whose families are fragmented in the diaspora of exile, code names, underground activity, people for whom a real home and attachments are something for others who will come after.

There were no more letters from the United Nations High Commission for Refugees. Occasional phone calls came with Aila's voice, deceptively near in his ear; far away, in countries she didn't name. After a few minutes he would pass the receiver to the one she was waiting for; although he no longer had it to his ear, standing by he could hear Aila's voice rise with excitement now that she found herself talking to her son.

When everything was forgotten, he dreamt of her: Hannah. A brief, brilliant dream precise as an engraving. Out of the steep dark of his sleep she shook each foot like a cat, as she always had, scattering drops of water while she got out of the bath.

The dream wakened him. He could not fall asleep again. There flashed and plunged behind his closed eyelids a broken sequence of men with white rags tied across their faces in torchlight, men on horseback carrying their flag with its emblem of the swastika, the deformed shape twisted once again to the same purpose. White extremists were rallying to that sign; blacks who had moved into white neighbourhoods were suffering threats and vandalism beneath it. And fear, fear.

An electronic cricket sounding in the quiet: he could hear the creaking whirr of Will's word-processor, printing out. At least the boy seemed to have turned studious enough, although business administration was not exactly the aspect of economics he himself would have chosen for his son. The boy, too, worked late night after night on whatever it was he was doing, since he'd bought the word-processor with money saved from part-time jobs he found himself. It was not possible to get up and go to the boy, tell him, I can't sleep, talk to me. But the silence was not the silence of the day, between them; Will was there, they were still together.

Although Sonny had been refused a passport for the compassionate purpose of visiting his wife and daughter, others were making the trip across the frontier for openly political purposes. White industrialists, churchmen, academics, liberals and lawyers: they were people belonging to professional and social structures within the law, even if they now pressed official confidence in them by tentatively stepping beyond it. Most never had had, nor sought, any contact with the liberation movement within the country. The instinct of a ruling class to seek out what it hoped might be the discovery of something of their own kind beneath a different skin and a different rhetoric ignored the opportunities to do so at home and led them to go abroad to meet the movement's leaders in exile, instead. For the feared future seemed to exist, already, there, outside the country. Perhaps some of its expected retribution might be won over, by pre-emption, before it arrived within.

Some came back in a euphoric state. The exiled leaders

wore lounge suits not Castro fatigues, they could small-talk over wine. Surely such people were not really revolutionaries? And even the Russians, who had armed them all these years, had turned out to be amenable to dining in Pretoria—in the end there is surely no deal so difficult, so unlikely, so obscured by tear-gas, punctured by gunshot wounds, so bedevilled by the explosion of land-mines and petrol bombs, by the preparation of lifetimes of imprisonment, the documentation of nights of interrogation, by the thundering of trucks moving thousands from their homes—no deal that, in the end, cannot be clinched in the course of a business lunch.

And meanwhile, let the police and army deal, in another proven way, with the strikers and demonstrators, the eloquent troublemakers, black and white, at home. And if they can't do it, there's yet another way of dealing: never discover those who finish off the troublemakers, killing from behind masked faces and shooting from moving cars.

At the same time as envoys of change on the white man's terms were flying back and forth, some perhaps secretly briefed by the government, several of Sonny's colleagues were getting travel documents restricted to certain destinations and valid for short periods. Some pragmatist in Pretoria must have calculated this could sweeten up the American Congress in its raucous calls for mandatory sanctions against the country. There was no logic—for anyone outside the Department of the Interior—to the decisions why this one should be let out on a string and that one should not. One or two were able to fly to Lusaka or London directly after being released from a spell of detention; the applications of others, like Sonny, were refused repeatedly. He had given up, for the time being, anyway. Assigned to responsibilities dealing with the crisis in black education, he was too busy to absent himself. And there were more and more disturbing happenings to preoccupy him; some in the area where he himself lived. At this house bricks were flung through a bedroom window; over the façade of that one, paint was splashed. Graffiti left its snail-trail of slime. Only a street away from Sonny's house a couple had just moved in and were arranging their furniture when a group of white men and women invaded the house and ordered them to leave. One bellowed at the husband: —This's a white suburb under Group Areas and there's enough of us to make you people get out. Even if it's made a free-settlement area we're not going to take any kind of *kak* law here, I'm warning you.— The wife said she was going to call the police; the group laughed, and tramped away. Little wonder they had laughed; the police told the couple they were occupying the house illegally: there were no grounds to file a complaint.

In the midst of these preoccupations one of the leaders took Sonny aside at a backroom meeting and informed him he was one of a small group called to consult in Lusaka. Travel papers had been obtained for all six comrades. Although nothing was said, he understood that leadership outside must have made it clear he was to be among them: a recognition beyond anyone's doubts about him, including self-doubt.

There was a difference between leaving the crisis for a family visit and being ordered to go as part of the movement's activity. There was a difference between stepping out of the plane before Aila, before Baby, as the one left out, left behind, coming only as a husband and father, and arriving as part of an official party, driven away to meet with the highest level of leadership in the hospitality of President Kaunda's presidential residence. In the cupboard where he went to look for a suitcase he came across the old carryall Aila used to keep packed for him in case he were to be detained. There was nothing suitable for this journey. He went down to the Oriental Plaza, where she had chosen her curtain material, and bought himself, on the recommendation of the shopkeeper who also was a comrade, a zippered bag with shoulder strap, pockets, and a combination lock.

When he came back from the trip Will was there at the airport to meet him. Will! Will, on the fringe of the crowd at International Arrivals who pressed forward, kissing grandmothers and lovers, exclaiming over babies, blocking the path of other passengers trooping sheepishly behind their trolleys. He felt himself break into the same proud, foolish, happy grin with which all the passengers faced home; someone must have informed Will that his father was coming back on this day and time. Will had come!

They stood before each other as if about to embrace. Sonny was babbling something, his free hand already feeling for the photographs in his breast pocket. Of course he could not talk there and then of the substance of the consultation with the leadership in exile; he had to confine himself to family matters pursued on the side. —They're in great shape—wait till you see—you should just hear your nephew sing, before he can even speak! Baby's keen to have you come up, I've got a whole long screed from her for you—

Will took the bag over his shoulder and walked ahead to the parking lot. —And Aila?—

Sonny seemed hurt by the interruption. —I'll tell you about that later. She's in Sweden. Just missed her by a day. Only one day. . .— He settled into the passenger seat and closed the door. —Now let's get home, my boy!—

His son put the key in the ignition and then turned his head

so that his gaze would be inescapable for either of them.
—They did it yesterday. Burned down.—

I was working Saturdays in a cinema, checking tickets at the entrance, and I came back to the house after the early matinee shift. That street is always livelier on Saturdays than other days; everyone off work for the weekend, and no school for the children. And Afrikaners and our people living there—everyone gardening or washing cars, the kids performing acrobatics with their skate boards and bicycles, the Afrikaners' visitors drinking beer on the stoeps, our selection of aunties and cousins and suitors being entertained indoors.

Not many people come to the house where he and I sleep. Baby and her friends don't giggle and drink Coke sitting on the steps. The cockroaches have to themselves the kitchen where delicacies were prepared. The rosebushes somehow have survived although nobody waters them. Most of the time the place appears to be shut up. But on this day the small space between the fence and the stoep was full of people and a crowd, thickening at the edges as men left tinkering with motorbicycles and cars to come up, and women joined them, and boys toted their skate boards towards the attraction, filled the width of the street. I could see only the backs of sheets of cardboard attached to staffs or hand-held on raised arms, tilted about above heads. Someone was ranting in Afrikaans but he had no loud-hailer and I could make out nothing against the restless approval of the crowd, a horrible purr of strange pleasure, a human sound I have never heard before, pierced by the shrieks of small children playing somewhere down among the legs. All white people. I don't know whether our own white neighbours were among them or not, the expression on their faces distorted them all alike. I'm confusedly aware that some of our people were there, on the fringe, there was a scuffle, someone was punched: there were others of our kind under whose eyes I passed where they stood, quite still, back in the cover of their stoeps, up the street. I walked on and entered the crowd, twisting my shoulders this side and that to make way, saying—I could hear myself!—*excuse me, excuse me, let me pass*—idiotically, still the well-brought-up young man, the way my mother taught us. The placards tipped and jiggled at me. OUR HOME WHITE GO TO YOUR LOCATION COMMUNISTS + BLACKS = END OF OUR CIVILISATION GET OUT KEEP SA WHITE. There was a crude drawing recognizably supposed to be him: the big, dark-rimmed eyes, the curled nostrils. It was slashed across with thick red strokes. I struggled my way to the front door and put my hands up, palm out, stiff fingers splayed, thrusting into those faces from which yells and shouts came at me like bricks and stones, thrusting them away from this shelter where he said he'd provide a decent place for us to live. The man who ranted was tramping, leaping up and down, green socks sagging over running shoes, bruise-coloured tattoos on the ropes of thick tense red calves and bulging red shoulders bare in a sleeveless T-shirt, huge swollen red face bristling with blonde hairs and sweat, tears of rage—I don't know. *Wat maak jy hier? Wat maak jy hier?* They were roaring at me, taking it up as a chant.

What was I doing there.

Yes, what was I doing there.

But I screamed: *This is my father's house.* And before they could decide what to do with me I plunged back, back into them again and fought my way out. Some police had arrived at last (the wagging tail of an aerial on a van, over there). I was pulled free, saved by one of the same kind I had opened the door to when they came to search that house, to arrest him, to take my mother away. They dispersed the crowd but didn't arrest anyone or seize the placards; and that Saturday night, while I slept in the bed of my current new girl, someone in the crowd returned and petrol-bombed the house, burned it to the ground.

I was glad to see it go.

The smell of smoke.

When I went with him to look at it, it was blackened bricks and timber, still smoking. A few of our people who had ventured out to stare stood back from us, as if in respect at a funeral. A kid was balancing himself on that plaster pelican—smashed—that had been a legacy from the white former owner of the property. The black policemen, sent after the fire brigade, to guard the place until there was some show of official investigation, tried to prevent us from entering what was left of the walls but were uncertain about their duty when he told them the house was his.

I followed him through shattered ice-floes of glass and soggy mounds of timber, clambered over contorted and melted metal, bent with him below the jagged shelf of lead ceiling that hung from a single support left upright. Your room, he said, making a claim for me, my life, against destruction, making sure I wouldn't forget. But there were no categories of ownership or even usage left. What had been the kitchen, the sitting-room, the places for sleeping were all turned out, flung together in one final raid, of fire and water, the last of the invasions in which our lives in that house were dragged and thrown about by hostile hands. He went poking at rubble with his foot and dirtying his fingers tugging away wet remains as if there were bodies to be found and rescued. He was breathing fast and loud in anger or close to tears; or both. *Sick, sick, they're sick* he kept hammering at me, only the onlooker and not the companion of his emotion. We emerged and our people who had dared to come out were still there, staring.

Their eyes fixed him. Their fear held them. I saw what it was—they expected him to have brought something out of what was destroyed. Something for them. He stood with blackened hands dangling open before them, he passed a weary gesture across his forehead that left a smudge he was unaware of. And he grinned. He grinned and his whole face drew together an agonized grimace of pain and reassurance, threat and resistance drawn in every fold of skin, every line of feature that the human face could be capable of conveying only under some unimaginable inner demand. It was very strange, what he brought them.

And then of course the old rhetoric took up the opportunity. We can't be burned out, he said, we're that bird, you know, it's called the phoenix, that always rises again from the ashes. Prison won't keep us out. Petrol bombs won't get rid of us. This street—this whole country is ours to live in. Fire won't stop me. And it won't stop you.

Flocks of papery cinders were drifting, floating about us—beds, clothing—his books?

The smell of smoke, that was the smell of her.

The smell of destruction, of what has been consumed, that he first brought into that house.

It's an old story—ours. My father's and mine. Love, love/hate are the most common and universal of experiences. But no two are alike, each is a fingerprint of life. That's the miracle that makes literature and links it with creation itself in the biological sense.

In our story, like all stories, I've made up what I wasn't there to experience myself. Sometimes—I can see—I've told something in terms I wouldn't have been capable of, aware of, at the period when it was happening: the licence of hindsight. Sometimes I can hear my voice breaking through, my judgments, my opinions elbowing in on what are supposed to be other people's. I'll have to watch out for that next time. Sometimes memory has opened a trapdoor and dropped me back into the experience as if I were living it again just at the stage I was when I lived it, so I've told it that way, in the present tense, with the vocabulary that was all I had to express myself, then. And so I've learned what he didn't teach me, that grammar is a system of mastering time; to write down 'he was', 'he is', 'he will be' is to grasp past, present and future. Whole; no longer bearing away.

All of it, all of it.

I have that within that passeth show.

I've imagined, out of their deception, the frustration of my absence, the pain of knowing them too well, what others would be doing, saying and feeling in the gaps between my witness. All the details about Sonny and his women?—oh, those I've taken from the women I've known. 'Sonny is not the man he was'; someone has said that to me: his comrades think it's because Aila's gone. But I'm young and it's my time that's come, with women. My time that's coming with politics. I was excluded from that, it didn't suit them for me to have any function within it, but I'm going to be the one to record, someday, what he and my mother/Aila and Baby and the others did, what it really was like to live a life determined by the struggle to be free, as desert dwellers' days are determined by the struggle against thirst and those of dwellers amid snow and ice by the struggle against the numbing of cold. That's what struggle really is, not a platform slogan repeated like a TV jingle.

He's been detained again. I wake up before it's light, these days, and I'm aware of him there, shut away. As if he were breathing in the next room in the house that's burned down. I've sent him this but I don't know if they'll give it to him. It's not Shakespeare; well, anyway. . .

4 a.m.
A bird sharpening its song against the morning
Furze of prison blanket mangy against the lips
Bird out there
Long ago we picked it up
Wired the tiny skeleton to make it bird again

Bird
Come, I'll hold you cupped in my two hands
Stroke your smooth feathers
Open the bars of my fingers and let you
Go!
Through the spaces of the iron bars
Fly!
Come, lover, comrade, friend, child, bird
Come
I entice you with my crumbs, see—
Dove
Sprig of olive in its beak
Dashes in swift through the bars, breaks its neck
Against stone walls.

What he did—my father—made me a writer. Do I have to thank him for that? Why couldn't I have been something else?

I am a writer and this is my first book—that I can never publish.

☐ **A SPORT OF NATURE**
Nadine Gordimer

Hillela, Nadine Gordimer's "sport of nature," is seductive and intuitively gifted at life. Casting herself adrift from her family at seventeen, she lives among political exiles on an East African beach, marries a black revolutionary, and ultimately plays a heroic role in the overthrow of apartheid.

354 pages *ISBN: 0-14-008470-3*

☐ **THE COUNTERLIFE**
Philip Roth

By far Philip Roth's most radical work of fiction, *The Counterlife* is a book of conflicting perspectives and points of view about people living out dreams of renewal and escape. Illuminating these lives is the skeptical, enveloping intelligence of the novelist Nathan Zuckerman, who calculates the price and examines the results of his characters' struggles for a change of personal fortune.

372 pages *ISBN: 0-14-009769-4*

☐ **THE MONKEY'S WRENCH**
Primo Levi

Through the mesmerizing tales told by two characters—one, a construction worker/philosopher who has built towers and bridges in India and Alaska; the other, a writer/chemist, rigger of words and molecules—Primo Levi celebrates the joys of work and the art of storytelling.

174 pages *ISBN: 0-14-010357-0*

☐ **IRONWEED**
William Kennedy

"Riding up the winding road of Saint Agnes Cemetery in the back of the rattling old truck, Francis Phelan became aware that the dead, even more than the living, settled down in neighborhoods." So begins William Kennedy's Pulitzer-Prize winning novel about an ex-ballplayer, part-time gravedigger, and full-time drunk, whose return to the haunts of his youth arouses the ghosts of his past and present.

228 pages *ISBN: 0-14-007020-6*

☐ **THE COMEDIANS**
Graham Greene

Set in Haiti under Duvalier's dictatorship, *The Comedians* is a story about the committed and the uncommitted. Actors with no control over their destiny, they play their parts in the foreground; experience love affairs rather than love; have enthusiasms but not faith; and if they die, they die like Mr. Jones, by accident.

288 pages *ISBN: 0-14-002766-1*